the moonflower couple

the moonflower couple

JOHN FAIRCHILD

DOUBLEDAY & COMPANY, INC., GARDEN CITY, NEW YORK

FOR JILL

*All of the characters in this book
are fictitious, and any resemblance
to actual persons, living or dead,
is purely coincidental.*

CONTENTS

MOONFLOWER

The scientific name Calonyction is a most appropriate one for this lovely flower, being a compound of the Greek words *kalos,* beautiful, and *nyktios,* nightly, and so meaning beautiful at night.

The moonvine is a nocturnal flowering plant, growing to twenty feet high in good soil, bearing large heart-shaped leaves and white, trumpet-shaped fragrant flowers to six inches across.

The flowers, very fragrant during warm summer nights, wither and die with the morning.

SOURCES: *Journal of the Washington Academy of Sciences February 15, 1945, Volume 35, No. 2.*

Wise Garden Encyclopedia, 1963 Edition Edited by E. L. D. Seymour.

1

PENSION

Catherine had invited Michael and Fiona for Tuesday luncheon at Madame Fleuret's pension, 8 bis, rue l'Université.

Catherine wanted Fiona to become interested in Michael Chase. That would keep her away from Paul Cain, the man Catherine hoped to marry. After graduating from Harvard Law School in June, Cain had gone immediately to Washington as a clerk to a Justice of the Supreme Court. Michael, after finishing Yale Law School in the same month, had decided to play and study in Paris.

Now Michael was standing next to a Norman cupboard, so warped the big door wouldn't close. Fiona took her seat next to Madame Fleuret, a fat woman with blown out, dyed red hair through which the grey was showing.

Michael quickly sat down next to Fiona. Catherine was pleased that her plan might work. Fiona was pleased too. She had met Michael five years before through Paul Cain, Michael's roommate at Princeton, and had seen him casually during her Vassar days, but now found him more grownup, more attractive.

"Michael, you've been here many Tuesdays as a guest. You seem to come and go as you please. Would you mind serving?" Madame Fleuret asked. It was easy for Michael to drop in. He lived next door in a big house lent to him by family friends.

"I will," Michael answered, defiantly throwing a torn napkin over his shoulder. He hoped Catherine and Fiona would laugh. He shuddered at the thought of Tuesday's menu: gristly blanquette de veau. He could still see the maid scraping the grey veal onto the plates.

Michael stared at the bottles of vin ordinaire, probably, he guessed, spiked with Algerian wine. He wished Madame Fleuret would give the signal to pour the bottle sitting nearest him on the scratched table.

Catherine spoke up. "Fiona, tonight we're going to a bistro with Michael. Why don't you come too?"

"I'd love to, but you know Father is alone at the Ritz. I wouldn't want to leave him."

Michael studied Fiona. He saw her long neck, her slender fingers, her fine body, and her shining brown hair falling to the shoulders of a snow white jersey dress.

Her bright eyes timidly took in the shabby room, sadly lit by the sunlight coming through the French windows and the rusted balcony rail. She heard the sharp clack-clack of people walking through the cobblestone courtyard below.

Fiona nervously fingered her napkin. With Catherine she never felt comfortable. They had been merely acquaintances at Vassar, but Fiona didn't graduate while Catherine did, with honors. Now Fiona was worried because Catherine knew she had left college her junior year, and if Michael also knew he might consider her stupid and flighty. She kept thinking, Catherine is frightfully intelligent. My grades were always below average and anything average I couldn't tolerate, so I went home to security, fun, and Daddy.

"Remember, students," said Madame Fleuret with a flick of her pudgy hands.

Michael poured a small amount of wine into his glass, tasted, and started to pour around the table.

Madame Fleuret continued, "You are here to learn French. After we close for vacation in August you can speak English." She bit into a big piece of bread and drank some wine.

André, Madame Fleuret's son, older than the others, rubbed his leg against Catherine's and filled her glass.

"Tonight again we will dance," André whispered into Catherine's

16

ear, as he adjusted his small, metal-rimmed glasses. Her black, too long hair was always falling over her brow. She kept pushing it back gently. André was the usual lumbering, sloppy Frenchman, with the short socks revealing his bare legs. He was a permanent student, intellectually stimulating and charmingly French.

Catherine moved closer to André. She spoke softly. "I've asked Fiona to join us, but I'm sure she won't. We'll find a way to get away if she does."

Madame Fleuret continued to talk to the room at large. "You must understand France to enjoy our culture. We are people tormented by years of war and hardship foreigners have never endured. You can't imagine the shame of being defeated and then occupied. When I lost my husband I had to struggle and make the best out of nothing. During the occupation André and I lay on our beds in pain from hunger. We didn't have the money to buy coal, or potatoes on the black market like those people below. You know, there were so many collaborators."

She rang the chipped gold bell. Paulette, the maid, could be heard shuffling down the hall to the dining room. She brought in the salad.

"Not bad," Madame Fleuret said, "but what a price for that tough meat." She knew Paulette had been getting her ten per cent from the butcher.

Madame Fleuret tossed the salad and then passed it to Fiona, who put a few leaves on her plate, still filled with meat. Fiona took a bite. The salad had sand. Michael helped himself, started to eat, suddenly stopped chewing. At that moment he looked at Fiona and they smiled. Their smiles were the first sign of any feeling and Catherine saw it.

Fiona stared at Michael's hands. They were small and narrow. Refined, she thought to herself. She liked the way his light blond hair hung over his ears. His lips were full, soft and round.

"We will all take coffee inside. Michael, please help Paulette clear the table," Madame Fleuret said as she got up and walked toward the salon. She wore a black crepe dress with a white lace bib collar. As she pulled at the double doors, her tight, clinging dress came up at the waist and away from her expanding bosom.

Michael put the napkin back on his shoulder and started the long

17

trek down the hallway to the kitchen. He refused to stack the plates. His mother had once fired a new butler because he had piled a butter plate on a dinner plate when clearing the table.

Fiona went into the salon with Catherine. "I would like to come tonight after all," she said. "You are so nice to have me."

"I knew you would when you saw Michael again. It's been a long time. I remember a weekend at Princeton. I was with Paul. You were down with someone else. André and I may go on to theater. You don't have to, though, if you don't want to," said Catherine in a blasé tone, pushing back her hair.

Catherine was a handsome girl with dark eyebrows, strong brown eyes, athletic legs. She had done a lot of riding at her family's place in Virginia before her parents had been divorced and both remarried, and she had been a leader on the campus.

Meeting unexpectedly in Paris, Fiona and Catherine had taken to spending the afternoons painting by the Seine and they laughed because neither could really paint. They found sitting along the river banks after lunch so relaxing and the early Paris afternoons, with the sun high in the cotton clouded sky, soft and gentle. And they talked of love and marriage. "I will marry a great man," Catherine said, as she held her head high. Fiona smiled and said, "I know you mean Paul Cain. Well, I will marry a great man for love." Catherine knew right away Fiona was thinking of Cain too. They painted until tea, when Fiona returned to the Ritz and Daddy.

In the salon, Madame Fleuret took her place in the high-backed Louis XIII armchair with the flowered tapestry worn to the canvas. She poured the coffee, heavy with chicory.

"Michael is staying behind. He wants to hear my professor's lecture at the Sorbonne," Catherine said to Fiona, who was ready to leave. "We'll see you later."

Fiona, noticing the dirty brass ball handles, closed the front door to Madame Fleuret's and started down the winding staircase—the steps worn, the walls flaky and peeling. How could Michael go there so often? She wondered as she rang the wall bell to open the big, black doors. She stepped over the door frame onto the Rue l'Université into the bright daylight.

She was happy. "Paris," she whispered and the thought carried her up the street. Far away at the other end of Paris another swan was swimming serenely in the Bois.

She walked slowly toward the Boulevard Saint-Germain, by the grey, bullet-scarred buildings with their high, black doors sealing in the secrets. She passed in front of an art gallery and stared into the window, first at her reflected face, then at a Braque lithograph—a large bird high in the sky, free in flight over the worlds, from white to yellow, then to bright warm orange. She thought of her father alone, waiting for her. She must hurry back.

Fiona entered the gallery. A tall man, leaning on a walking stick, came to her. "May I help you?" and his tired, used eyes brightened just for that moment when he felt her beauty.

"The bird, your Braque, is it a lithograph?" she asked.

"Yes, but better than that, an eau forte originale," and he lifted it from the window.

"I love it," Fiona said, taking the lithograph. "Could you send it this afternoon? You see, it is for my father, a present. What should I leave with the concierge?"

"In dollars I would calculate about four hundred."

"Our address is Hotel Ritz, Place Vendôme side, Jardin Apartment 8A-B. Thank you," she said, quickly leaving, delighted she had thought of her father and not just of tonight.

She crossed Le Pont de la Concorde over the Seine and midway turned to look out over the winding, rolling river. Up a way there was the corner under the leaning tree where she and Catherine often painted. But now, a big brownish black barge floundered like a whale in the quiet water.

She saw the highly varnished cabin and the oversized rudder and long tiller securely tied. The fresh, clean tricolor flapped from the flagpole and the lady of the barge was hanging out the captain's wash, right in the middle of Paris.

As she pushed the white revolving door to the Ritz her foot sank into the thick white rubber mat. Fiona stepped inside and immediately the concierge, in chocolate brown uniform with gold keys on each lapel and brass buttons, rose from behind his light mahogany desk and bowed: "Bonjour, Mademoiselle Stephenson."

She walked down the long, narrow Ritz corridor lined with per-

19

fume, antique, and clothing shop cases, securely locked and guarded by a middle-aged woman with tea-colored hair, who was sitting spread out over a Louis XVI stool, reading a magazine. She nodded casually, as though thinking, that girl is too young to buy.

Fiona approached the elevator at the Vendôme side. The concierge announced: "Mademoiselle, I believe your father is in and he has the key." She looked at herself in the mirrors as she stepped into the honey mahogany elevator. The operator moved the brown wood handle with polished brass head and the car went up.

Fiona did not knock. Daddy always left the door open. She entered the large living room. Mr. Stephenson, a nattily dressed man in a navy, double-vented blazer, was on the telephone, his back to Fiona. He stood straight, surrounded by a smoke haze coming from his black and gold cigaret holder.

"If the publication is for sale, I'm willing to pay a good price, but you must work directly through my agent.

"No, impossible for me to keep all of the present personnel. I must run things my own way and with my own people." He gave a flick of his cigaret and the ashes missed the blue porcelain ash tray.

"Think about the proposition and ring me tomorrow before we leave for London."

He hung up the phone and turned around: "Darling, where have you been all afternoon? It's almost three-thirty."

She went over to her father and putting both arms around his neck stood on her toes and kissed him on the cheek. "I'm sorry to be late, but I walked back from the pension. We had so much fun and I saw Michael Chase."

Fiona held her father's hand. His blue eyes fixed on her and she knew it was the moment to ask.

"Tonight I'm going out to dinner with Catherine and her friend André. Michael will be there. May I telephone them to come here first for a drink so they can meet you?"

The hall porter knocked at the door. "Oui, entrez," said Mr. Stephenson. The porter came in with a package and Fiona immediately took it from his hand.

"Daddy, this is for you. I saw it in a window on the way back here and I couldn't resist."

20

Mr. Stephenson looked at her. He could forgive everything he knew. She was spoiled, but beauty was worth spoiling. There could be no problems for her—not the problems he had faced growing up with money but without the right social position. He had the power and he knew it and used power well to buy the publications he wanted, but he was always concerned with his social position. Martha, his wife, took care of that. Mrs. Stephenson was from a fine Philadelphia banking family.

He walked to the high French door and opened it all the way, pushing back the red damask curtains. Fiona followed him out onto the balcony. Below were the Ritz gardens—red and white geraniums, pale purple hydrangeas, white and deep purple petunias in beds and planted high in white wrought iron stands. Fiona and her father looked down at the ladies having tea. She thought, such a bore, all those ladies sipping and stuffing gooey cakes into their mouths while the young waiters rushed back and forth over the crunchy stones.

They went back inside and Fiona, tucking one leg under her, sat down on the blue silk satin Louis XIV sofa. She let her black patented, gold buckled shoe drop to the dark blue carpet. Mr. Stephenson went over to a marble-topped side table, took a cigaret from his gold case and sat next to Fiona. She looked straight into his face, her brown eyes dancing. "I'll ask them to come in an hour and I thought we could have a little champagne and then be off. It might be late, Daddy, so please don't wait up. We'll be going dancing at Jimmy's. They have the best records and all the young group in Paris will be there."

"Well, have a good time," her father said smiling, but a little sadly.

She kissed his cheek, jumped up, and went into her bedroom. She opened the gold leaf cupboard and took out two dresses. She held the black linen one with a white pussy cat bow up to her body and studied it in the closet mirror. "That's it," she decided. She put the dress down on the pink satin bedcover and lay down beside it to call the pension. She would tell Catherine to come to the Ritz.

2

TOGETHER

Michael and Fiona dined well at a Left Bank bistro. They let André and Catherine go on to the theater. It hadn't been difficult to do. André and Catherine wanted to be alone too.

Michael and Fiona had enjoyed the wine, a strong Beaujolais, heavy and fruity in flavor. She thought Michael "divine." He thought Fiona delicate, refined, educated, and civilized to the point where she could be in his words "useful."

They finished their café filtre. Fiona added her second lump of sugar, stirring slowly—anything so the evening would never end.

"Please, a poire brandy," Michael said to the waiter, "and make sure it's Williams. Swiss pear brandy smells as fresh and sweet as pears in the sun."

"Daddy drinks it," Fiona answered, "but I find it strong."

"Have one before we go to Jimmy's."

Seated behind her cash box, the wife of the owner of the bistro—fat and used from hard work and that extra apéritif—thought to herself, what a beautiful young couple. They surely will be married soon. At that age, I was hardly a beauty. If I had been, maybe I wouldn't have ended up in this place, adding up bills between sips of vin rouge.

Fiona found it difficult to talk to Michael. She remembered what her mother had said, "Be careful and choose wisely. You can select the man you want to marry. You must be proud of your husband and feel he is superior to you. Marriage today is not all love. The man and wife are a team working for one common purpose." Fiona had never thought through her mother's lecture on marriage, but suddenly she saw in Michael love and power. She lived in that special world where power was there, always taken for granted, but love she knew was hard to find. She remembered her sister's wedding, the most "in" social event of the year in the small Connecticut church where all her friends were supposed to get married. One of the young lady guests was stung by a bee during the service and the ushers carried her out nearly unconscious. As the allergic reaction closed up her throat, she gasped for air. Fiona was horrified to think no one had asked later on if the girl had reached the hospital in time. Everyone was too busy with the wedding to worry.

The next day Fiona learned the girl had died. The death from a bee sting had been a bad omen for Fiona's sister, Elizabeth. Two years later Elizabeth divorced her husband, saying, "Because he was a bore." They must have been bored with each other in the beginning. How stupid then to get involved, Fiona thought, as she looked across the table at Michael.

Michael had his plans for that evening with Fiona and his plans for his future. He had done well at Yale Law. Four years at Princeton and then Yale for law. That was the right course to follow.

He finished his poire and put the glass on the table. Fiona had taken one sip and was getting to like it, the perfume more than the alcohol.

Michael felt the pear brandy going to his head. He remembered the day before flying to Europe, his father had discussed his future, that "big, bright future," were the words he used. Michael imagined himself a new, young Kennedy. Like the Kennedys he had the wealth, the looks, and the education to succeed in public life. There was no reason not to run for public office. His father and Uncle John and the whole family had contributed heavily to the Democratic Party. Michael was sure that the aggressive, new young breed—and he

23

considered himself part of this breed—would carry on. Fiona just might be the one to fit in.

"This has been a marvelous day for me," Fiona said to Michael, looking at him the same way she had looked at her father four hours earlier. "I'm in love with Paris and the way the city bubbles with the French. Every time I walk down the street I have a special feeling, as though I'm more alive."

Perhaps, Michael thought, Fiona was too naïve, too innocent. He had been to Paris many times. In his own mind, he was a man of the world. She was too much a sweet jeune fille. Michael could not think then of anything to say to Fiona, not even the obvious. He didn't want to make a mistake now.

"The check, please," he said quickly and he was ready to get up and leave. When uncomfortable, Michael was always impulsive. Try the next thing, move on to something else was his solution.

They left the bistro and stepped out into the cobblestone street. Michael had rented a black Cadillac limousine, so out of place in the narrow Paris streets. It was waiting for them. They got in and Fiona sat closer to Michael than she had really planned. Suddenly they were very alone in the back seat as they turned the corner onto the boulevard and sped past the young evening crowd out on their zooming motorcycles. Fiona found it exciting, the girls on the back, holding on so tight to the boys' waists. It was almost embarrassing to be in a big Cadillac. Michael would never take to motorcycles, she thought, as they pulled up to Jimmy's.

He was nervous about getting into the club. You had to be a member, or introduced, as his French political friend had told him when he had introduced Michael.

The club sat catty corner on a narrow street just off the Grand Boulevard. The doorman, sighting the Cadillac, immediately opened the door. "We are full tonight, Monsieur, are you a member?"

Michael answered with a strong oui. He was furious the doorman would dare ask him. Now he would have to worry about a table and about getting in, because there were couples standing in front of the black lacquered wood door. Michael and Fiona took their place in line.

"I'm sure we will get in. I've been introduced," he said, taking her hand. A small door opened and a fat-faced woman looked out. She looked like some mad sorceress, Fiona thought. Michael pushed his way in front of the line and rapped on the little door. It opened again and the same woman stared straight at him and quickly shut the door. His face reddened and he returned to Fiona, taking her hand. Three people in front went in and only then did Michael get up his courage.

"Je suis ami to Monsieur de . . ." The last name faded away in his faltering French. The big door opened and the woman looked out again. She saw Fiona was well dressed and admired her belted dark mink coat. She beckoned Fiona. Fiona went, taking Michael by the hand.

Inside it was dark and smoky. The record was turned up full. "J'ai envie, j'ai envie." Over and over again the man sang, "J'ai envie."

The young waiter in tight black pants and a red bus boy's jacket took them to a dark end of the room where they sat on red velvet stools, jammed next to a kissing young couple. The girl was right up against the wall, holding her friend close. It shocked Fiona, but Michael was blasé. He had expected Jimmy's to be warm and intimate. As the waiter put two glasses, two green Perrier bottles and the silver ice bucket, with silver tongs rattling inside, on the small, round table, Michael noticed the bottle of Scotch was Johnny Walker Red Label. He was annoyed they hadn't been asked to choose their own brand.

The crowd danced closely locked together, round and round, in contact with the "boom bah" beat. The women, in short black dresses, shifting high above the knees, clung to the well-tailored men. Entranced, they danced, the young so beautiful, the old hoping they were still beautiful, but everyone thinking they were with it, everyone glad to be in with the right crowd. Tonight they were all securely in love.

At the opposite end of the room, around a circular red and gold banquette, sat the celebrities: a painter, who looked as gaunt as his paintings; a woman novelist, who looked savagely decadent and who stayed most nights until the 4 A.M. closing; a dress designer, with his pretty male companion; a loud singer, on hand to hear her latest

25

record; the young, blond grandson of a famous French general, cuddling with the singer.

Marianne, the owner of Jimmy's, hovered over her celebrity banquette like a busy chicken. The crowd came hoping to be recognized by Marianne, who made a specialty of snatching handsome young boys away from the young girls. "I show them real love," she told some of her customers. In her black, white, and red apartment where she lived above the club (hallway black, living room white, bedroom red), she wined and dined the international set and the élite of Paris and the world. It had become chic to be recognized by Marianne, who came from a Marseille fishmonger's family.

She boldly sent out invitations to the young boys for one o'clock lunch. "Half an hour for apéritifs, one hour for lunch, followed by one hour of love." Her savage charm and coarseness excited the rich and social, young and old alike.

Fiona and Michael didn't dance right away. They settled into the music, the smoke, the body beats, and sipped Scotch and Perrier. Fiona pushed her hair back over her shoulder and moved closer to Michael. He felt her nearness. He loved her perfume. St. Laurent's "Y", he thought. His mother wore the same scent. He admired her slender neck, the way she tipped her delicate head toward him. He had a desire to take her hand, which was resting next to his on the banquette.

"We must dance," he said, smiling at her.

Then he took her hand firmly and they made their way through the crowd onto the dance floor. He moved in closely, holding Fiona tightly. She liked the way the palm of his hand kept pushing her closer and closer. Her head touched his and she turned it slowly, brushing her face across his lips. Michael sensed they were being admired, making him feel even more romantic. Fiona enjoyed being held in his arms.

"Boom, bah bah, rock and rock—boom, bah rock and love, love, zoom," around and around, faster and faster. Fiona was dizzy; Michael, excited. "Boom, bah bah, rock, rock, rock." The music stopped and Michael put his hand on Fiona's head and pushed her face into his chest.

"It's so wonderful. I love every minute. Let's go on and on," Fiona said softly.

They stayed late. Michael off the dance floor became serious.

"It's a shame you left Vassar when you had only one more year," he said to her and he poured them both another drink.

"I was bored. Really bored with all those girls," Fiona answered, looking onto the dance floor. "I wanted to live," she added as an afterthought and turned back to Michael.

"Are you living now?" Michael asked her rather cynically.

"Tonight. Yes. A little," she said, looking into his eyes.

Michael was determined to find out more about her. "Well, what do you want out of life anyway? What's your idea of fine living?" he asked, hoping to put her on the spot.

Fiona hesitated. She said, "To enjoy all, all of it with someone else. If I love, I'll protect and help him. I'll love strongly and devotedly. You know what I mean."

Michael nodded.

Fiona stroked her hair and continued. "His career isn't that important to me. If we love enough and are free to live in our own way, we won't make the mistakes of our parents."

"My parents didn't make any mistakes," Michael said.

"I don't mean mistakes. I mean not to conform to all their standards. I'm not going to follow the group like Mummy and Daddy. They see the same people all the time, because they're the right ones to see. It gets to the point that all their friends start to look and act exactly alike. Just like my friends at Vassar. They conformed. Conformity leads to boredom. And I won't be bored. If you conform long enough, it's too late to make a change."

Michael frowned. "It's different with me," he said. "I want so much and I've thought a great deal about getting everything. I have a duty to perform. I feel people in our position, with our breeding, you know, the civilized (a word he borrowed from his mother and father) have a responsibility in public life. I want to enter politics, perhaps later the foreign service, where I can give the best of myself to my country." He almost said, to the world, but caught himself just in time. To give himself to the world would sound rather pompous. Paul Cain had always kidded him about being such a pompous ass.

The Johnny Walker Red Label was now half empty. Fiona's eyes, filled with smoke, were smarting. She thought Michael, as she had heard, aggressive; almost too handsome, to the point of being beautiful. She imagined him a Greek god, blond longish hair falling over his ears, a fine, slender body. She liked his long legs and the way he had entered the room at the pension with hands behind his back, resting on the double vent of his suit; like Prince Philip in the newsreels, she thought. Michael was so sure and secure about himself for a young man. She had never met anyone quite like that except maybe her father. Fiona wished she could share in this security.

They danced, barely speaking, for two hours, as one body. And they continued drinking. Michael thought it now all rather corny. He was holding Fiona's hand under the table. Could he ever be in love? He thought love didn't exist. Fiona wanted so much love. Michael could not let himself go. There was still so much to do, and he wasn't sure about her being the right one for him. He refused to play the lover's role, but took another drink and still held her hand.

Jimmy's emptied out. Marianne disappeared with a young man, a sign for the waiters to start closing down.

Fiona and Michael stepped out into the Paris early morning. It had just rained and the wet streets reflected the car lights moving through the night.

"Let's walk home, Michael."

They started down the long boulevard, hand in hand. He put his arm around her waist. Her head dropped to his shoulder.

"I won't be seeing you again," Fiona said, lifting her head off Michael's shoulder. "We're leaving tomorrow for London. Daddy has a business deal."

The boulevard was empty except for the cars.

"I will see you again. Soon I hope," Michael answered.

"When?" Fiona asked.

"Back in New York. Sometime in the fall, I suspect," Michael said.

Fiona thought "back in New York" sounded so far off.

Michael dropped her hand and quickened his pace. "Now I'm sorry I let the car and chauffeur go. We'll have to walk."

28

"Good," Fiona said, moving closer to Michael. She wanted to put her arm around his waist and pull his body in to hers.

Michael felt her closeness. He smelled her perfume and could see the glow in her dark hair. They talked softly to each other, as if someone might be listening. There was no noise, only the cars splashing through the water as they passed. At the intersection, the drivers nervously flashed their headlights, then sped on.

"I'm sorry the evening is over, Michael," she started to say.

Michael took her hand again. They were now heading down the Boulevard Saint-Germain. Michael was so pleased he knew Paris well enough to guide them home.

Soon they would be passing the Rue l'Université where Michael lived in an exclusive "hôtel particulier" classified as a historic monument by the French government. His family's friends were away in Biarritz, so Michael had the whole "hôtel" and some of the staff to himself.

Would he ask her up? She wanted to know, even though she wasn't sure what she would say. She squeezed his hand tightly. His hand was soft.

"I'm tired. Can we stop?" Fiona said, heading toward the curb, where she dropped to the straight, long wooden bench where Parisiens during the day waited, watching alive Paris pass them by.

A young couple zoomed around the corner on their Vespa. The girl clung on tightly to his waist and kissed the back of his neck. As they went down a narrow side street, the brakes squeaked and the scooter came to a stop. Fiona heard the kick stand go down to the pavement with a scrape. The girl was off the scooter and her arms still around the man. They kissed up against the wall. She giggled and the laughter bounced off the tall building across the street. The man reached out with one hand, pushed the buzzer and the door opened. They went inside.

"What are you watching?" Michael asked.

"Over there. They're in love," Fiona answered.

Michael started to laugh. "You know who that is." And he was still laughing.

"Who?"

"André and Catherine. They're just getting back." Michael stood in front of Fiona, who sat curled up on the bench. Her shoes lay in the dirt. Michael leaned down to her and, looking at her intently, placed both hands on the sides of her head. He pulled her head toward him, into his waist. She felt his belt hitting her forehead. He quickly sat down on the bench and spun her around. He kissed her neck and ran his tongue under her ear lobes. His lips were on hers, and his arms pulled her in close. The palm of his hand was on her back, pressing.

"You're hurting me, Michael. You're hurting me. Please, Michael. Not here."

He didn't let go. His right hand dropped to her legs, caressing up and down her thigh. Fiona fell back.

"Michael, not here. Please." And she looked over his shoulder to the grey building with the big black doors that she had closed at lunch time. She saw herself spread out over the boulevard bench. Her hair was mussed. Michael forced her head back and again and again placed his lips on hers.

Fiona turned sideways and pulled away. She was off the bench, leaving her shoes turned over in the dirt. Michael grasped her from the back around the waist and held her.

"You feel so warm, Fiona. I want you now." And he was kissing the back of her neck. "Now. Let's go to my room."

Fiona put her hands to his, removing them and turned around to face him. His eyes were fierce, his lips contorted.

"You look like some wild beast. You've had too much to drink," Fiona said calmly and she moved back from him.

"I want you," and he followed her. "And you want me, Fiona. You're excited. I can feel your body trembling when I touch you. Come here," and he held out his hands.

"Let's go back to the hotel," she said. "Daddy will be waiting." Fiona clutched her shoes and bending over, put them on, holding onto Michael's waist. Her hand was slipping around his leg.

Michael knew he had triumphed. He was satisfied that he could have Fiona. It needn't be now. Later would do, if he so decided.

He took her by the arm and they started walking down the boulevard. Michael was tired and kept turning his head to look for a taxi.

They passed the café terraces, with their wicker chairs piled up on top of each other. The gaiety, the intrigues that had gone on hours earlier would begin all over tomorrow.

Fiona thought of Jimmy's—the music and dancing so close to Michael. The words, of, "J'ai envie, j'ai envie," ran through her head.

"There's a taxi. There's one," Michael yelled, running away from Fiona. The taxi stopped and the driver rolled down his window. "Rue Cambon, Hotel Ritz," Michael said. The driver nodded his head.

They were inside, speeding along the Quai. Fiona leaned forward, straining to see the barge she had seen earlier in the day. "There's where we paint. Where Catherine and I paint," she said, pointing out of the window. The breeze felt soft and fresh on Michael's face. Night air was so much cleaner, he thought. She looked up into the cloud covered sky. Fiona wanted to see just one star. She looked down into the river, black, silent, except for the clumsy barges passing through the sleeping city. The cabin lights and the running lights flickered into the water, and the flags on the barges flapped.

"Wait, please," Michael said to the cab driver at the entrance to the Ritz. Michael bounded out of the cab, followed by Fiona. He took her arm and led her to the door. He kissed her on the forehead.

"Good night," he said.

"Good night, Michael," and Fiona went through the revolving door, up the two marble steps, as though she had been floating on air.

"8 bis, rue l'Université," Michael told the driver, and put his feet up on the folded jump seats. He smiled to himself, pleased, so pleased with his success. He thought of Catherine, back at the pension, but would she be with André? She had gone with him. They were together, possibly now they were in bed. He should have taken Fiona then, but good judgment had made him wait. He was proud of his power to resist.

He climbed the pension stairs and unlocked the door. Catherine had given him a key. He tiptoed down the hall to Catherine's room, stopped, listened, and turned the knob. The door was locked. He heard the movement in the bed, rustling and surprised whispers.

Michael returned down the hallway, trying to walk gently on the creaking floor boards. He opened the front door. Groping for the switch in the dark, he lit the depressing stairwell. He went down cautiously and was soon out on the street alone with two cats scurrying away over the cobblestones. He rang for the concierge at the "hôtel" and the door buzzed and swung open just enough for him to get through. He closed the big door with a bang, which resounded throughout the courtyard.

He took the elevator to the third story, got out into the hallway leading to the study, which was all done in red velvet.

He usually read, but not tonight, so he went straight into his bedroom. The light was on and his pajamas and dressing gown were out, folded meticulously on the turned-down bed. He took off his clothes and lay down nude. He thought of Fiona, then Catherine. He didn't sleep right away.

Fiona looked into the mirror. Her hair was tossed about and her cheeks red. She smiled at herself and whispered, "Propriety. The hell with propriety." She undressed and went back to the mirror. She felt her breasts, turned sideways, and patted her buttocks. She straightened up, put her legs apart and threw back her head and danced around to the music playing in her mind.

She went to the bed and grasping the pillow with both hands rolled over onto her stomach and pushed her body into the mattress.

3

APART

The next morning Fiona and Mr. Stephenson left for London. Mr. Stephenson was concerned about closing a deal to buy an English fashion magazine. Fiona was looking forward to a weekend with a young Englishman.

She had written Michael a sentimental and gushy letter that night after he had left her at the Ritz. She didn't want him to think she was all that frightened of him.

They boarded Air France Flight #812 at Orly for the forty-five-minute flight over the channel. During a quick luncheon and Taittinger champagne Fiona tried to put Michael out of her mind.

"What are you thinking about? Last night?" Mr. Stephenson asked. He knew Fiona well enough to expect that she was always in love, or dreamed of being in love. He had seen her often melancholy as she was now.

Fiona looked out of the window. The plane was surrounded by clouds. She couldn't even see the wing in the sky. Eerie, she thought to herself, terrifying, suspended up here in this aluminum cigar box. She felt panicky. Her father reached over and held her hand.

"See," he said calmly, "we are going down."

"The clouds are on top of us, all around us. Will they ever end?

Look. There's the sky. It's so blue. How marvelous," Fiona said. She saw the bright green English countryside below, dotted with red brick houses, one right after the other.

They flew over the red chimney tops and touched down at London airport.

She had forgotten about Michael. She was in England and as the plane taxied up to the terminal Fiona saw a black Rolls-Royce station wagon standing by the strip. There her Englishman, Richard Talbot Ross, was waiting for her.

Fiona spent a chaperoned weekend at a ghosty English country house in Sussex. They rode through the woods, picked roses, and swam in the manor house indoor pool. After the swim, they had strong, marvelous tea and watercress and cucumber melded into white butter on thin English bread. Then it was time to dress for dinner, which was served solemnly in the great hall by footmen. Maybe she would like living in Europe. There was a certain refinement and respect for the past that appealed to her.

Later, as she slipped into the big four-poster canopied bed, she adored the idea that her scratchy linen sheets had been warmed by the maid with a warming pan. She thought this life could be hers for the asking. But actually Fiona couldn't imagine herself rattling around such a big place, watching after the garden, the kitchen, and the upstairs maids. And she didn't really like the damp stone house with the thick, century-old clinging ivy.

She was sure Ross wanted to marry her. Fiona had been told by her father that Englishmen, even when married, spent most of their time at the club. She didn't like that idea and expected her husband to be at her side at all times.

Returning to London airport to meet Mr. Stephenson for the flight back to New York, Fiona sensed Ross wanted to talk to her, but he was so reserved and pathetically shy that he just couldn't get the words out.

"I'll miss you," he said and turned to look out the window.

"I had a delightful weekend, Richard, and I won't forget being with you," Fiona answered.

"When will you be back?" he asked hopefully.

34

"Probably sooner than you think," Fiona answered with an air of mystery in her voice.

He clutched the leather hand pulley as the Rolls rounded the corner and went into the tunnel under the airport runway. Fiona reached out with her hand. He held it just for a minute until they came out into the daylight.

The Rolls came to a stop. The chauffeur was out of the car quickly to unload the luggage from the folding back rack. Richard moved over closer to Fiona and she was about to reach out again for his hand. He looked into her eyes. She answered him by stroking his hand.

"Fiona. Fiona, darling. Here I am," Mr. Stephenson said, tapping on the window. He tipped his black bowler and opened the door to take her arm. She was out of the car and Richard Ross dutifully followed them to Gate 7 for boarding.

Mr. Stephenson shook Richard Ross's hand and walked ahead down the enclosed passageway. He thought Fiona would want to linger behind. Instead she held out her hand. She said good-bye quickly and ran to catch up to her father.

Bored, Fiona returned to her rarified routine of cemented-together Manhattan. About the only new news was that Willy Mackintosh had redecorated her mother's apartment in new colors, mostly browns, with a smattering of paisley fabric here and there. This was a temporary arrangement, because her mother planned a new town house which wouldn't be ready for a year. Willy had the brilliant idea, or at least Mrs. Stephenson thought so, of hanging the paisley on curtain rods all over the walls so that the sitting room looked something like an Arab tent. All her mother's finest Louis XVI signed pieces had been redone in the applegreen color so popular with Willy this month. He had found on Second Avenue some old Venetian glass mirrors and had hung two together over the fireplace. Mrs. Stephenson liked everything in pairs.

Fiona told her mother the temporary arrangement looked divine, but thought to herself she would one day use her own decorator.

Bernadine, Mrs. Stephenson's maid, and Henry, the valet, were in attendance as usual, but Henry, who served breakfast, for some weeks now had been giving Mr. Stephenson a Doriden sleeping tablet at 8 A.M., instead of his B-1 vitamin tablet.

"Henry has been warned by your father never to make a mistake about his pill again," Mrs. Stephenson said to Fiona, as they drank their fresh mango juice at a small breakfast table set up next to her mother's canopied bed. Fiona sniffed the white roses in the white Lowestoft creamer. Fiona admired the tiny flower bouquet design on the creamer, so nice with the white roses, she thought.

"Mummy, I think you are looking well. We missed you in Europe."

"I would have loved to have been there, darling, but you know how demanding my life is. I'm trying to fix up the house in Antigua, the new town house, and you know Brooks Farms takes so much of my time. Now, tell me about yourself. Daddy reports you saw Michael Chase. A nice family. I know his mother and father only vaguely."

Fiona looked down at the table. Until this moment she had dismissed Michael from her mind. "He's nice enough, but I won't be seeing him again."

Mrs. Stephenson put down her sickly orange mango juice. Slightly alarmed, she said, "Darling, did anything happen between you?"

"Mummy, really, let's not bring sex into it. Times have changed. I've told you before."

Mrs. Stephenson knew well enough there had been no change from her day.

Mrs. Stephenson was considered by many as the leading social hostess in New York. By the chic crowd, she was looked upon as the chicest. By the detractors, she was chic only because she was beautiful and had the money to make herself more beautiful. She was tall, thin, tiny boned, with rich, auburn hair. She had looked upon Fiona as an ugly duckling and refused to accept the fact that her own chic crowd considered Fiona not only attractive, gentle and nice, but the most eligible catch in all of New York.

Fiona envied her mother, especially all the fuss made about her when she went to the four in French restaurants, the three "La's" and the one "Le." Mrs. Stephenson always got the best banquette in the corner, where she could see everyone and be seen. Dressmakers, hairdressers, artists, writers, painters, and conductors all

36

sought Mrs. Stephenson's patronage. The fashion magazines and even the stodgy New York *Times* clamored for interviews. "What will you wear to Ascot, to Lincoln Center?" "Who makes your clothes?" Her mother was asked every question except was she happy. Mrs. Stephenson never had time to think; she was too busy doing what she felt was necessary to keep her New York's social leader.

She broke away when her migraine throbbed and retired for a week or two to the British West Indies. There she shopped the boutiques and redecorated the house. Her latest success, photographed in a fashion magazine, showed her "Full Moon" beach house with red lacquered walls, the black stone floor scattered with orange, black, pink, and bright blue cushions. Guests sat on the floor and dined off low Philippine bamboo tables. After dinner, they moved out toward the sea and rocked lazily in straw hammocks. Then a steel band arrived. Tall torches placed among the red, white, and yellow hibiscus plants lit up with an eerie orange glow the artificial tropical lagoon where the guests sometimes swam and played into the morning.

Mr. Stephenson was flattered by his wife's fame for chic parties. Fiona once heard her father during a quarrel with her mother say, "Good parties are good for my business." This thought revolted Fiona.

Mr. Stephenson was demanding of his wife's time and insisted that she run their three houses as he ran his office. Servants were expected to serve at all hours. Meals were perfect and guests, no matter how many times they stayed at the Stephensons, never had the same course twice. Mrs. Stephenson set up a filing system so that she had a record of when she entertained each person last and what they ate, complete to wines, vegetables, and hors d'oeuvres. The Stephensons entertained at least three nights of the week at home and were out the other nights. Her social secretary had Mrs. Stephenson's engagement book blocked out three months in advance.

Fiona had figured her existence was going to be different. She would expect the same luxury, but she was determined her life would be filled with close personal relationships with her husband, children, and friends.

When they'd finished their coffee, Fiona said, "Mummy, will you be needing Jonathan and the car all day? Because I have some errands to do. I thought I might go to Albert's and have my hair done for tonight. You know, he does the most amusing false braids and for me he's doing them much longer."

"Take the car, darling. I have lunch with Homer at La . . . . . at one and the decorator is coming before. Homer's new book is supposed to be on its way to being a best seller."

Fiona didn't like Homer, or his book, because he had spent one year tooting about it at every dinner party and had gotten many social ladies in New York to help put it across. Homer talked in a deep, somber voice. He knew everything about her mother's friends and was their confidant. They all felt safe with him. Fiona looked upon him as the court jester to her mother's world, but then he really had more influence on the women than they on him. Fiona thought Homer looked like a lanky toad, but with his certain best seller he would be a croaking frog.

Fiona couldn't wait to leave the breakfast table. She was terrified her mother would insist that she lunch with Homer.

Fiona went to her room to read the paper. She would take her time, lingering in the morning—she liked that—and fix herself up before going to Albert's.

"Darling, I've changed my mind," said Mrs. Stephenson half an hour later, in Fiona's bedroom. "I'll be going with you to the hairdresser. Daddy and I have that dinner tonight for Homer and Max, that Hollywood producer who wants to negotiate for his book."

Fiona didn't like the idea of her mother going to the same hairdresser. She feared her mother might copy her hair style. Why didn't I keep my mouth shut, she thought.

Mrs. Stephenson's day began. She had a half hour with her secretary fixing up social engagements, arranging the sitting "map" for tonight's black tie dinner; then another fifteen minutes with the maître d'hôtel for the wine and another meeting with the chef. Fiona had heard her mother doing the same orderly things now for years. Nothing seemed to change. Even the flowers from Mary Lester's on Park Avenue were always white roses and phlox.

From the country house, Luigi, the head gardener, brought in every other day "personal" flowers—sweet peas, lilies of the valley, garnette roses, hyacinths, anemones—to be arranged in small antique glass and porcelain objets.

"You arrange the flowers beautifully, Luigi," said Fiona as she passed through the living room on her way out.

"I've been well trained by your mother," he answered, as Mrs. Stephenson came into the living room wearing Benjamin Franklin glasses. When she saw Luigi and Fiona she took them off and put them into the pocket of her red silk blouse, worn over her stark white pants.

"You're still wearing your morning costume, aren't you, Mummy?" Fiona laughed.

"It's the only place to wear pants—at home for my morning chores," Mrs. Stephenson said in a positive tone.

Fiona knew enough not to argue. Her mother was definite about all matters of taste, especially fashion.

"See you tonight, Mummy. Good-bye Luigi," Fiona said cheerily, as she went out of the door and into the elevator. She breathed a sigh of relief to be out of the house. The routine is getting me down. I've got to escape. The trouble with people like Mummy is that they are afraid to live. They always think something terrible is going to happen to them. If they took a chance, it could be something exciting, wonderful, she thought to herself, as Jonathan, with hat in his hand, held open the door of the Jaguar.

4

THE GAME

Catherine stayed in Paris longer than she should have. The football season was on. Harvard was playing Princeton that weekend and Paul Cain never missed that game.

Catherine had thought of coming home, but delayed to avoid the football season. She hated the game, so American, so downright boring, not at all attuned to her intellectual, refined interests, as she had told everyone, including Paul Cain.

But he wasn't going to the game alone. He had called Fiona and she had accepted right away, because she liked Paul and she couldn't wait to escape her family. They were getting so much on her nerves, Fiona was in the mood to marry just to get out from under her mother and father's wing. She had told herself to be careful, but hadn't she been careful for a long time now?

Paul planned to fly up to Boston and meet Fiona at the hotel on the Common. He had told her Friday night that Michael would be taking the early special train and he might "look you up." This idea whetted Fiona's appetite and intrigued her. She realized that she hoped Michael would be still interested in her, even passionately interested, as he had been in Paris. What a fool she had been to run away from him that night. She remembered the boulevard bench, her shoes in the dirt, and Michael holding her tight.

Fiona was sitting in the parlor car when Michael walked through. She immediately swung her chair to face the window. She pretended not to see him. But he spotted her right away and leaning over the chair, whispered in her ear, "Where have you been? I've been waiting."

She really looked sensational, he thought. She wore a red chemise dress and a Somali leopard coat, leopard boots, and her smooth hair hung straight down her back, so shiny and soft, Michael wanted to touch.

Michael decided then that he had to have Fiona that weekend and he was sure that he could. She still appealed to him, just as a piece of candy does to a little boy. He had seldom been refused anything, and he remembered that night in Paris very well. He'd never had any difficulty attracting girls—or doing what he wanted with them—and there was still something special about Fiona.

He knew that Fiona was going to Paul Cain. That made her even more tempting. All is fair in love and war, he thought to himself. He was jealous of Cain's success. He had always done better than Michael, who had Cain's accomplishments listed, like some job résumé, in his mind: a better Princeton Club—Ivy; editor, Harvard Law Review; now a job clerking in the Supreme Court.

Michael resented Cain even though he called him "a friend," and attributed Cain's success to the fact that Cain's father was Senator Willard Cain, Democrat, Massachusetts.

Michael suffered from his middle class, midwestern family background—and from the fact that his father—this last part hurt the most—persisted in being a big small parts manufacturer to the Detroit automobile industry. His mother, at a *very* young age, had had a fling at Hollywood as a starlet.

It would be something to take Fiona away from Cain. And besides, he really was strongly attracted to her. Maybe now she was ready and the right one for him.

Fiona now pretended to be furious. He had never answered her letter. Who did he think he was anyway? She too had no doubts about her attractiveness. "I'm not going to be alone," she said, looking fiercely at Michael. "I'm going up to Cambridge to spend the weekend with Paul Cain. As you know."

He rang for the porter. "I would like this chair."

"But you can't, it's taken," said the porter.

"I'm sure you can arrange to have the person moved," and Michael slipped him a five-dollar bill.

Fiona was amazed and secretly pleased that Michael had taken such quick action.

"You haven't called me at all, Michael. You have bad manners. I've been told so by a number of people." She made up that bit.

He ignored the remark and rang the bell. "Let's have a drink and make up. You know I planned to get hold of you soon. Really, I've thought a lot about that night at Jimmy's.

"Two very dry martinis, Tanqueray Gin if you have it, or Beef-eater."

"We only have prepared mixes," the porter answered crisply.

It was Michael's way to order, not to suggest.

The drinks came. Fiona took a big sip and then picked out the olive and swallowed it. She was nervous that Michael had taken over.

The train raced on past New Haven. It was a bright, clear, crisp American fall day. The leaves were just starting to turn.

Fiona looked out across the way at the glistening railroad track and their silhouettes together in the roadbed. Michael swung his chair so close it touched hers. As the train took the long curve outside New London, their silhouettes disappeared.

Michael finished his drink and ordered two more. "I feel like champagne and music. See, Fiona, you've lifted my tired spirits."

She had forgotten about the weekend already. She had forgotten about Paul Cain. Michael had taken over. She accepted the second dry martini from Michael, who said the prepared mix wasn't bad at all, but nothing compared to his.

The second martini humbled Michael and made Fiona weaker and stronger at the same time.

She thought of leaving a message for Paul at the hotel, to tell him she wouldn't be coming for the weekend. She rationalized it was better for Catherine and Paul that she didn't see him. She would tell Paul her mother wasn't well and she had to return to the city.

Michael and Fiona brushed legs. She didn't move her chair. She

42

smiled sweetly, almost innocently, and then looked straight into his eyes.

Michael knew it was the right moment to say, "Let's forget our plans, let's go to dinner at the hotel, then maybe the theater. We can leave this weekend to the undergraduates and be alone with each other. This is our weekend."

They were almost at the station. Fiona did not hesitate. She had broken away for the first time and felt free from her family. She was no longer smothered with the boring comme il faut life of her parents. She was ready to be savage.

Michael had stayed many times at the hotel with his family. He only had to pick up the telephone from South Station to have the same suite and the same flowers his father had always arranged for his mother.

The hotel receptionist immediately recognized him. They got into the big elevator. It smelled of Flit, Fiona thought. They went to the twelfth floor. They didn't say a word to each other and both couldn't wait to have the manager, who insisted on showing the suite, leave them alone. He opened the door and Fiona saw two large vases filled with long-stemmed white roses mixed with white phlox. The living room was large and overlooked the park.

Fiona walked to a window and lifted the white shade. So Boston, old cloth shades, she thought.

"I'm embarrassed," she said forcefully.

"About what?" Michael answered in a worried tone.

"About what to tell Paul," she said, looking out at the park.

"I'll take care of that," Michael said, going quickly to the phone next to the overstuffed chair near a window.

He picked up the phone and at the same time reached out to take her hand.

"Reception, please. I've an important message for Paul Cain. You know him, of course," Michael said, looking at Fiona. He shook his head and put his hand over the receiver. "They don't know him," he said with delight.

Michael went on, "Please tell him Fiona Stephenson phoned to say she couldn't make it. And, yes, say she's frightfully sorry. Make sure he gets the message. He will be looking for her."

He hung up the phone and went over to Fiona.

Two bottles of Taittinger brut champagne, 1955, rested temptingly in silver ice buckets. Michael opened the first bottle himself. Fiona unzipped her bag and rang for the maid, who arrived immediately. "Please, would you mind unpacking this case." The maid first was startled to think such a young lady couldn't unpack her own bag, but the manager had told her earlier, ". . . all the discreet service they need."

Michael filled the champagne goblets and took the two glasses into the bedroom. He put his down on the table and gave Fiona hers, gently putting his arm around her waist, just as she took a sip. "The bubbles tickle my nose," she said, moving in toward Michael. He couldn't kiss her, the goblet was touching her lips.

Fiona pushed his hand away from her waist as she slipped into a big purple and white tulip chintz armchair. She kicked off her shoes, bit into the glass and fixed her eyes on Michael. Following Fiona to the chair, Michael sat at her feet. He took her foot, felt her slender ankle and put his lips to his goblet and finished the champagne.

She thought she had planned her scene perfectly. She was playing the part of the temptress. Michael thought he had planned the scene even better. He was the seducer. He had seduced many times before. He had never failed in love.

Fiona put her hand on Michael's head and ran her hand through the thick blond hair, digging her nails into his scalp. Michael was startled, "Hey, that hurts." And he quickly got up from the floor, lifted Fiona into his arms and carried her to the bed with his lips on hers. He lowered her dress below the breast. He kissed her and took the dress farther down, still kissing her.

She was breathing heavily. Her mouth was open, her tongue rubbing her lips. Michael took off his clothes and sat down next to her on the bed. Fiona lay nude.

They were together for two hours in a deep sleep, their bodies satisfied. Even Fiona's perfume had a different smell. Her hair was spread over the pillow. Michael awoke her by stroking her toes with his foot.

He went into the living room. He snapped a white rose from the stem and carried it to her on the palm of his hand. He knelt on the floor. They were face to face, their eyes locked together. Fiona saw the rose and Michael's face so close.

"It was wonderful, divine, darling. I love you," Fiona said.

Michael didn't respond. He smiled, got up off the floor and went to the phone and ordered dinner. "Caviar, Iranian if you have it."

Michael returned to the room, put on his clothes as if it were any other night before dinner.

Fiona quickly got up off the bed and went into the bathroom and ran water for a bath. "Why don't these maids clean out the tub?" she called out to Michael, who was finishing off the first champagne bottle and preparing to open the other.

The door buzzer jarred Michael. He let in the waiter, who pushed the wobbling cart, with a bouquet of red roses, through the door. A mound of caviar in a big blue tin, trimmed toast, chopped onions, egg whites, yolks, and Russian vodka smothered in ice, all ready to be served.

"Harvard lost again, twelve to three. It was a dull game," the waiter told Michael.

5

ENGAGED

Fiona had imagined all the beautiful dreams about proposals. She never had thought Michael, or anyone else for that matter, would ask her to marry the way he did it. But then, wasn't that half of Michael's charm? He acted so quickly and went all the way.

They were coming back on the train after the weekend in Boston. The same colored porter was in the parlor car on the return trip and he remembered them. A good omen, Fiona thought. Michael didn't even recognize the porter. He was too busy thinking about the weekend and especially Saturday afternoon at the hotel. After they had made love, he had pulled up the window shades and looked out into the park lake. Two swans swam majestically pressing together. They looked right that way, always together, swimming back and forth across the lake. Somehow then he knew Fiona belonged with him, was, indeed, already his.

"It's not going to be like the last time when we said good-bye?" Fiona asked, interrupting Michael's private thoughts.

"Not at all," he answered. Michael knew she was prodding him to say he loved her. He refused. That would be too banal.

They paused and sipped their drinks.

"What about tonight. Are you free?" he asked.

"Of course, if we are going to be together alone," Fiona said, swinging her chair around to Michael.

"And the rest of the week? Every night and maybe even for luncheon. Are you busy?" Michael added coyly.

"All the week," Fiona said, playing the game.

"We will have to make it formal if we are together that often. You know how they talk in New York," he said thinking of the expression on Cain's face when he learned that they had been in Boston.

"Do I interpret you to mean?" Fiona asked, trying to be blasé.

"Yes, you do interpret me correctly," Michael said mechanically.

"When?" Fiona asked.

"That's not up to me. That's up to my bride," Michael said and he reached out to take her hand. He kissed her fingers and rang for the porter.

Their engagement would not be announced officially until after Christmas, but for a few hundred intimate friends of both families La . . . . . , one of New York's smartest watering and eating places, had been reserved for a Thursday night in early December.

Fiona looked over her Paris dress sketches from couturier Yves St. Laurent and was delighted she had selected back in August a white silk organdy with embroidered navy polka dots. The dress had two ruffled layers just above the hem and was promised for delivery for the winter season. Fiona had telephoned Paris to ask them to finish the dress in time for their party. She planned to have her hair done by Albert with a longer than usual braid intertwined with real daisies.

La . . . . . has pea green walls, middle class Montmartre Utrilloish paintings, red velvet banquettes, good French food, and a Swiss headwaiter who never stops smiling. George, the headwaiter, and Monsieur Lafitte, the owner, weren't a bit worried about the menu; Mrs. Stephenson had seen to that, but no one could decide where to put the orchestra, The Knockers, from Helen's Cellar. Fiona insisted the party "swing" for her young friends.

It began at eight. The florist had just finished the floral arrangements—on each table garnette roses and daisies in Napoleon brandy snifters and long-stemmed white roses in every corner of the restaurant.

Michael and Fiona arrived with Fiona's parents. They had been drinking dry vodka martinis at the Stephenson apartment and everyone was still tense.

The Stephensons had grave doubts about the marriage. Mrs. Stephenson thought Fiona was going beneath her social strata. Mr. Stephenson, a self-made man, considered Michael immature, untested, too sophisticated for his years. But wasn't that true of that generation? They grew up before their time.

Mrs. Stephenson entered the restaurant with a white ermine coat draped over her shoulders. Mr. Stephenson had a white nosegay in his lapel. Michael wore his new double-breasted dinner jacket, received just that morning by air mail from his London tailor.

"Shall we check our furs, darling, or leave them on?" Fiona asked her mother.

George, the headwaiter, smiled and bowed and smiled again. "Bon soir, Madame Stephenson." Monsieur Lafitte rushed out of the kitchen. Mr. Stephenson greeted him warmly, "You are so nice to let us have the restaurant." Monsieur Lafitte nervously held his hands together and smiled at everyone.

"A little Dom Perignon to begin the evening," said Mr. Stephenson.

"Thank god I did the seating arrangement this morning," Mrs. Stephenson said, sitting down on the nearest banquette and letting the ermine fall to one side. "I have a frightful headache again."

"Sorry, darling, do you want another aspirin?" Fiona asked, pushing her braid back over her shoulder. She had made sure the daisies were still attached.

Michael paced nervously up and down looking at the guest cards. The Cains had been invited too, but they were having a party of their own in Washington. Michael took the list from the headwaiter. Geraldine and George, friends. Gerry was active in all sorts of theatrical causes, the angel for struggling artists. George, a doctor, had a unique social position in New York because of his Boston family background. New England and right, thought Michael. Homer, the writer, sitting next to Mrs. Stephenson. That figured. She always had Homer nearby. He talked and gossiped and kept her amused.

Michael looked for Uncle John's card. Uncle John, the leader of the Chase clan, even told Michael's father what to do. Uncle John had made the fortune and kept making millions more through shrewd investments. He was the only person in the family who terrified Michael.

Fifteen minutes late the guests started arriving. Homer checked his red-lined cape and cane, took several short, dancing steps, embraced Mrs. Stephenson, kissing her on both cheeks and said, "Darling, darling, how wonderful." He gently gave his damp hand to Fiona, looked admiringly at Michael and whispered in his ear, "What a perfect marriage, my dear boy, such a beautiful joining of forces. Of course, she's divine."

The Chases arrived. Mrs. Chase was dressed in a yellow and purple flowered Mainbocher sheath. Her ruby earrings dropped heavily from her ear lobes. Her dyed blond hair needed retouching. She had been drinking again. Fiona could see Mrs. Chase's mouth drooping to one side as she kissed Mr. Stephenson. "Really, you are sweet to do this for the children. We're so thrilled about Michael. He is a fine boy, you know," she said to Mr. Stephenson, who was finally rescued by Mr. Chase.

Both fathers went to the bar.

"It's a fine marriage," Mr. Chase said. "You know we have great plans for Michael. I am sure after he works in Senator Borden's law firm he will be prepared to run for political office and win." Mr. Chase was anxious to enlist the support of the Stephenson publications for Michael's career. Mr. Stephenson was a Republican and resented those people with money who had deserted to the other side. A product of the big, rich machine, he thought to himself.

"My daughter will not hinder his career. As a matter of fact, she will help him to get elected. Remember the Kennedys. Look what they did together. Jacqueline Kennedy was always at his side, in public anyway," he said with a snide smile.

Mrs. Chase had changed to martinis and had already finished one. She sat down next to Mrs. Stephenson and looked her over thinking, she's so damn chic and so superior. Homer gave a sickly smile and moved away a little. "Darling," said Mrs. Chase, "what are we going to do about their apartment? Something with a lovely view of the river would be just the thing."

Mrs. Stephenson had already decided on the apartment and Fiona had selected the decorator. Fiona had gone out of her way to use a decorator her mother had never employed.

Mrs. Stephenson got up from the table to greet the guests. Mrs. Chase sat and sipped, "Tell me, Homer, who is the lady arriving in the chinchilla wrap and those emeralds? I hate chinchilla. It's so vulgar."

Homer Breadcraft ignored that remark, but said, "Tell me, Mrs. Chase, about your days in Hollywood."

"What days in Hollywood?" and she stammered, "I have never done any acting at all."

Just at that moment Michael arrived. He had been seating Uncle John. Michael heard Homer say "Hollywood." He blushed and leaned down, kissed his mother and took her hand to steady her. "Now Mother, don't you think we had better have some dinner?" Mrs. Chase adjusted her left earring, twisted her mouth to one side and said acidly, "Perhaps we had better manger." Homer Breadcraft knew he had made his point.

Michael and Fiona had hardly spoken to each other. They didn't have a chance, they were so busy circulating. "They really are a divine couple," from table 29. "She's beautiful, so young, but her mother seems hardly happy," table 4, right in the front. Michael and Fiona met briefly. He brushed his hand against hers and then they both moved on.

They paid their respects to Uncle John, who sat propped up in a corner. He had argued with the headwaiter about the wine, Montrachet, 1960, chilled too quickly, and he suggested Monsieur Lafitte pay attention to the temperature of his wine cellar. Uncle John wore thick-lensed glasses in thin silver frames, which kept slipping down his nose. Each time he took a bite of the mousse au sole swimming in champagne sauce, he pushed his glasses back up.

"You're lucky, my boy, to have this girl," he said to Michael and Fiona. She didn't like being called a girl. "Now, Michael, if you get to work in that Borden law firm, there's a bright future for you. Don't get too spoiled with all these parties, fine food, and being mondain. This merry whirl can't go on forever," and pursing his lips together he took a long drink of wine.

They have their problems already, he said to himself with relish, as Michael and Fiona moved on to table 25. The orchestra started up and played on until three in the morning. Michael and Fiona went home separately, too tired to say more than good night.

6

PLAYHOUSE

The engagement was announced solemnly in the New York press, which proceeded to make an unprecedented fuss about the wedding. Fiona's wedding dress became the source of great speculation and the social world, those few of the élite invited to the wedding, which was to be held in a small Connecticut church, were busily planning their own wardrobes. Bergdorf Goodman was the clearing house for who was wearing what.

Michael and Fiona had received their duplex apartment from Mr. Stephenson as a wedding present. It was on Fifty-seventh Street and overlooked the East River. Added to Michael's already fine art collection were a Giacometti, a Miró, two Braque oils, and a fine Sam Francis, which was so large it required a special wiring system to be hung on the walls.

The decorator had decided to do the apartment in bright colors, many different Brunschwig chintzes, some especially designed in England. Their pale yellow bedroom was furnished with a light beige rug, a massive Louis XV black desk trimmed in gold metal, and, in the center of the room, a fine four-poster canopy bed. The canopy was blue, white, and red flowered chintz, lined in bright yellow glazed chintz to match the curtains. Michael found the bed through an agent who had bid for it at an auction in Georgia.

Michael and Fiona spent two months combing New York's antique stores. One month before the wedding the twelve-room apartment was completely furnished and only the terrace garden was left unfinished. The landscape architect had not come up with the right plan for the terrace, which needed a great deal of work because water leaked through to the floor below.

They never took time to pause and reflect. They were too busy buying and going to parties. They would start out with everything, an apartment filled with the finest furnishings and paintings and decorated to perfection. They were never concerned with what an object cost. They only saw what they wanted and they knew it could be theirs. They never took the time to think what would be left to do when they settled down. They both had an insatiable desire to own objects symbolizing elegance, taste, and security.

Michael's dressing room was lined with beige and white mattress ticking. He had borrowed the idea from a Paris apartment. The George II mahogany clothes horse was placed discreetly next to a small black leather couch. His black riding boots were so shiny they reflected the mustard-colored tea cannister lamp on the Hepplewhite library steps. A Vesey glass table in front of the couch was filled with silver fish, some with precious stones in their eyes. The rest of his fish collection was in the library, encased in a red velvet book shelf. Michael had not yet found the right lighting and was in the process of putting in glass shelves, the better to show the fish. He was born under Pisces, the twelfth sign in the zodiac.

Fiona's Armorial Lowestoft collection (mostly wedding presents), vivid blues, whites, oranges—plates, platters, cups and saucers—were on her library shelves.

The only problem in the library was the Louis XVI mantel, purchased at a Salle Drouot auction in Paris. The stone mason and the chimney man had installed the mantel after widening the fireplace, which coughed black smoke. Michael had told them to do anything to make it work.

Michael and Fiona both had the taste and the education to know the best and they did not rely entirely on the opinions of decorators, or antique dealers, but spent time reading up on the history of fine objects. Only for his art collection did Michael consult Paul Dernay of the Metropolitan Museum.

Michael took interest in Fiona's trousseau. He had definite ideas on how she should look at all times. Fiona had a tendency to dress to suit her rebellious mood. She was mad for short skirts, the English look (loving hands at home clothes) now all the rage. Michael wanted Fiona to stay within the bounds of safe, expensive Mainbocher staples, the traditional socially sure fashion for years. Fiona argued she wouldn't dress like Michael's mother, who had no style, but instead she wanted her own style. Fiona was on her way to becoming a fashion plate. She had already been noticed wearing the innish fashions at the three "La's" and the one "Le". It amused her to be photographed by the press, but secretly disturbed her mother, who had never dreamed of being in fashion when she was that young.

Before the wedding Michael and Fiona were in a sense married. They had made love, but not too often. That was perfectly normal in this day and age. What was abnormal was that their house was already built.

Fiona had once mentioned children to Michael. He merely shrugged his shoulders and said, "We aren't ready for them yet. We have to wait five years, until we get settled. The right time will come when we can start a family." Fiona placidly accepted his answer.

They discussed his career. Michael made it clear from the beginning that Fiona would have to work hard for his political success. She was perfectly willing and her interest in pushing her husband was more than normal because she really had nothing else to do. Her house had been built, charity balls and benefits bored her, and they couldn't spend all the time at parties, although they both did enjoy parties with the right people.

Before the date of the wedding, Fiona and Michael played house in the dressing room of their own apartment, and always before going out they would meet there over a drink, to discuss the plans for the evening.

One such evening, Fiona came in the room, walked over to the large pedestal English globe and with two fingers spun the world

54

around twice. Michael was already drinking a martini. They both had dressed earlier at their parents' apartments and then met at their new home. Michael removed his dinner jacket and changed into his white piped and initialed black silk dressing gown and his monogrammed red velvet bedroom slippers.

Fiona stood at the globe and looked down at Michael. "May I have a martini, darling?" and she adjusted the ruffled collar on her short, white organdy evening dress. Her braid was tied with a tiny red bow.

"Really, the apartment is divine." Fiona was rambling on in her bubbly way.

"But it's not all finished. It's taking such a long time," Michael added casually.

"Don't be silly, Michael, we've done the whole thing in a couple of months. What could be quicker than that? Just wait until I get Luigi to come in and help me with Mummy's flowers." Fiona kept talking.

As he checked the seaming of the beige mattress ticking on the wall, Michael interrupted: "You mean you're using your mother's flowers? Haven't you got the imagination to select your own?" He scowled.

"Where can I get fresh flowers like Mummy's?" Fiona asked.

"Go to a good florist in New York. Any good florist. You've got to know, to have your own style, even in flowers," and Michael finalized his order by sitting down on the sofa and looking straight at Fiona.

She put his riding boots away in the closet. "That's where they belong. Not out here," she said.

"I like them outside. Do you mind? They belong out in a man's room," and he removed them from the closet.

Fiona could see Michael was in a bad mood.

"You know," she began, hoping to distract him, "Catherine called today. She and Paul are marrying a day after us. Isn't it divine? They're getting married too."

Michael hated the word divine. So pretentious, he thought to himself.

"Well, isn't it divine?" Fiona said again.

Michael shrugged and answered. "I expected they would when she came back from Paris. What a pity. We'll be in the tropics, far away from another boring wedding."

His face reddened and, as always when he became tense, the back of his neck broke out in red spots.

"What's wrong, darling, were you fond of her, or something? You always said she was a bit horsey and kept talking about her horsey legs."

Michael turned away and walked toward the window. "I've got to tell you something, Fiona. It's silly, I know, to get upset, but I learned today Cain is running for the House from New York City and he's expected to win."

Fiona didn't respond immediately. She stood looking blankly at Michael. She knew what Cain's running for the House meant. Michael had wanted to be the youngest member, but Cain had beaten him to it.

"Well, darling," Fiona said with a sweet smile, "the way we're acting you'd think he was a Republican who'd defeated us. Our day will come."

Michael couldn't even think of the wedding now, which was a week away, only of Cain and that he was going to marry Catherine, who, with her family connections and fortune, certainly would be a great help to his career.

Fiona took a long sip of her drink. "Think, we'll be off to the West Indies alone and I'm sure when we're there all this will be far behind us. I long to take off my shoes and relax. I don't think this wedding will ever be over. What's the plan for tonight?"

"We're going to Beebe and John's for cocktails and I think Senator Borden will be there. I asked John this morning if the table could be arranged so that you can be next to him."

Fiona sighed. "He's such a bore."

Michael banged his glass down on the table and shouted, "For god's sake, Fiona, it's not going to be the last boring dinner you're going to have to attend."

"I know," she said softly, "but we spend our evenings always with older people and all we talk about is politics and world affairs."

Michael didn't answer her, he just continued drinking, then, looking at his watch, said, "It's time to go."

56

He slipped out of his dressing gown and changed back into his tuxedo. He left the slippers on the floor and the dressing gown spread over a couch. Pierre and Mary, the couple they had hired, would fix the room.

Fiona couldn't forget that her friend Catherine was going to marry a probable future Congressman. And one day he would be a Senator, she was sure. She remembered Catherine had always said she would marry an important man. Fiona decided she was going to work harder than ever for Michael. She took Michael firmly by the arm and they left the apartment.

7

COUNTRY LIFE

The next morning Fiona got up early, dressed in her riding clothes, and at nine was on the Connecticut Turnpike speeding at sixty miles an hour to the Bay Ridge Hunt Club. She wished Jonathan, her mother's chauffeur, would go even faster. She slid down into the back seat of the black Jaguar with red leather seats and tried reading a fashion magazine.

Fiona looked forward to riding at the club, but she dreaded luncheon at Michael's sister's suburban home, complete with swimming pool, jungle gyms, two ponies, bird houses, and a swarm of children —three boys and one girl, her nephews and niece to be.

As she read the magazine, she thought, I will telephone this morning and agree to the interview. They had wanted to write Fiona up as one of those beautiful people. She had been slightly concerned. The photographer also wanted to do four pages on the interior of the new apartment. Fiona found it a bit odd to photograph their new apartment before the marriage. Somehow, it meant bad luck. But then the editor, Mrs. Lallie Pentcheck, had assured them the pictures wouldn't appear until months after the marriage. Michael agreed to the photo story because he was naturally proud to show off his new home to the magazine's sophisticated subscribers, many his friends.

Uncle John had warned him at luncheon not to play the rich man with great taste too much, because this role could nauseate the public. Fiona and Michael rationalized that a certain amount of publicity was needed now.

At the stables, Fiona got out of the Jaguar, walked briskly across the field, slapping the riding crop against her leg, and went into the club office.

Miss Howard, with her hair tied in a bun, sat behind a desk with a cigaret dangling from her mouth. She was about seventy, always had been a Miss and liked it that way. She was manager of the club and spoke with an English accent.

She didn't bother to look up when Fiona shut the screen door. She had seen the Jaguar arriving and didn't feel there was any reason to make a fuss over "this young girl" just because she had so much money and, really, because she was just too damn beautiful. She went on smoking, dropping ashes on the paper where she was adding up figures. She never did get the bills out on time and then if the members didn't pay immediately, she got after them.

"Good morning, Miss Howard," and Fiona emphasized the Miss.

Miss Howard looked up from her work, nodded and said, "Good morning." She went back to the addition, took a deep puff on her cigaret, saying, "Yes, Miss Stephenson, Terence is ready."

Fiona paused at the door. She thought Miss Howard would at least say something about the wedding. She let the door bang as she went out to the stables.

"Good morning, Jim. I'm ready for a good ride."

"Miss Stephenson, Terence is in fine shape this morning. He's some horse."

Fiona walked up to the first stall, opened the door and stroked Terence, a chestnut gelding. He pawed the straw.

She led Terence out, quickly mounted without the steps and was off, first into the ring to get the feel of Terence and then out into the open field.

Fiona felt as free as the wind on a horse. She loved the control she had over an animal so beautiful, so powerful. She let Terence out into a gallop, her knees and legs pressed against the warm, moving body, and they took the first fence of the outside course.

Miss Howard turned from her desk and couldn't help but admire Fiona's riding style. It was a fine sight to see a beautiful girl riding so well. That girl really has everything, Miss Howard thought to herself and turned back to her work.

Fiona rode for an hour. She thought, if only Michael would learn the discipline and perfect control that goes with experienced riding. Michael's only association with riding were those shiny black boots in his dressing room and they had never been near a horse. He disliked most women who rode and always said riding was for mannish women. It made their legs like Catherine's—and Fiona smiled to herself because she knew her legs were perfect.

She returned slowly to the club. The older women, the dedicated riders, the ones Michael couldn't stand, were out for their morning ride. They were all dressed in shiny boots, ratcatcher shirts, English jackets. They rode side by side, each leg brushing against the next rider. As Fiona passed, they nodded stiffly, an instructor doffed his hat and Terence turned his head to take a look at the other horses.

Fiona slid down and handed the reins to the groom. Soon she was in the Jaguar speeding over the private club road, with the dust billowing up behind.

Michael's sister, Georgette Jordan, dreaded the visit as much as Fiona did.

Georgette was plainly pretty, with a cherubic face, red hair, ginger snap freckles and blue eyes. When the Jaguar drove up, she had just been talking to the private school headmaster. Her four children had been raising a fuss on the bus. He had suggested that possibly the Jordan children had a basic psychological problem and certain insecurity at home, perhaps a lack of love and Dr. Henrod, the school psychiatrist, ought to be consulted.

"Well, what was so serious on the bus? I don't think pea shooters and shooting paper clips with rubber bands really so bad." She hung up the phone in a huff and turned to Mary, the colored maid, who was listening the whole time as she blew the dust across the table.

Georgette continued to the maid, "Last winter he called me up because Veronica stood in the corner of the ice rink and didn't skate. They made a big thing about that and said it wasn't normal. I asked

60

Veronica and she told me she didn't like to skate and hated the cold ice. I told her to go on hating skating and that finished that."

Mrs. Jordan hadn't bothered to change for Fiona. She had on overall red pedal pushers, red sneakers, with holes on the left foot and a white Brooks Brothers button-down shirt.

Fiona got out of the car carrying a crocodile dressing case and rushed up to Georgette. "Darling, it's marvelous to see you. Everything looks so pretty in the garden and you're looking so well." She wondered if Georgette ever went to the hairdresser. God she looks a mess, Fiona thought as she went into the front hallway. "The house is divine, darling." Fiona hated modern architecture, especially with all the goldfish bowl glass. "I see you've bought lots of new things. That Lowestoft teapot is superb. Where did you find it?"

"Right here in town," said Georgette in a bored tone.

Georgette, like her brother and the whole Chase family, was an avid collector of objects. She was a compulsive buyer of anything that pleased her fancy for the moment.

Fiona asked to be excused. She wanted to change from her riding clothes and wash up a bit.

She went to the powder room, closed the door and took out a grey dress with a tiny white bow at the neck. She put on the dress, brushed her hair back, looked at herself in the mirror and thought her coloring high and pretty, as always after riding. She lipsticked her lips with a new pale pink, Dior Number 23. She took a quick look around the powder room, dark blue velvet carpeting, dark red toilet fixtures, fresh daisies (she put one in her hair), and yellow walls, the same shade as in our bedroom, she realized. Of course, we had the same decorator. I must be careful next time, she said to herself. She left the room so hurriedly she forgot to remove the $159.95 Bendel price tag from the dress.

Georgette was sipping a Campari with twisted lemon peel and she handed Fiona a drink. She saw the price tag on Fiona's arm, but said nothing. So did Mary, the maid. Mary looked knowingly at Mrs. Jordan. They both smiled.

"Well, I suppose you're getting all ready for the wedding. I understand there are to be more than five hundred guests. You know we

61

had seven hundred and fifty to ours and it was too much. It's a problem seating all those people," she said.

Fiona sat down in a yellow and purple flowered chintz chair. The colors were so vulgar and bright. It crossed Fiona's mind Georgette's taste was a bit Hollywood like her mother's.

"The seating, you know, is no problem for Mummy. She has Henry, who has a fabulous memory, just perfect for our wedding reception. We aren't having a tent. If it rains, Brooks Farms is large enough to take the guests inside. Mummy has Willy doing the decorating. Masses of white, blue, and pink wicker chairs are to be scattered out on the grass terrace, so that little groups can gather. You know, folding chairs look so commercial, like a business party. We're decorating the trees with long white silk streamers and blue and green porcelain balls, some with lights inside. The servants are wearing white and blue uniforms to blend in with the decorations. Mummy really is giving her all to make our wedding special. She wants the animals—the horses, the sheep and goats—grazing in the distance. Anemones, or roses, white roses, are to float in the pool. You know Mummy's aversion to swimming pools. She's always trying to fill them up with something beautiful."

Georgette looked at Mary, who was still listening and pretending to clean.

Georgette thought her husband Peter was right. The Stephensons were so efficient it was scary. They did everything perfectly, with so much work. She finished her drink and went to the bar and poured another.

Georgette secretly resented the social life of Michael and Fiona. She loved her rambling suburban house filled with animals, two Great Danes, two Siamese, and a rare St. Vincent parrot. Peter, who was in charge of stockholder relations for a steel company, kept telling her she wasn't made for New York's social life, but she read with envy about the wonderful, gay parties in the social columns and never missed Eugenia Sheppard.

Fiona sat quietly observing Georgette, all of the time thinking she couldn't lead this square, regimented suburban life. Georgette looked tired and so harassed.

"Your mother and father," Fiona began hesitatingly, "have been

62

so sweet to us. They've helped us decorate the apartment with so many beautiful things."

Fiona, lighting a cigaret, realized she was wearing the Bendel price tag and tore it off.

They ate luncheon outside on the terrace next to an Italian fountain.

"Darling," said Fiona, "we really haven't had a chance to know each other. There are so many things we should do together. For a long time I've been waiting to ask you about Michael, when you were children. He tells me he is terribly close to you and you know how much he loves you."

Georgette picked up her fork and knife and cut the avocado pear filled with chicken salad right down the middle. "Of course we adore each other. We had to stick together you know. Mother was so difficult. Finally Michael went off and left me holding the bag. You know Mother's drinking hasn't been amusing.

"Daddy was so busy making money and running to New York for playtime that he ignored all of us. I don't mean he isn't a kind man. He's generous, always giving us presents, big presents—understanding too, but he doesn't understand our problems. He hasn't time to. Maybe he would rather forget all troubles."

Fiona had never heard Michael talk this way about his mother and father. She knew Mrs. Chase drank, but then Michael had always said she had been the perfect mother, "doing everything we wanted her to do."

"Funny," said Fiona, "Michael seemed to adore his mother and got along with her so well."

"Of course he did. He was never there and when he was, he bossed all of us. I am sure you're going to see what I mean." Georgette got up from the table to get the coffee.

While Fiona was visiting Georgette, Michael was attending the annual meeting of Chase and Company, the family's investment firm.

The meeting was held in the board room. They met with their financial advisors to discuss the past performance and future of their world-wide investments.

It had been an excellent year. They had passed their budget by fifty per cent in earned income. The Chase firm was staffed with twenty-five specialists to guide the family on how best to use their money. They had a small research department, so keen that large public investment houses and banks watched carefully to see what Chase bought.

Alvin Merriweather, a principal in the firm, but not a family member, had just finished reading the complete report. Michael, attending the meeting for the first time, was bored. He looked around the mahogany paneled board room, silver water cannisters at each end of the table and baccarat glasses at each place. He scribbled on his black leather pad one arrow after the other in a continuous line. Picasso and Miró oil paintings lined the walls. The two artists don't belong together, Michael thought. ". . . and we expect to see over a million shares of Alliance Chemical and then we will reinvest in Crude," said Mr. Merriweather, blinking through his glasses and droning on like the civil servant to the family he was. And besides, Michael thought, the picture frames should be thin, stainless steel, not those pretentious heavy French frames, which no one used today, except Uncle John, who looked a little bored with the meeting himself.

Michael was convinced he could never enter the family business. He now knew that Wall Street wasn't for him.

Michael's father didn't say a word. As usual, he let Uncle John handle the funds and rarely did he advise on how his own money should be invested. He nervously fingered his pencil and from time to time drank from the water glass. Hubert Chase had accepted the secondary role to Uncle John. His car parts business was booming. He had all the money he would ever need and only one desire: to see his son succeed in public life, and for this purpose he'd use his fortune to back Michael.

He looked upon his son as a young god, truly given to the country to serve. He respected Michael's intelligence, was proud of his every move, and could not see him doing anything wrong. He had never disciplined Michael and had allowed him to dominate all their lives. Before Michael attended Yale Law, Uncle John had warned he would flunk out.

Uncle John had been wrong. Michael's grades had been excellent. Mr. Chase also remembered how Uncle John had cautioned him about sending Michael to Paris.

That's the wrong place, even for a summer. He should start work right away before going into the law firm. A government job, that would be easy to arrange.

Mr. Chase looked over at Uncle John, who was slouched in the black leather chair, with his arms resting on his well-defined stomach. He smiled to himself when he remembered Uncle John had said, "Michael is living too well, too soon. He'll be bored before he's middle-aged."

Now Hubert Chase held his hands together on the inlaid table and looked across admiringly at Michael. He was so proud and so pleased. He had but one worry, Michael's high blood pressure, but the doctors assured him there was no cause for concern. The blood pressure did keep him out of military service and for that they were all thankful.

Mr. Merriweather concluded his report, paused briefly, took off his glasses, rubbed his left eye and said, "And, may I say again, it's been a fine experience working for this firm and with such a fine family."

Uncle John thanked Mr. Merriweather, rose from the table quickly and went out of the room followed by his brother, who had trouble keeping up. Michael paused to let Mr. Merriweather go ahead. Mr. Merriweather only bowed and held out his hand and Michael went first, secure that in his first meeting with the firm Mr. Merriweather had recognized Michael's authority.

They took the tobacco leather covered elevator to the ground floor and went out into the street where a black Mercedes 600, with a small back window closed off with shade, stood at the curb. The New York license plate was JB 1118.

Michael, his father and Uncle John climbed into the back seat. Uncle John carried his French pigskin gloves in his left hand. He was never without them in the street. They symbolized the old days when he had been First Minister to France. They were off uptown to Le . . . . . for luncheon. They arrived at Fifty-seventh Street quickly. Uncle John pushed his way through the revolving door, stopping short inside, only to be bumped by his brother.

Henri Rouët, owner of Le . . . . . , shook Mr. John Chase's hand firmly, bowed to his brother and ignored Michael. He escorted the three gentlemen to a small table in front of the bar.

"Why this table, what about my usual table, the round banquette over to the side? Didn't George, my secretary, reserve?"

Michael was secretly pleased his uncle didn't get his table.

Monsieur Rouët, a big, heavy set man, with a small, tough-looking mouth, handed the menu to John Chase as much as to say please sit down and be quiet.

"Sorry, but the table was reserved for a party of four."

They all sat down. The waiters brought the cold lobster, flown in the night before from England and the sommelier uncorked the Muscadet.

Monsieur Rouët hovered over them just long enough to show he was interested, even though he hadn't been able to give the Chases the best table.

Uncle John wished he had ordered a dry martini ahead of time. He fingered his wine glass up and down and then turned directly to Michael.

"Now about that political career of yours, my boy. Your father and I are prepared to go all the way. I have contacted the important factions in the party and the top men seem quite ready to get together to help you. They realize, of course, they will get substantial backing from us, but, up until now, they have been completely subservient to Cain. The Cains are in and we are not and we've got to face the facts. The Cains are more powerful, they have money too and have used it well."

The revolving door turned and in stepped Senator Cain and Paul Cain. Michael was the first to see them. He gained control of himself quickly. He knew they would stop by and speak. Uncle John poured more wine, snapped his finger for the sommelier and ordered another bottle. As Monsieur Rouët was rushing to greet them, Uncle John stopped him, "The fresh mayonnaise is superb, just enough vinegar." Michael's father turned uncomfortably in his seat and let his napkin drop to the floor.

The Cains approached. "Well, gentlemen, it's nice to see you here all together," the Senator said, leaning on his black cane with the golden eagle head, "in my favorite eating spot."

"Hello, Michael. You're looking well and happy. You should be, you've got Fiona. Send her my love and tell her she really missed a good weekend," Paul Cain said with a twinkle in his eye. The Chases were all standing and shaking hands with the Cains.

Mrs. Cain and Catherine arrived later. Catherine spun out of the door and into the eyes of all the men. She looked ravishing and as she brushed her hair back from her eyes she smiled gently. She saw Michael first and came over to him. He got up and took her hand. He did not kiss her, but wanted to. Uncle John, struggling up from the table, reluctantly put his wine down. Mr. Chase stood there, his face reddened and his mouth frozen into a permanent smile.

"How wonderful to see you. We can't wait for the wedding, but you really are the naughty ones, escaping to the West Indies before ours," said Catherine, as she made her way to the other table.

The Chases all had the same thought. Where would the Cains stand on Michael? Would they see to it he had a chance to rise in the party, or would they see to it that Michael burned out like a fifteen-watt light bulb?

Most likely the Cains, unconcerned about Michael, and supposing all along he would try for some political office, considered the chances for success remote. Paul Cain had already laid plans for his campaign and *his* chances were excellent. The Chases knew they had been outmaneuvered. Michael was smart enough to realize that through his father, Paul could exert some control on Michael's political future. If Paul won, it would make matters even worse. The waiter interrupted his anxious thoughts.

"A poire, Monsieur?" he asked.

"Yes, thank you," and Michael knew he shouldn't. His head already ached after the white Burgundy.

The Chases lingered over the pear brandy and coffee long enough to make sure the Cains would leave first.

Paul escorted Catherine to the revolving door. They stopped, turned back and waved to Michael. How confident they looked together, Michael thought. One by one the Cains went through the door out into the bright daylight and to a great future, Michael begrudgingly admitted to himself.

Michael returned to the apartment after the luncheon for a short nap. The Cains were pounding in his head and he couldn't sleep. He waited impatiently for Fiona to return from the country.

Fiona came into the dressing room. Michael thought she looked tired and couldn't help comparing her with Catherine. Catherine had seemed more sure of herself, gayer, although not as beautiful. At least Fiona is more beautiful. That thought satisfied him.

"Well, darling, did you have a nice, successful day? How was the riding?" he asked perfunctorily, not at all interested.

She answered in the same tone, "Everything was fine. I had a nice visit with your sister. And how did it go with Uncle John?"

"Oh just fine, successful meeting and good luncheon." He didn't once mention the Cains.

They were going out to dinner.

8

TROPICS

Michael and Fiona felt they had really been married three months before the ceremony and walked through their beautiful wedding, dull and prearranged to the nth degree.

Michael said the reception was "never to be forgotten."

"It's a shame we were so tired. We couldn't enjoy one minute. There were too many people to see and all at once they were all over us," he said sitting on Fiona's bed.

They were spending the wedding night at Brooks Farms in Fiona's room, the blue room, where she had grown up.

Fiona was in the bathroom, undressing, and the water was running into the bathtub.

"Do you really have to take a bath?" he asked. "You had one this morning. I've never known anyone who bathes so often. And besides it's our wedding night."

Fiona didn't hear him. She was immersed in a bubble bath and the water was still filling up to the top, the way she liked it.

Michael looked around the room. So damn much blue. Depressing he thought and he realized the same blues were in their apartment. He looked down at the blue bedsheets. I wonder if she decorated the room herself. Probably Willy.

Michael paced the floor, tying and untying the knot on his blue dressing gown. His blue pajamas lay spread out on the bed. The water was off now. He could hear Fiona moving around in the bathtub. He imagined her immersed in white bubbles up to her chin. Damn it. Is she ever coming out, he asked himself. He smiled, took off his dressing gown, let it drop to the floor, and ran to the bathroom door and burst in. Fiona giggled and started laughing. "Don't," she said, "you can't, the water will overflow all over the floor. Oh Michael, darling Michael." Michael reached out with his wet hand and slammed the door.

The next morning they left for Kennedy Airport in the Jaguar.

As Jonathan sped toward Kennedy to catch Pan American flight #229 direct to Barbados he looked into his rear-view mirror at Fiona and Michael. He saw them, each on one side of the car, looking blankly out of the window. What could a young couple about to go on their honeymoon be thinking? He remembered his and recalled how frightened he had been.

Fiona was sure of one thing. It was time she and Michael got away together to gather their thoughts. She knew neither one of them had been moved to love, or even compassion for each other, except for that one time in Boston. She thought of last night, the wedding night, the bathtub. Well, that really had been funny, a joke, not terribly satisfactory.

Michael stared out of the window at the burned-out grass along the highway. He couldn't imagine four weeks with Fiona on a twenty-acre island.

The island had to be fabulous. He had checked with Miss Pentcheck, the fashion magazine editor. She said it was the latest place, exclusive, divine. "So divine, my darlings," she had told Michael and Fiona at luncheon. "Once you are on that little silvery plane, shining in the sun, that you take from Barbados, you step into Paradise. You're cut off from the world. The telephone, a hand cranking model, never works." But what would they do there, Michael was thinking, as they approached Kennedy Airport. He put his hand to his mouth and decided. We will prepare ourselves for the future, our days ahead when we will be working.

Fiona wondered if she really had been that attracted to Michael and wouldn't it be disastrous to find out he was not really a good lover. She remembered her mother developing migraine when her father made romantic feints.

Jonathan drove up the Pan American ramp, swarming with Puerto Ricans, emplaning for those mass San Juan flights. They were all screaming, dragging their children and baggage around in every direction. Fiona couldn't face fighting the mob.

"Sit darling, it's going to be all right," Michael said softly to Fiona. "We will be taken care of."

A young man with a bushy mustache, dressed in a black blazer, came up to the car. "Chase party?" He spoke through the window to Jonathan.

He went to the back of the car, opened the door and introduced himself.

"I am here to assist you, courtesy Pan American. Please get out and we will check your baggage immediately." Fiona followed Michael out of the car, shook hands with Jonathan, who could say only, "Enjoy yourself, Miss Fiona. Sorry, I mean Mrs. Chase," and he smiled.

Michael directed the baggage. Fiona admired the way he looked: really handsome in his silver buttoned Edwardian double-breasted blazer, light blue cotton shirt and red and yellow bow tie, grey flannel cuffless trousers, black buckled John Lobb slippers.

Michael and Fiona pushed their way through the Puerto Ricans, who seemed noisier than ever. "Their flight has been canceled and they are so furious they've stopped us from boarding all flights. We called the police. It's been some mess today," and the Pan American man mopped his brow with a blue handkerchief.

"Mrs. Chase, you go right upstairs to the Clipper Club, take the private elevator at the bottom of the spiral staircase and we'll meet you there. They are expecting you. Possibly a cooling drink or a cup of tea will relax you before the flight."

Michael weighed in the eight heavy suitcases. He shook hands with the Pan American staff and his Sky Cap, like the perfect politician at work, and went upstairs to the Clipper Club to rejoin Fiona, who was sitting watching the big jets load.

She was glad to see Michael. Up there all alone looking out the

71

window, she suddenly became dependent on him. She had great fear of flying, but had never told Michael and she didn't intend to now.

"For old times' sake, let's have a double martini," she said to Michael, who was quite shocked at the word double.

"What old times' sake?" he snapped back, knowing full well Fiona was thinking of the train trip to Boston.

On the plane, First Class seats were reserved for them. They fastened their seat belts and waited for the takeoff.

"Darling, I can see you loathe flying. The thing to do is to keep busy reading, or doing something."

Fiona reached down and pulled out of her chocolate brown Gucci bag a canvas, needle, and multicolored wool threads. "This is my new pastime," she said to Michael, "needle point. I thought the rug would look wonderful next to our Queen Anne desk." She put the needle in the canvas, drawing the wool through for the first stitch. "A symbol of our marriage," she said, teasing Michael.

The plane waited in line behind the TWA flight and then turned slowly onto the runway: the screeching roar, the ground moving faster and faster, up and then suddenly a drop down, up again and a sharp turn to the left. As they went through the clouds into the bright blue sky, Fiona realized she was clutching Michael's hand.

Her hand is damp, thought Michael, she really is frightened. He realized how dependent on him Fiona had become. It made him feel stronger, even superior. He knew she would be willing to do what he wanted, and obedience, for him, meant the perfect wife. They ordered their martinis and as he sucked the smooth steeped-in-gin olive he smiled at Fiona, who leaned over and kissed him.

They flew south out over the water. After lunch, Michael and Fiona dozed. She woke up first. She had been having a nightmare. She didn't have them often. She dreamed Michael had refused to marry her, but there he was now, right next to her. She wanted to kiss him again, but the stewardess came with tea.

Michael didn't dream. He was tired, but happy to be away from family and friends. He had thought he was independent, but it dawned on him now that he wasn't. Uncle John's final words were, "We are behind you, Michael," and Michael thought to himself, I should be thankful. Look what's going to happen to me. I have everything. He took Fiona's hand.

The plane made the approach to Barbados low over the windward side of the island. The sea was choppy and the heavy cloud cover moved fast over the water. The trees were permanently bent forward fighting the trade winds blowing across the runway. As the plane swooped down, water flew up. It had been raining. Just beyond the silver wing tip in the lush green field, Fiona saw a black cow grazing. The cow munched away. The plane was just another big, noisy bird.

She felt relaxed and happy as the plane stopped and then took the slow turn around, heading back up the runway to the Barbados airport, where the pink, white, and red oleander swayed with the wind, their green leaves shining bright from the showers.

They were met by the Pan American district manager, who moved them quickly through customs. He had met many VIP's in his day and had always told them, "You know, in the West Indies things slow down. We aren't in a rush to get here and there." Fiona liked his sunburned face and Scottish brogue.

They walked through the airport waiting room. It was deserted except for a few West Indians between planes, slumped in the highly varnished, slatted seats. Fiona passed a door with a sign above, "Children's Playroom." She stopped, opened the door and said, "Michael, let's take a look." Inside they saw a crib with a mildewed mattress and propped up against the headboard, a little black doll with white button eyes.

They boarded the LIAT Avro 748 Jet Prop for their island paradise destination forty-five minutes away. The stewardess passed fresh orange juice and ham and cheese sandwiches on the locally baked bread. It was good.

Below the clouds, the sea looked grey and sad. There was little sun, only now and then rays came through the heavy rain clouds, which moved swiftly onward. The plane came down, made a quick pass over an island with a mountain hump in the middle, and soon they were on the runway between two mountains. Fiona thought the wheels had skimmed the sea before they touched down on the black macadam runway, not much longer than the driveway at Brooks Farms.

"We're here," said Michael. "Let's keep our fingers crossed."

They went through the island customs and got into a taxi. The driver said his name was Mike. Their luggage followed in a second taxi. They drove ten minutes along winding roads built into the island hills. Fiona had never seen such foliage, bright green, dotted with bright red and orange flamboyant trees, exotic enough to make her want to stay.

They went down a steep gravel and sand road. The driver shifted to low gear just in time as they headed out on to the dock. He made a sharp left turn, honked the horn five times, three short, two long.

"Is this it?" Michael asked, concerned.

"Yes, sir," said Mike, smiling, his chocolate face lighting up and beaming from white to white teeth.

Across the water, about two hundred yards offshore, Michael saw the hunchbacked island they had flown over. Nestled into the side, on a black and white sandy beach—symbolic he thought—were shingled, native huts, clustered close together, like some village.

"That's the hotel, over yonder," said Mike, all teeth again.

A tiny white boat, with blue top and frayed canopy, started from across the way and in three minutes docked.

"Darling, how does it look?" he said quietly to Fiona, who held her hand over her forehead and looked windward out to sea.

"It's beautiful, Michael. A paradise, just as you said."

"I mean the hotel. What do you think about it?" he snapped back.

"Well, let's wait till we get there and see."

The captain of the battered boat held out his hand, helped Fiona down the steps and under the canopy into a side seat. "Welcome to the island, Mum. I'm Robert the captain and will take you across."

The engine hadn't stopped. It continued to turn over, but instead of putting the throttle forward, Robert, who was barefoot and dressed in white unbuttoned shirt and rolled up white pants, reversed the engine. They were aground and Robert, not the least bit embarrassed, passed by Michael and said, "Excuse me, sir, seems

74

we have a problem." He jumped out of the boat and into the water, gave a big heave ho and was back in the boat.

Michael looked around the unpainted boat, the motor exposed to the sea air put-putting away as they headed across, at times making half circles on the sea, coming back just in time to point toward the other side. As they approached, two of the high globe hotel dock lights went on. The globe and bulb were missing from the other light post near the water.

Maybe we shouldn't even bother to stay, Michael thought when they'd landed, but Fiona was already at the end of the dock looking at the stoned-in aquarium. She watched a big blow fish attack a lobster hidden in the rocks and then two large turtles pulled, one by one, the lobster's feelers out. The lobster lay dead at the bottom of the sea and all the fish joined in.

Michael followed Fiona down the narrow stone path by the beach and past a rock garden of deep brownish, purple, and light purple plants: jump up and kiss me, a brilliant cyclamen pink and lavender-white, queen of flowers, so light and fluffy. On the right was the hotel dining room, with its glass louvered windows open to the sea air and down below, the bar, with big swinging Mexican wicker baskets covering the lights, heavy dark green and purple glass fixtures, swinging with the trade winds.

The barman, in unbuttoned rainbow striped shirt, didn't look up. As they passed by a large cage, a parrot said, "Ha, ha, ha." Fiona stopped. "Look Michael, it's just like your sister's parrot." The bartender looked up and pointed. "That's Bebe. She comes from the mountains right over there."

Led by a native who introduced himself as Caesar, they came to their own tiny hut. The cone-shaped ceiling with large beams was made of purpleheart wood. The walls were stone and one side was covered with wicker straw matting.

Fiona took off her shoes and with her toes touched sea shells gathered from the islands and pressed into the stone floor—so cool and warm at the same time. She dropped to the bed, held out her arms to Michael and said, "Darling, I adore this place. It's charming. I won't ever want to wear shoes again."

"Yes Mum, you're right, Mr. Fraser, he's the owner, doesn't want the guests wearing shoes at all. This is a place to relax and enjoy the sun," said Caesar, as he brought in three bags. He carried Michael's attaché case on his head.

Michael sat down on the flowered bedcover and put his head back on the olive cushions. He pulled out another, a green and blue striped cushion, and rested his head on the stone wall. He opened the sweet pine, hand-hewn louvers and the air rushed in through the banana trees and elephant-ear plants surrounding their new home.

Two tall drinks in deep blue glasses, with candy cane straws, stood on the bamboo table. Michael handed a glass to Fiona.

Fiona and Michael sat on the bed drinking. They were really alone for the first time with no place to go.

Fiona admired the bouquet sitting on the low bamboo table. She leaned over and breathed in the white ginger, mixed with rose of Sharon, cyclamen, and red turk's cap.

"How heavenly, better than jasmin, so strong it almost goes to my head."

"Darling, it's the drink, not the flowers," said Michael, going into the bathroom. On the counter basin a plastic ice container held a butterfly tree branch, blooming red and pink flowers.

He carried the container to Fiona. The place wasn't bad at all, he thought, and decided to go to the bar and bring back more drinks. He took off his shoes, went back into the bathroom looking for the bathtub, opened a woven bamboo door and stepped outside into the shower. He was startled to be standing alone, about to undress, looking out to sea. A bamboo fence up to his shoulder screened him from the beach. He undressed, stepped into the shower and turned on the water. Fiona came into the bathroom with a cake of Guerlain soap she'd brought and laughed at Michael standing nude. She rushed in with her clothes on, wrapped her hands around Michael's neck and kissed him, first on the cheek, then the eye and then the mouth. "Now we're even," she said, throwing back her head and laughing.

Michael dried himself with the light blue towel, printed with dark blue tropical plants. Good taste, like Porthault's, he thought to himself. He put on his bright red linen slacks and slipped over his head a pale blue and white striped T-shirt. He stuffed his dark glasses into his pocket, opened the woven bamboo closet blinds and pulled out a pair of beige doeskin sandals. He sat down on the bed and bent over to buckle them.

"You're getting fat already, darling," Fiona said, coming out of the bathroom with a pink towel around her head. "You can't even do up the sandals," and with that, Michael gave a big tug backward on the buckle and the grass rug slid across the floor.

"I'm off to the bar to get you a drink. There are no phones or buzzers around here, you know."

He stepped out onto the stone terrace facing the sea. The waves lapped at the wall and just enough spray came over the top to dampen the footpath. Michael looked up into the ink-black sky, dotted with millions of bright stars. The big dipper never looked so clear. He passed by the cottage and the elephant-ear bushes and banana trees rustled in the wind. The tiny pebbles crunched under his feet. The lights high up in the waving coconut trees guided him to the man-made lagoon, winding its way around a tropical jungle. So tempting for swimming.

He continued down the pebbled path to the bar and the maids, with their little caps and striped uniforms, in chorus said, "Good afternoon, sir," and Michael returned the greeting with "Good evening."

He crossed an arched stone bridge next to lush green baby paw-paw trees and went up two steps into the bar. The bartender was shaking a drink for a lady in a big orange straw picture hat. A black scarf, attached to the brim and tied under her chin, held the hat on. She wore a black printed bathing suit with a low fishnet back cut to the coccyx.

"Carl, please, another Bruce He Haw with a triple vodka," she said to the bartender in a proper British accent, and when she saw Michael approaching she swung around on the orange imitation leather bar stool. "Ah, Mr. Chase, we have been expecting you." Her eyes were small, but very blue and boldly penetrating. "May I offer you a drink?"

"Thank you," said Michael, a bit taken aback, and she was still staring as she crossed her legs and started to light a king-size cigaret with a small gold lighter. "Oh please, let me," said Michael, taking the cigaret lighter out of her hand. He felt the soft skin and saw that the nails were perfectly polished bright crimson red. She put the cigaret to her lips and Michael flicked the lighter. Nothing happened. Again he flicked and then a third time. "It must be broken," and she smiled. Carl scratched a match against his white nail, put his black hand up to protect the flame and lit the cigaret.

The lady must be beyond middle years, Michael thought, but still elegant, civilized, and charming.

"And now, the drink," she offered a second time.

Michael couldn't answer immediately, because he recognized the lady—Anita Boutell, the great English actress, winner of two Academy Awards and considered one of the élite of the film and theater world. Michael remembered that Fiona's mother and father knew Miss Boutell well. She had spent weekends at Brooks Farms.

He was about to say he had enjoyed her last picture, where she had played an aging Southern lady who had been raped in her Pullman sleeping car. He caught himself in time—he'd just treat her like anyone else—and he ordered two daiquiris with a dash of Angostura.

Miss Boutell finished her drink, put the round mustard-colored glass down and slipped off the spindly bamboo bar stool. She's not so tall, Michael realized.

Miss Boutell thanked Carl and nodded to Michael with a twinkle in her eyes. She crossed over the bridge onto the path and past the Philippine straw hammocks, strung up under thatched roofs. Soon she was on the beach and in the water.

Michael returned to the cottage bearing drinks and freshly roasted, ground island nuts. He had been eating along the way.

He walked into the room and felt Fiona's warmth and presence. Even the room looked different. The large white ceramic lamps, with mahogany necks and Japanese grass cloth shades, were on, and below each lamp Fiona had placed bouquets of flowers: lavender and white queen of flowers, yellow and red hibiscus, red and white frangipani and pink and white oleander, all mixed with drooping lime green, mustard yellow mottled leaves.

Through the door Michael could see Fiona brushing her hair with a silver brush and, as she went on, her hair seemed to become even more brilliant. She wore a blue, yellow, and red circled Pucci blouse and white pants to just above the ankle. She was barefoot. Michael didn't have to tell her. He took off his sandals.

"I met one of the stars. Anita Boutell. Very attractive and charming. As a matter of fact she bought us these drinks."

Fiona was unimpressed. She had seen these theater people so many times at her family's and her only thought was would the island be quiet with these people who liked to dance and drink all night.

"I don't want to see anyone. Just swim, eat, and sun. Have our little drink before lunch and dinner. I don't even care about the mail."

Actually, Fiona was concerned. Michael had been on the island two hours and he was interested in others and not enough in her, she thought to herself.

It was now dark. Mountains of clouds rolled across the sky. The palm trees and the elephant ears tossed nervously. The tree frogs and the cicadas started their beat music.

"Another drink?" he asked, sliding open the door to the terrace to look at the rain clouds gathering overhead.

"Not for me," Fiona answered coolly, twisting her braid around. She wanted to stick a ginger flower in her hair, but couldn't bear to disturb the bouquet.

Michael was gone for another drink, or to see what was going on. Fiona got up, went out on the terrace and watched him walking up the beach. Suddenly he stopped, turned around, and started running back.

He ran up the steps to Fiona out of breath.

"What's happened?" she asked. "Are you all right?"

"It's that blasted donkey. When he saw me, he started waving his tail, put his ears back and charged. I looked around. He opened his mouth and yawned."

Fiona laughed, "You're just like a little boy. He wouldn't hurt anyone."

They went down the beach together. Fiona led Michael the roundabout way to avoid the bar, where Miss Boutell sat with friends. They passed a fern-filled pool and sat at a bamboo table. Miniature

Hong Kong hurricane lamps, with dark-colored stained glass shades, flickered in the dining room cut through a large boulder.

Plants were growing out of the rock, green against the grey stone. Through the louvered glass windows Michael and Fiona looked out to the sea and the main island, filled with many lights climbing up the side of the mountain. A seventy-foot schooner, black, with gold trim (so 1900), and a small white yawl were anchored in the harbor. They turned with the current. The hotel boat putted back and forth, its bright red and green running lights fading into the sea.

As she made her entrance into the dining area, the trade winds blew Miss Boutell's long, white Mexican wedding dress with its big, lacy sleeves. She swept across the room and, as she got to her table, turned quickly around and said, "Now darlings, where shall we arrange ourselves tonight?" She took her place in the middle, put both elbows on the table and looked straight ahead at Michael's table for a moment and then became engrossed in conversation with the three men who were with her—actors, Fiona assumed.

"She doesn't seem very friendly," said Fiona teasingly. Michael ignored the remark, and kept staring, hoping Miss Boutell would look at him again.

"The dinner isn't bad," Fiona said, trying to break the silence between them. She was eating freshly baked pumpkin, cucumbers, and sweet white yams. "Michael, have you ever had cristophine?"

"No," he answered.

"Well, you're eating it now," she said, pointing to her plate.

Michael looked over at Miss Boutell.

Fiona turned her head away from Michael and stared at the big rock wall.

"What's wrong?" he asked.

"Nothing. Nothing at all," she said, brushing her fingers against her cheek. She turned back quickly. "I want to leave. You stay here so you won't miss anyone."

She got up from the table, pushing the bamboo chair back across the stone floor. It made such a high screech, Miss Boutell looked up from her table with an icy stare and so did her companions.

Fiona quickly left the dining room. Michael got up, his chair screeching too on the stone, and followed her down the steps and out onto the beach.

They each got into a hammock under the thatched roof, their heads down and their feet up. The sea was silent, the breeze constant, gently washing over their faces.

"What's wrong with you anyway?" Michael asked in a severe tone.

Fiona didn't answer. Already he's bored, bored with me, she thought. He'll be bored with the island tomorrow. She turned her head and looked out to the water. If only we had some communication, she thought.

Michael continued talking: "We might as well get this straight. You're not going to possess me. I'm not your little dog on a lead."

"No, you're not," Fiona said in a voice sounding completely resigned. She put her fingers into the sand and gave a push. She wanted to go higher and higher, faster and faster.

Michael went on. "I know you're jealous already of that actress. She fascinated me, so what? You don't think I want to sleep with her, do you?" His hammock was still.

Fiona was still swinging. She had trouble hearing him. "What did you say?" she asked.

"Well, aren't you interested?" he shouted.

"In what?"

"In me." Michael was becoming exasperated.

Fiona jumped off the hammock and went down to the sea. She removed her shoes and looking up at the moon, almost full, waded in the water. Michael followed her with his shoes on.

I might as well be alone, she sighed to herself, and make the best of it. Oh what a divine night. Heavenly. And she was at the end of the beach walking barefoot over the stones, happy just now to be away from New York and Mummy. Though she missed Daddy.

They returned to the cottage which had just been sprayed to get rid of the insects. The striped curtains were drawn tight, the beds turned down to dark blue flowered sheets with a pale blue background.

Michael pulled the curtains back so they could lie in bed and see the sea and sky. The moon breaking through big clouds made a sparkling carpet across the water. Fiona opened the louvers, closed by the maids when they sprayed, to let in the night air and they soon slept.

From across the way came the piercing sound of a flute, carrying a West Indian tune. Then, other musical sounds from a guitar and the deep throaty groan of a bamboo tuba. The band was coming to the island on a boat. They landed on the dock, struck up again, marched off the dock and into the bar.

Michael rolled over in bed.

Fiona was dreaming, deep in a tropical sleep that anesthetizes. Banana trees, coconut trees, madly flapping against the sky, making dark shadows like monsters' arms and feet reaching out into the night; a droning Greek chorus of tree frogs and cicadas; a piercing cry of the flute; snakes, fish, barracudas, conger eels; clouds, snake lightning into the stormy water, a roll of thunder; the slash of the sting ray's deadly tail into flesh and Fiona was awake screaming.

She looked out of the window to the sea, rushed out of bed and immediately shut the sliding door. "It's the wind, the darn trade wind. It makes me so nervous. First I'm hot, then cold," she said, falling back on her bed exhausted.

The bamboo band played on, over and over again, "When the Saints Go Marching In."

Michael reached over to touch Fiona. Her brow was wet. "Darling, what hit you? The dinner and the drinks must be too much. Damn that music! I thought this was supposed to be a quiet place. We are going home tomorrow if this keeps up," and Michael sat up in bed, hitting his head on the table.

The flute, through the open louvers, played back, "When the Saints Go Marching In."

The next morning, Michael and Fiona got up early and went in to breakfast.

Miss Boutell, black picture hat, pink bandana under the chin, pink bikini, was sipping her coffee at the counter. She was perched on a high stool, her face buried under the thickest black-framed dark glasses Fiona had ever seen. In back of Miss Boutell was Bruce, the donkey, sticking his nose into the small of her bare back. She slowly turned around and casually fed Bruce a piece of her toast.

"Good morning," she said cheerily. "Hope we didn't keep you

awake last night. Mr. Fraser told you this was a quiet place. Well, it really is. Don't think all of us theater people are really that bad. Last night was the first night we raised such a rumpus. You know, we were playing tag in the pool. Imagine grownups like us playing tag, but then we had been drinking."

Miss Boutell gave Bruce another piece of her toast.

"We really didn't mind," said Michael. "We were a little bit tired after our long trip from New York." Michael had hoped Fiona would say something, but she just got up on her stool and drank her orange juice. Fiona was furious that her sleep had been disturbed.

Miss Boutell left the breakfast room and went to the beach for her early morning sea shell hunt. Fiona liked doing the same thing and was a little put out to think Miss Boutell would comb the beach before she could get there. The beach was so short, there certainly weren't going to be any shells left, Fiona thought. Already the beach boy was there, raking up the stones, shells, and rotted coconuts, which he gathered in little piles to be picked up in a pail and carted off.

One of Miss Boutell's companions—he was John Printz, he said —pulled open the warped beige door.

"Frightful noise last night. We must apologize, all of us acting like a bunch of monsters. Such a racket. It won't happen again," and he got up on his stool and ordered pancakes with bacon. Fiona took in all of Mr. Printz. He was tall, dark-haired, thin and young in the face and to the shoulders, but his stomach was hanging over his navy bathing trunks. Fiona thought he looked very English and the usual actor type, with his long black hair arranged just so to fall over his large ears.

Miss Boutell came back into the breakfast room, followed by Bruce. "Good morning, darling. Did you sleep well?"

"Awful," said Printz, screwing up his face and putting down his knife and fork. "Terrible headache all night. Must have been that dreadful wine you bought in town at the supermarket."

"Poor darling. Why didn't you take my liver salts?"

Michael was amazed to think the island had a supermarket.

"Darling, you are always complaining. No one asked you to drink it," Miss Boutell said and she took a deep draw on her cigaret to finalize the statement.

"I'm off to town to do a little shopping."

"My god, not again. You must have bought out the damn place by now," said Printz.

Michael was fascinated with this domestic scene. Fiona was only bored.

"I'm going to get the bird, if I can persuade that man to sell it."

"What are you going to do with a bird in London? Who is going to take care of it? I'm not. That's final," and Printz slammed down his coffee cup.

"I will take care of it. Think of how wonderful it will be to have a rare parrot. He's so beautiful—the colors on the wings just like a rainbow woven in silk."

"The damn bird will die in the fog and cold. Let's be serious. No bird, Anita."

Miss Boutell ignored his remarks and from the way she was standing at the door, her legs firmly in place, Michael and Fiona knew she would get her bird.

They left a half hour later, all together in the yellow Peugeot 403 station wagon. Michael sat in front, Fiona in back with Miss Boutell. The two ladies barely spoke. It was hot outside and the red seats burned their legs.

Fiona couldn't bother to speak. She hadn't come on her honeymoon to go shopping. What a fool she was to tolerate Michael's whims. He always had to be with someone else—to flatter his ego. He made such a fool of himself.

They sped along, past the green hillside, dotted with orange and red flamboyants and almond trees giving shade to scrawny cows. Fiona wanted Michael to see the colors in the trees against the green grass. He went on chatting to Miss Boutell.

The driver honked at the natives walking barefoot along the pot-holed road. Two older men and a woman were repairing the surface. Fiona wondered if they could possibly ever finish the job. The woman held the pail of bubbling tar. One man spooned it out with a brush and the other man pressed the tar into the hole.

They did Miss Boutell's shopping: pink dress material with pink polka dots, pink fabric for sheets, blanc to blanc wine, Gorgonzola cheese, straw mats, liver salts and the parrot. Michael named him Little Vincent.

As the taxi jogged along, Miss Boutell held the bird on her lap in a special basket. She took off the lid and the bird stuck its head out. "Oh you sweet little darling," she said, holding the bird up to her mouth and kissing the beak. The parrot nibbled on Miss Boutell's lips. Fiona hoped the parrot would bite.

As they reached the top of the hill, Fiona saw an old wooden house, overgrown with weeds. Fallen coconut trees, decaying in the sun and eaten by ants, littered the front path. Outside, a handpainted, rotted sign read: "Ever Ready Funeral. Latest fashions. All kinds of caskets."

"How dreary," Fiona said to the others, as they all looked out the window.

The driver turned around and laughed. "We enjoy ourselves every minute here, because we all know we are going to go," and he honked his horn three times as they passed the road pavers still working under the noonday sun on the same only half-filled hole.

9

PARADISE LOST

"A drink. Come now, after that trip in the hot, broiling sun, you must be thirsty," Miss Boutell said as though Fiona and Michael wouldn't refuse. They were just getting out of the boat and Michael was holding Anita's hand to help her up on the dock.

"No, thank you," Fiona said, as she climbed out quickly, avoiding Michael's helping hand. She ran down the dock and stopped next to John Printz, who sat dangling his feet over the edge into the aquarium. "Come on over here, Anthony, let me give you another rubdown, old boy," he said to the big turtle, who kept swimming away and back again for another rub. He pulled the stick out of the water and, looking at Fiona, said, "Well, I see you've got the damned bird in the basket." Fiona nodded and ran off the dock and onto the beach. The parrot stuck his neck out and the lid fell off.

Michael followed Fiona down the beach to the cottage. He so much wanted to have that drink with Anita.

He lay down on the terrace redwood reclining chair. He adjusted the blue canvas cushion under him, picked up his drink, ordered before they left, and looked out to sea. Small waves left a sheet of spray as they broke over the reef. The water close to the reef was emerald green, patched with deep blue and a long stretch of brownish green. Way over on the other side, green hills rolled down onto the beach. On the top of the highest hill an old abandoned stone sugar mill, surrounded by huge breadfruit and almond trees, commanded a view out to sea and the small Grenadine Islands, strung together in a chain. The highest mountain on the island was shrouded in a ringlet of clouds and farther to the north dark sheets of rain headed toward the peak.

Fiona sat down on Michael's chair. He moved his legs and his feet touched the hot stone floor.

"It's so fantastically beautiful, so much more real than what we have been thinking and living all these months," said Fiona seriously and somberly.

"What do you mean? That we haven't been living in reality?" Michael said firmly.

"No, not exactly that. It's that we seem to be spinning here and there, always with people, never getting down to what counts in life. I know that sounds banal, Michael, but it's true," and she paused as though she had trouble expressing herself.

"What do you want from all this life?" he asked.

"I guess we really have everything. I never thought we had too much, but I am beginning to wonder what we'll be doing five years from now. We'll have seen a lot and done so much in such a short time. Sometimes I'm frightened that there won't be anything left. Except maybe you will be the one person I will always have," and Fiona leaned back into Michael's arms.

"Darling, you forget we have responsibility. I know we've had the material things, but now we must try and work for others. Our job is to help others, to work for our cause."

Fiona got up and moved to the small bamboo chair. She had hoped Michael would say something wonderful to her. Why didn't he say he wanted always to be with her? Instead, all he wanted was to be admired by the whole world. She was worried that Michael was so concerned with impressing others and suddenly Miss Boutell's image crossed her mind.

"Look at Anita," she began and Michael was pleased Fiona now thought in terms of "Anita" and would warm up to her.

"She's got everything in life, success, beauty, and she still has to

87

waste her time buying and shopping, running here and there. She wants to please the whole world too. I hope you don't want to be an actor," and she laughed at her own remark.

Michael was incensed. He put his drink down and walked across the small terrace. He sat on the wall and looked right at Fiona.

"You don't understand, you silly girl," he started and Fiona interrupted.

"Please don't call me a silly girl."

Michael continued: "I don't want to please the whole world. I want to be somebody, make something out of all this mess. We are rich. We have power. What good is it if we don't put it to use? I can't see how you can compare a public figure serving the public with an actress."

"What's the difference?" Fiona asked in a tone meaning she didn't think there was any difference.

"We, as public figures, have responsibility to see that the world functions smoothly, that poverty is eliminated, that children are schooled and people are free to vote. You know, all that a democracy stands for."

"Is that what a democracy is?" Fiona asked, adding cynically, "Then why doesn't Uncle John give up some of his money to help the masses? The last time I saw all of you together, you, your father, and Uncle John were talking about how you could save on taxes by selling something or other."

Fiona went on: "Look at the attitude of the Kennedys. Great as they are, they're still imperious. Their tentacles reach out everywhere. Their power is enormous."

Michael interrupted, "They deserve everything they have. They have sacrificed themselves to become public monuments."

"But," Fiona continued, "is that the way the new democracy works?"

Michael looked at her and said, "Yes."

"What's happened to the pioneer days," she asked, "when any man, poor, uneducated, could go west and get to the top? I think we have to reassess our values, or the country will destroy itself. The pioneer spirit is gone. The power spirit, the power personality has taken over and I hate the power society we live in. We're heading down the road to mediocrity, uniformity."

"Fiona, you're a silly girl. You don't understand a thing about government, taxes, even democracy. You had better stick to your needle point and running my house." He walked into the cottage, yelling back, "Let's go to lunch. I want to talk to some intelligent people."

Fiona quickly went down the steps onto the beach.

"Where are you going?" Michael shouted after her.

"I don't want any lunch. Go flirt with that middle-aged actress. You belong together, always wanting to be in the public eye." She ran down the beach and jumped into the first hammock she saw, wrapping herself up inside so no one could see her. Michael wouldn't go to luncheon without her.

The hammock dragged in the sand with the weight of her body. She lay still and listened to the trade winds blowing the sand around her.

What was wrong with her, or was it with both her and Michael? Why didn't they get along? Or was she just too unreasonable and Michael too sure of himself and not at all sympathetic to the problems of others? She remembered the old workers tarring the road in the broiling sun. She had been the only one in the car to notice them.

She put her hand in the sand and gave a push. What are we all striving for anyway? The people on the island seemed happy with the everyday, simple life. They had so little, still they laughed, played, and even joked at death. They did have natural beauty, still unspoiled—the sea, the sky, the sun. Yet she and Michael, sitting outside on the terrace drinking, hardly admired the view. There was no feeling of true love, or any understanding between them. Fiona started to cry and the sand in the hammock mixed with her tears to scratch the side of her cheek.

Bruce, the donkey, nudged her hammock with his wet nose, opened his mouth showing what few teeth he had left and yawned. He let out a loud "He haw, he haw," and Fiona started to smile.

She got up and walked along the wall, the water spraying up from the coral onto her feet and looked out to the island of Bequia, floating majestically, so green and within touching distance. What a beautiful day, Fiona thought. How could I be so unhappy?

Soon she was at the end of the wall, almost at the tip of the island, near the windmill. The day was so clear she could read on the tail of the windmill, as it followed the wind, the trademark: "Made in USA, 1900, Armco, Chicago, Illinois." Below, the rusty pump went up and down monotonously, bringing the sea water into the lagoon swimming pool. Better an exciting life, full of unexpected changes and even high emotions than the humdrum grind of living, she thought, as she started up the steps to the top of the island.

Halfway up, exhausted and hot, she caught her breath on a stone seat, carved with the signature "By HBL, 1966." Fiona admired the way the seat curved gently around the coconut tree trunk, so the view out to sea was undisturbed.

She continued up the path, which now turned into stone and dirt. Near the top Fiona saw a squad of natives stripped to the waist, in bathing suit trunks and undershorts, cutting away at the rocky cliff. Their bodies were deep black, shiny in the sun, with sweat pouring over their muscles.

The natives worked in teams of two. The first man knelt down in the stones, his legs apart, and with his fist held the spike. His partner, with a wide swing of the hammer out above the head, struck with great force. A large piece of rock spun around in the dirt, then fell on its side at their black, white-soled feet. Fiona's eyes were fixed on their firm black bodies. She was stimulated by the idea of men breaking rocks from a wall of stone. If only Michelangelo had sculptured this, all in black marble, wouldn't it have been magnificent? She admired their well-formed bodies.

Mr. Fraser was talking to a small and frail white boy. Fiona looked into the boy's face. He was terrified. Fiona nodded to the boy. He must be about seventeen, she thought, as she turned to Mr. Fraser.

The boy went up the hill to join the other men. He was the only one among the natives to wear a shirt. They put down their hammers and the men who were squatting got up, dropping their spikes. Some sneered and others laughed at the boy.

90

"What's going on? What are they going to do to him?" Fiona said pleadingly.

"A little trouble," Mr. Fraser responded, wiping his brow. "They are kidding the boy because he's the only one with white skin working with them. He's a common laborer, like the rest. He works in the quarry, carries cement on his head and breaks rock, but they just don't like him."

"But what are they yelling out at him?" Fiona asked. She could see the boy was suffering humiliation. He held tightly to his spike.

"They are saying he's got a girl friend, black, I imagine, who is a whore and she sleeps with all of them because he's not good."

The boy started yelling back. His English wasn't as heavily accented as the natives' and Fiona caught the words, "She's good, she cooks for me and does my wash and I love her."

"You see," began Mr. Fraser, trying to calm Fiona, "he's an English boy. There are a lot of them here who work like the black native common laborers. They live in their own little district over there. They sometimes intermarry with the blacks and no one thinks anything of it. But this poor lad wanted to quit last week, because the other workers tormented him so much. He went home and told his wife he was going to quit, but she made him come back. They needed to eat."

Fiona turned away from the quarry and started down the hill. Mr. Fraser followed. Fiona looked back at the boy. He held the spike to the rock and his partner raised the hammer to strike. The blow made a sharp, piercing noise. Fiona trembled. The piece of rock fell away into the dirt and as she turned around, the boy placed the spike farther up the rock to start another strike.

They reached the bottom of the hill and Fiona returned to the cottage.

"Are you ready for lunch?" she said cheerily.

"I'm glad you've decided to eat," said Michael sarcastically. He assumed she had slipped temporarily into one of those feminine moods, so aggravating to all men.

They didn't go to luncheon. Michael read aloud a letter from Uncle John.

Fiona already had forgotten about her quarrel with Michael. She

91

had forgotten about the English boy on the hill. She thought it wonderful Michael was at last confiding in her. He read from the black embossed stationery:

My dear boy:

What we thought has finally happened. It should come as no surprise to any of us. Young Cain is forging ahead, hands down. The New York Times devoted a feature story, saying he is the bright new light in the party. Young Cain cleverly enough has denied all attachments to his father, the Senator. You can see where I have underlined, young Cain makes it clear he represents the new, vigorous generation of thinkers and while he respects his father's opinions, he does differ on many important ones. Namely, the question of Vietnam. Cain is bold enough to say he doesn't believe the American public is getting the real facts on Vietnam, nor is Congress, a popular thought among many today. You can read the enclosed clipping yourself.

Catherine, now his wife, is being described as an elegant and vital part of the new, young team. She has started campaigning vigorously, opening new playgrounds and, alone, except for newspaper reporters, walked through Harlem streets talking to the people.

The Times concludes that from all reports young Cain is off to a late, but good start. There seems little doubt he will be elected and naturally, from the story in The Times, you know the paper will support him.

Michael put down the letter and for the first time with warmth in his eyes, said, "Well, it isn't all that bad. He hasn't won yet."

"But look how clever Cain is," Fiona interrupted. "He almost disavows his father, stands on his own two feet and even goes so far as to disagree with him on important issues. I would say that's smart politics."

Michael had to admit to himself Fiona was right. He said, "Smart maybe, but it could rebound on him. The voters could say he's too young and inexperienced and an upstart to be thinking on his own so soon."

"I think you are wrong, my darling. Remember the Kennedys—

their youth. And remember that word vigor. Outward honesty made a big hit with the public and went right to the voters' hearts. They won hands down. Their youth and independence carried them a long way. Cain is the same type of politician and I'm sure he is going to have a big success."

Fiona went out on the terrace. "The sun is divine. And we worry about Cain. It's so far away."

She came back and took off her bathing suit. "I'm tired. I need my nap," and she looked at Michael as if to say a nap could be an inviting idea. She slipped into her full-length, white cotton batiste negligee. She walked toward Michael, the negligee blowing in the breeze, the blue bows tied casually, all the way to the floor. She smiled sweetly and almost reassuringly at Michael and lay down on the bed.

Michael lay there looking at his wife, so fragile and delicate. She has fire burning in her heart and a kindness to others, he thought. Michael knew he lacked her tolerance. She was beautiful, her hands so fine, her fingers long and slender. Her arm was outstretched. Michael held her hand and ran his fingers up and down her smooth nails. Her long hair fell over the pillow. He remembered Boston and he thought of Ophelia. He wanted to touch her all over, but she was sleeping now. Her lips, without lipstick, opened a pinhead, her nose, reddened at the tip from the sun. The long dark lashes, still. She smiled softly, the same smile she had given Michael before falling asleep.

Michael only wished he could rest free from his need to find something more, to prove himself, to reach for what—power? Where would he finally find his peace? How could he be satisfied? What else would he want?

He got up off his bed, paced the room, turned back and looked at Fiona and disappeared through the curtains onto the terrace. Soon he was on the beach. He walked back and forth. If only he could get Cain out of his mind. He dug his left foot into the sand, leaving an imprint, but as quickly as Michael made his mark, a wave washed it away.

He reached the end of the short beach and turned to start back in the other direction, but saw a fat man smoking a pipe coming toward him. His drab, grey shirt hung out of his Bermuda shorts. Michael could tell from the smell of the tobacco it was an inferior grade.

Michael walked to the water to escape him.

"Afternoon. Fine day. What we came for, isn't it? Lovely island. I suppose you're like me. Ate too much lunch, didn't you now? We can walk it off," and now he was next to Michael.

"Like sea shells?" asked the man. "Hilda and me, we have quite a collection up by the wall over there."

They went up to the cottage wall. The shells were lined up neatly.

"You see over there, my little friends the ants have done their work well."

Michael looked over and saw the wet shells crawling with thousands of red and black ants.

"I use them ants to clean off my shells and they do a great job. That's life isn't it, always someone using someone else to get the damn job done. Someone taking advantage of someone else. Basic in nature, I guess," and the man snickered, relishing his own words.

Michael was repelled by the idea. That's the philosophy ruining the world, he thought, walking away in a huff.

Michael realized he had never accepted the truth about life. He lived in some sort of dream world where he moved people as easily as he had rearranged the furniture in the new apartment. He always forgot that his money, or the money of his family, made manipulating people easier. Only once had he been shocked about having too much money. Paul Cain, his roommate at Princeton, had lived off a meager allowance even though his family had sufficient money. One night they had been drinking together. Michael shuddered when he recalled how stupid he had been. They were talking about fixing up the room, where to arrange the book shelves and how to place their desks in the study. Michael said, why not get some new book cases built and besides, their desks were pretty crummy anyway. His roommate, incensed, yelled at him and the words still rang in his ears, "Why, you rich bastard, you don't realize how much more fun it is to make something out of nothing. All you do is spend your god damned money all over the place and you think that buying this and that takes care of everything. Well, you're damn wrong," and in his

94

rage Cain broke his glass in the fireplace. Since that time, Michael had become sensitive about his wealth and even though he had an uncontrolled desire to buy, after spending a large amount of money he felt nauseated, but his sickness was temporary, because the next day he would be tempted again and buy more.

Michael saw Anita at the far end of the beach. He couldn't resist going to her. She was surrounded by three little girls and Bruce.

"Oh, please, Miss Boutell, before we leave, your autograph," said the little girl with the thick glasses, and handed Anita a bouquet of wilted red and white oleanders, mixed with shiny green leaves.

"You have been so nice to us, Miss Boutell, we are going to miss you and I am going to be writing you often," said the older girl.

She looked up from the autograph book at Michael. He could see Anita was about to perform. She stared out to the sea, to get inspired, Michael thought. Then she raised her hands to silence the girls.

"I want to tell you a story," she began, stroking the donkey's back. "See how Bruce's light fur is darker along the back and across the neck." And she traced the sign of the cross on the donkey's back.

"Do you know why?" Miss Boutell asked the children.

The children and Michael shook their heads.

"You remember when the Virgin Mary was traveling on the road to Bethlehem, just before little Jesus was born. She first asked a camel for a ride. The camel refused. She then asked a horse and he said he was too tired to carry them to Bethlehem. Then she asked the donkey. He took them willingly. Jesus afterward blessed all donkeys with the sign of the cross on their backs, just like Bruce's."

Michael stood silent, amazed at the tenderness of the story. He was as moved as the children, probably even more because he had never seen Miss Boutell as a warm, gentle person, only as a hard-driving, great dramatic actress. Michael looked into her blue-green eyes, which were brimming with tears and realized she had played a great scene—a real scene at that.

The sun was now high in the sky, its rays beating down on the beach. Miss Boutell pulled her hat down over her brow and looking at

Michael said, "My, but it's getting so hot I think it is time for us to take a siesta."

Michael had no intention of sleeping. He watched Anita go out into the water with her hat still on. She dipped gracefully between the waves, then ran out quickly and right up the beach to her cottage near the windmill. The three girls were left standing alone with Michael and he didn't know exactly what to say so he headed up the beach after Anita. He walked over the stones and onto the path next to the wall. Before he realized it, Michael was standing right outside her cottage watching.

Through the full-length sliding glass doors he looked straight into her room. Anita was standing in the middle of a straw rug powdering her naked body.

Then she sat down at the small dressing table, pulled out a mirror and brushed her hair with a silver brush. She looked at herself closely in the mirror, stretched the skin across her forehead and gave a pat under the chin, smiled forcibly at herself, got up from the table, immersed herself in more powder and disappeared in a talcum cloud onto the bed. Michael was sure Anita had seen him watching.

He ran back down behind the wall to their cottage. He went through the curtains, looked down at Fiona, sleeping, fell to his knees and kissed her neck. She moved over on the bed and Michael lay down next to her.

In a moment they were kissing, their lips open and stretching for each other. Color rose in her neck. She was a-blush. Her buttocks were soft at first, then firmer. He thought of Anita powdering herself. Michael writhed with delight, his mind moving with greater desire than his body. Then they stopped to preserve the desire, to extend that moment. Fiona looked into his eyes, dropped her face to his. He pulled at her hair, pushed her head down hard onto his chest and quickly retained control, pushing her over on her side. They were locked together again. Then, that moment, half pain, all ecstasy, "More, more, more," Michael groaned breathlessly.

He lay on the bed, his right arm stretched languidly over Fiona's back. Her hand was off the bed, the palm turned back. Suddenly the heat of Fiona's body turned cold and sticky.

96

Her head was to one side, the long neck twisted, like a swan floating.

Fiona lay there on the bed. She watched the sky go grey. A sheet of gentle rain sprayed the island. Two rainbows arched and dipped far away into the sea.

Michael was looking now. They saw the rainbows fading into space. "What a pity we didn't see them form. I only heard the soft rain," Fiona said, going into the bathroom.

Fiona took the arched, beige cake of soap smelling of jasmin. As she stood in the shower looking out to sea, the strong jasmin covering her body reminded Fiona of Mummy.

Fiona could never quite get Mummy out of her mind. She kept thinking she really didn't love her. It was only fear and conscience that kept her close. She never consulted Mummy about what she would do. Fiona knew exactly what guidelines Mummy had set up for her and she slavishly followed.

Fiona turned up the water. She liked the psst shower noise and the hot and cold beating down on her. The strong spray felt like millions of pricking thorns. The small amount of pain was pleasant. Just part of my sensuous nature she thought, raising her face to the spout.

Fiona looked out over the water. Raining sheets skimmed across the sea. The soap dropped to the floor and she let it slide across the crude stone to wash into the drain. The rain poured off the roof. Fiona turned up the cold tap full and stood surrounded in water. She shivered. She turned down the hot water. I'm testing my physical strength, my will power, she thought to herself. Her hair dripped. She pulled it back hard, wrung out the strands until her scalp pained.

Her love with Michael half an hour before had been warm, certainly not passionate. She wanted more. Michael would have been shocked at the idea of "more," Fiona thought. He would have called it undignified. It wouldn't have suited his pose. Then, too, she was supposed to be refined. Mummy had always told her to be. If only she could escape from what she was supposed to be. People just don't understand me, she thought as she came out of the shower and returned to the bathroom. She regained her composure as she brushed her hair till it was almost dry. At each stroke, one idea came over and over again. I have got to be myself. I have got to show myself. I want to be identified, recognized as being by Mummy, father, husband, friends. The *some* in somebody was more important than the *body*. Michael has his responsibility, but I have mine too, even though I am a woman. I must express myself. I can be aggressive. Remember Boston, when I took Michael. I did the leading that day and I can do it again.

"Darling, you are brushing your scalp too hard. It's red. Stop," Michael said as he came into the bathroom. He looked tired, his eyes were red and bloodshot. Fiona put the brush down and looked into the mirror. I'm fresh, feeling wonderful, she thought.

She is still a jeune fille, Michael thought as he turned on the hot water.

Fiona had the urge to go right in after him and turn off the hot water and stand there with him in the cold. But she remembered Michael really didn't have that kind of sense of humor.

He was so damned serious about everything and she could never get through to him. There never seemed a moment when they could talk about their importance to each other. When would they let out their true feelings? Fiona wondered if her mother had ever communicated to her father. She knew he didn't communicate with her mother. He was always too occupied with business. He brushed aside serious questions of relationship.

Michael had his principles, that was true, and fine ones, Fiona supposed, about helping the common man and putting big money to use to help the common man. But she knew that what really counted was the inner strength in a man whose identity in the eyes of his family and others was unique, even daring. All great men, she felt, had dared to assert themselves in times of danger. Our existence, she thought, is perfectly secure. We have all the security that money can buy, but you still cannot go to the bank to buy security within yourself. There always lurked some hidden danger in life that would come upon you unexpectedly one day. Then there would be the attack and you would have to fight. Fiona had always feared that she wouldn't be able to fight an enemy. She also feared security would lead to boredom. Perhaps that explained her desire for sensuous

98

pleasures. She felt her appetite for sex increasing and Michael, she knew, would only begin to awaken her. What could be the ultimate? What would come to her later? This thought excited her. Already, on her honeymoon, their security was almost boring. She longed for stimulation. She longed for some sort of excitement, some sort of challenge that they could take on together. And they weren't going to find that challenge in the tropics. Fiona longed to begin living. Their life was really just starting.

She put on her salmon and white print full-length caftan, bowed on one shoulder. She was about to fasten her big white snowball earrings spiked with gold, but at the last minute changed her mind. I look just too sweet, she thought. Instead, she got into her white tight fitting Pucci pants and zipped up with a strong, sure tug. She slid open the door, banging the handle against the aluminum frame and said, "Michael, hurry up. It's time for a drink."

She went outside. She stopped next to the moonflower vine growing out of a red earthenware pot.

"Michael, quick. Look it's the moonflower. The blossom is growing, coming right out this minute. It smells. It's so beautiful. Look at it grow," just as we should she thought to herself.

Michael came out of the door, wrapped in a towel. He went over to Fiona, putting his arm around her waist. "Yes, I know, darling. I've seen the flower. It comes out now, about six, and will be gone by tomorrow morning."

Before sunup, the moonflower blossoms wilted, hanging limply, almost dead, to the vine.

10

NEW YORK

The telephone hadn't stopped ringing. At least Fiona thought it
hadn't stopped. They were back in New York—home, living,
breathing New York. Fiona had her wish. She was stimulated, or, as
she lay in bed eating her breakfast off a delft tiled tray, so pretty
with the tiny blue daisy print Porthault sheets, she was at least busy.
So busy she hadn't yet had lunch with Mummy. Today she would
meet Mummy and Fiona wanted to look her best.

It was unusual for her to worry about how she looked at luncheon, but now that she had appeared in the fashion magazines it was
a challenge to look her best and especially to look fantastic when
lunching at La . . . . . with Mummy.

Fiona took her hard toast from the English silver toast rack, put
butter on and covered it with English marmalade. She liked the bitter marmalade and had told Pierre the butler to tell his wife Mary
to put only Cooper's on her breakfast tray. Michael wasn't eating
toast these days and no sugar in his coffee. He was watching his
waistline. He hadn't liked the picture in the fashion magazine. He
had admitted to Fiona he looked older and certainly fatter than his
wife.

In the back of her mind Fiona wanted to prove today at luncheon with Mummy that she was no longer an ugly duckling. Fiona had reached the point where she was going to show her mother that marriage and her new life had made her a different person, and she was determined to free herself from her mother. She was even ready to challenge her mother on her mother's own grounds of chic, in, and all the other social powers that she had watched her mother hold supremely.

The telephone rang.

"Madame, it's Mrs. Signatelli. Should I say you are at home?" asked Pierre.

"Thank you, I'll take the call."

"Hello, Marella. I've heard the news. Fabulous, sounds absolutely marvelous. What a superb idea for the ball. We would be delighted to give a dinner before. The apartment is divine. Michael begins next week in Senator Borden's New York office. He'll be some sort of administrative assistant. The Senator seems a nice enough man, brilliant, I guess, wonderful for Michael's future. Yes, I do know his wife."

Fiona paused on Senator Borden's wife. She was allergic to her brashness and vulgarity. I know Marella is just waiting for me to say something wrong about her, Fiona thought, and changed the subject.

"We did see the Cains. Catherine looked marvelous. Paul slightly harassed, but you know he's a political animal. We all hate big parties like that, rather impersonal, but I guess everyone was there. No, Mummy just came back into town today. I'm seeing her for lunch. I know she's fantastic. Everyone tells me how beautiful she is. Yes I did see that picture in the papers. I thought she looked her best.

"Please, not another luncheon. They'll be there together? Oh, I see, only Catherine. I couldn't imagine Paul going to a ladies' luncheon, but I suppose in politics you have to be every place."

Fiona thought she had better go to the luncheon, especially if Catherine Cain was going to be there.

"Marella, yes, darling, if you really think the luncheon will be amusing and that I could help, I'll arrange to go. Really, I must get myself together before meeting Mummy. Good-bye."

Fiona stayed in bed reading the morning newspapers. Michael kept telling her she must be well informed on national and international affairs. She was frankly bored reading the New York *Times* foreign news coverage. What should she care about events in New Delhi or Cambodia and what de Gaulle said in Paris? Not that she wasn't concerned with the world's happenings, but her real interest, and she admitted it quite openly to Michael, was in the social and art life of New York. Mixing with these people excited and stimulated her mind, but politicians continued to bore her, and sometimes dismay her.

Too often she found politicians without conscience, real conscience that is. Outwardly they followed moral principles if they thought it politically expedient, if it would help their public image. Uncle John had already started on Michael's and Fiona's image and had warned that if they spent their whole time partying and going to first nights, the public would wonder if Michael ever did a day's work.

Fiona was making it a custom to set aside a half hour, while sitting in her bed under the canopy, for meditation. She said it was her plotting time to lay out the day's work and the evening's fun. But she thought a great deal about Michael. She hoped he would recognize that he couldn't just echo the words and copy the ways of others more powerful than he. Michael had to assert himself, to cut out his own path for his own career. Surely working in the Senator's office should firm up his ideas. She didn't ever want to admit it, but she feared Michael had become mentally as well as physically flabby. He seemed ambitious but actually lacked an aggressive drive, a determination to lead. He always followed, preferring not to struggle, and never realized that his success would depend on being recognized as an individual. Michael still believed that power came only through money and Fiona could not bear the thought of being merely the typical anonymous young lady at the side of her handsome, rich husband who represented nothing more than good fortune.

She threw off the sheets and stuffed her feet into her bunny rabbit slippers. They felt so soft, warm and cuddly. She had fifteen minutes to get to the hairdresser and one hour there before meeting Mummy.

Twenty minutes later, Fiona was in the checker cab on the way to Albert, the hairdresser. It was a hot New York day. Why did people seem to rush more in the heat? she wondered. Probably only to get out of the steam bath streets and into the cool, air-conditioned buildings. Suddenly New York went inside, when outside the sun was burning bright. And inside the millions of air-conditioning machines purring away killed the smells and noises that are New York.

"Hot enough today, lady?" said the cabby, driving with one hand and mopping his brow with the other.

Fiona always liked talking to the cab drivers. "It *is* rather warm, but I don't mind. I just keep busy." Fiona knew this was almost a lie. Keeping busy going to the hairdresser and to luncheon with Mummy, all air-conditioned, she thought.

A bus in front discharged a black oil cloud and the smell from the fumes filled the taxi.

"What do you do to keep busy on a day like this? If I were you, I'd stay inside. But all you ladies are out shopping, running around in the hot streets. I'd love to be home with a beer, watching the Mets on TV."

Fiona wouldn't tell the driver that she was going to the hairdresser and then to luncheon with her mother. That would really sound silly.

The cab stopped in front of Albert's mansion.

"Let me put you right at the door, lady. Just sit back and relax. I'll get that man in front to move," and he put his hand on the horn. "Get out of the way. Can't you see I'm trying to get in there? I have a lady in the car. She's in a hurry. Come on, move before I call the cops."

"Never mind, I'll hop right out here, or I'll be late," and Fiona opened the door. She gave the driver a forty-five-cent tip, more than she had intended. Fiona was relieved she didn't have to answer his last question: "And what do you do to keep busy on a day like this?" The words sat in her head as she went up the marble steps into Albert's.

Fiona hated the hairdresser's. Such a waste of time and all the phony chichi, all for the sake of beauty.

The ladies in their dark glasses were shopping in the "Après Nous Boutique" next to the red carpeted grand staircase. They all had

Albert's look, natural flowing hair. They bought scarves, cosmetics, all sorts of beauty aids in the boutique, out of an urge to buy just something as a reward for sitting under the hot dryer. So they walked up and down in the boutique, looking. They felt glamorous again, with that symbol of security, dark glasses, down over their eyes so as not to disturb their just set hair. Funny, thought Fiona, as she continued up the red carpeted stairs, how we all come shrouded in scarves, and when we go out we want everyone to see the change. There's something about hair and having it done.

Fiona went to the third floor where Albert had his private salon and where he trained his assistants who eventually were transferred to the floors below to practice on the less important ladies who were happy enough to pass through Albert's hallowed doors of beauty.

Willy, the decorator, had reconditioned the mansion and changed it into a hairdresser's dream. He had been determined to take Albert's out of the realm of the usual brothel look of the traditional hairdresser. The idea had been for the client to relax in a civilized beauty spa. Fiona buttoned up her leopard print smock and took her place on the bamboo chair and waited for Albert to make his entrance. Albert did more than the in social ladies' hair. He lived within their refined, confined world. Mummy had warned Fiona not to confide in him. Albert didn't try to fish for their little confidences, but it just happened, sitting in the beauty mansion for several hours a week where there wasn't much to do except be pampered, the best of the ladies let forth with their innermost secrets.

Fiona this morning was pleased to be given the private room where Albert took his most important clients. Of course, this honor hadn't come overnight, but rather quickly for Fiona since she had "made the fashion magazines" and was, as Bette the red-haired manicurist said, "a comer."

Albert, a wispy, soft spoken man with sharp brown eyes, was behind her as they both inspected Fiona in the mirror.

"You are looking wonderful, Mrs. Chase. Your hair is in fine shape after all that sun. It's getting that amber glow like your mother's. I think we will do it the same way, 'natural,'" and he pulled the comb through the top.

Albert was tired. He had just returned from a Cape Cod party where one of New York's leading hostesses had asked him as hairdresser and as friend. Fiona had heard about the party and was more than curious to know who had been there. Rumor had it that all the Kennedys had gathered in the dunes around the Cape Cod village and it had been a reunion for their closest friends, including some members of President Johnson's cabinet. Michael had longed to be asked, but they had not been.

It was not unusual for Albert to be invited, and in this case the hostess of a certain age had more than just a hairdresser interest in Albert. She found him attractive and delightful company. Like many ladies, she was left with her money, a husband who was always elsewhere, but many houses with their fine gardens, her wealthy friends and, as she told her analyst, in spite of all seemed always alone.

Fiona sat silent. She liked the way Albert was now brushing her hair. It wouldn't take long before he started telling her about the party.

Albert was dressed in a double-breasted, pin-striped grey business suit and, except for his highly polished black shoes with shiny brass buckles, he looked like any young Wall Streeter. Albert never carried a comb in his pocket; instead there was a red silk paisley handkerchief.

The hairdresser's look was taken out of his room. The art magazines, *L'Oeil, Connaissance des Arts, The Tatler, The Connoisseur,* were stuffed into the black bamboo rack next to France's *Paris Match.*

Albert moved back and forth across the waxed parquet floor, getting in close to Fiona and then moving back as he worked over her hair. She shifted in the small chair. The blue and white needlepoint cushion, a gift of one of his clients, dug into her back.

"I just arrived back this morning from the Cape. Mrs. Miller gave a wonderful party for the Kennedys, about seventy-five people under a tent in her garden. The flowers were incredible. It was the first time I have seen formal planting in and out of the dunes."

"I've heard about the gardens," Fiona said quietly, hoping Albert would go on about the party.

105

"Of course, because your mother and father were there," he added nonchalantly.

Fiona had assumed her mother had been invited. It was just like Mummy not to tell me anything, she reflected, because she still thinks I'm a little girl and not invited to the same places.

"I just sat there and marveled at the flowers in the dunes, one row and then another rolling into the blue, blue sea. You know everything in the house is blue. I guess it was Mrs. Miller's blue period when she had the house done."

Fiona nodded and Albert continued, "They arrived in private planes from all over. The cabinet members flew in through the fog and I guess they had to sneak out of Washington. It was eerie seeing all those government people paying respects to the Kennedy clan. The Washington group left early to get back to the capital before the President found they were out of town," Albert said smiling.

Fiona wanted to ask if the Cains were there, but she continued listening, knowing full well Mummy would tell her everything at luncheon.

11

MUMMY

Mrs. Stephenson's secretary had forgotten to reserve. It didn't make much difference at La . . . . . They just took the best table away from someone else over the protests of Mrs. Stephenson.

She came into the restaurant and they looked up from their tables. They knew who it was and they knew they were eating in the right place today. They were secure because Mrs. Stephenson by being at La . . . . . made the restaurant very in.

Mrs. Stephenson had just been to her hairdresser around the corner from Albert's. She had been an Albert customer, but there had been a falling out after one of the manicurists leaked some information about what Mrs. Stephenson would be wearing to a White House reception.

"Really, Monsieur Leland, I didn't want to take this table. I just can't imagine my secretary, Mrs. Anthony, not phoning you ahead. I'm meeting my daughter and we decided on your restaurant this morning."

"Madame Stephenson, it is always such a pleasure to have you. Now may we order you an apéritif? I hope you enjoy your luncheon," and Monsieur Leland bowed out of the picture and snapped his finger for the waiter to bring a Campari on the rocks with a twist of lemon.

Mrs. Stephenson had wanted to look her best for Fiona. She was thinking they really saw so little of each other and now that Fiona was married, they would be even more apart.

Fiona opened the door and stopped at the bar. She hesitated. She knew her mother would be at the best table on the left. Mummy is looking beautiful, Fiona thought. Her white linen dress with black sash casually tied at the waist, her white kid shoes and white bag, so right for a hot day. She's so cool and collected, so well put together on the brown leather banquette. Mrs. Stephenson was smoking and her long black and gold cigaret holder rested on the ash tray. She picked up the cigaret and Fiona saw her mother's long fingers and her ring—a cabochon ruby—as she took a puff and let the smoke come out slowly around her. She picked up her glass with the bright red Campari and drank and looked around the restaurant. She knew most of the faces in the outer room, which was really the only place to sit. The outer room was furthest from the kitchen.

Fiona approached the table. "Mummy, oh Mummy, how wonderful to see you, darling. I was just watching you from the door. You look divine. You never seem to change."

Mrs. Stephenson moved over on the banquette and took Fiona's hand and kissed her gently on the right cheek. She's changed, marriage has changed my darling, she thought to herself. She's suddenly a woman.

"Darling, how's Michael? Is he well? Did you enjoy yourselves? I assumed you would be back soon. It gets frightfully boring on an island for weeks on end. I find the heat wearing and it makes me moody. You know your father can never stay still any place and he loathes the sun."

"Mummy, it was wonderful. We're really so happy. I think we're going to enjoy every minute."

Mrs. Stephenson thought Fiona, as usual, was running over with enthusiasm. It was charming, all that enthusiasm.

"We just swam, ate and drank, and completely relaxed, but we felt we had to get back to find out what's going on. We've got to work, not just play."

"Why should you? You have a lifetime to work. Look at your father, he does nothing else but work."

108

"Yes, I know, Mummy, I realize that. Sometimes I think he works so hard he forgets about you."

"It can't be any other way for us, darling. You see, I married your father because I admire him so much."

Mrs. Stephenson sipped her Campari. She was shocked at what she had said, that she had married Walter because she admired him. Ridiculous.

Fiona continued, "But what do you admire? I don't understand."

"I admire his power, that he can make things go. He's a genius at creating. The whole idea of his publications, they are still the prime influence in the world. Imagine what he can do through the publications. It's not the money, we have all that. It's not the material things. It's the idea that your father stimulates the thoughts of many people. He's a sort of taste maker. Although I don't believe in one taste. I think it's an effrontery to say so-and-so has good or bad taste. Who is really the one to decide?"

"I agree," said Fiona, completely taken back by her mother's seriousness.

Mrs. Stephenson wanted to tell Fiona that power and creating didn't have anything to do with a happy marriage. She just couldn't.

"Mummy, I hope you don't mind, but I've wanted to ask for a long time."

"Please do, anything you want."

"With Daddy so busy," Fiona began, "where does that leave you? I mean, you have your houses, your social life, your friends and, of course, the family."

Mrs. Stephenson was hurt that Fiona had put the family last, but she had to admit the family came in that order.

Fiona went on, "But aren't you ever lonely? Aren't you sometimes frustrated not being someone else? I don't mean someone who you think is better, but just for a while, wouldn't you want a career, or to, say, be an artist?"

Mrs. Stephenson could hardly answer. She had never thought of being anyone else. She had never even thought she would be better off if she had lived differently. The thought had never entered her head. She was the way she was. It was all there for her. Everything was set. It could never be any different.

109

"Well, you see, darling," she answered Fiona, "I have your father. He takes up most of my time. I play my role for him. I admire so much everything he does."

"But how can you share his life? It seems to me all you're doing is running his house beautifully and waiting for him to tell you what to do," Fiona said.

"Fiona, I don't think you can expect much else from a woman. She has to play the secondary role, be part of a team working together. Let's have some luncheon."

"I'm sorry, Mummy. I'm only turning to you for help. I don't understand, I thought you'd help. You know we've talked all around about living, but we haven't touched on the real problem. That's love," and Fiona smiled kindly at her mother.

They ordered luncheon. Dover sole grilled with a mustard sauce. Fiona could hardly wait for the headwaiter to leave. She wanted to pursue the subject of Daddy. She had opened a side of her mother she had never realized existed.

"Mummy, you see love is so important to all of us. To know that we're appreciated somehow, that a man cannot do without us."

Mrs. Stephenson twisted the ruby. "But men can do very well without us. They don't need us. There is always another woman ready and very available."

"Other men are available to us, too," Fiona answered firmly.

"Yes, but your conscience, your position, your children make it difficult for a woman. You are dependent on your husband. I'm sure you will see what I mean. I need your father, he gives me security. I don't mean the money. I mean he's always there to arrange for me."

"But, Mummy—love, don't you have that?" said Fiona raising her voice.

"Darling, security is part of love. A man provides security."

"No, I don't mean security. I mean love—sex is a big part of it, so is understanding, stimulation. I need all of them," Fiona said emphatically.

Mrs. Stephenson paused. She wished the sole would arrive. "Darling, sex is more important to some. I quite understand. My stimulation comes from your father and what he does."

110

"You mean you are stimulated when you're alone talking about business, people, and even the weather?"

"Yes, we have our understanding together. Your father decides what we do. We usually do what he has planned."

Fiona thought their life sounded dreadfully dull.

Mrs. Stephenson went on, "You are going to find that you have a certain role. That is important. You are quite exceptional. I don't mean you are gifted. But you are entering into that special world, I suppose you would call it society, although I hate the word. You are expected to act accordingly. Entertain well, be chic, aid charity, know everybody important, and observe all the standards we live by and I now enjoy. I know sometimes they may seem false, but these values are part of us, of our group. We can't deny them—or change them. And sometimes they're a good influence. That carries me forward."

Fiona asked, "How can you enjoy a false life—anything that's false?"

"I once decided to forget those standards, to try to live an ordinary sort of life. I did for a time. But then I got bored. I had nothing else. I just couldn't settle down to the bridge club in Connecticut and the dances at a country club. Maybe you would have wanted all that. But like you, I wanted to be exceptional, a leader, like your father."

"I understand," said Fiona, looking around the restaurant to see who was watching them.

"I try hard to be gracious, charming, because I want to be admired. You see, Fiona, I haven't really had the love you hope to have. So I've had to settle for what I do best. And I struggle just like everyone else, even with all the security in the world."

"Mummy," Fiona said taking her mother's hand, "I understand now. I do."

"No, you really don't, Fiona. You see, I never dared take a chance. I was too frightened of losing my security. I was too frightened of your father and I know he takes advantages often. He knows I fear what others will think. I'm a big front."

"He sounds so horrible, Mummy," Fiona said.

"No, he is not horrible at all. He just doesn't understand that I

111

want to provide love and warmth. He rejects it. He's too proud. He's too strong, too sure of himself. I've failed. I can't communicate to him. We're overburdened, both of us, and driving ourselves on to I don't know what. Yet we won't let go ever. Our pride is too strong."

"And what makes Daddy so aggressive?" Fiona asked.

"I suppose it's his background, coming from a middle class, midwestern family," Mrs. Stephenson answered.

Fiona thought of Michael's family. I guess they might be called rich middle class, she figured.

"Your grandfather worked hard, starting his first newspaper in a small town and he gave it all to your father, who really made it grow. But your father was never made for the small town. He dreamed of bigger things. It took him ten years to expand, but then he reached that social impasse where he wasn't quite all the way there. He needed help." These last words seemed final. Mrs. Stephenson did not want to go on.

The waiter arrived with the two Dover sole, golden brown and sprinkled with parsley. He presented the fish to Fiona and her mother on the large silver platter.

"Would Madame prefer that I prepare them?" the headwaiter asked.

"Oh yes, please do," said Mrs. Stephenson.

The headwaiter took the knife and with one stroke cut the two sole right down the middle.

"That's where you came in, right, Mummy, to shore up Daddy's social position? I thought so for a long time," said Fiona.

Mrs. Stephenson didn't answer.

The headwaiter cut the sole at the sides and lifted hundreds of tiny bones away from the flesh.

"I suppose I did help, darling. I knew he needed me then. But now he has accomplished almost everything and I am not that important any more. The struggle is over."

Fiona lifted her head high and looked around the restaurant. It was like a goldfish bowl, everyone staring. Fiona knew they were staring. But wouldn't it be awful if they didn't look. Fiona realized Michael needed her too, just as her father had used Mummy.

The headwaiter finished deboning the last sole. He lifted out the backbone and the small vertebrae, all perfectly in place. The sole lay neatly pieced in quarters on each white plate with four perfectly shaped small white boiled potatoes. The waiter spooned out the thick, yellowish mustard sauce. By then, Mrs. Stephenson and Fiona were not at all hungry.

12

MICHAEL

Fiona was too tired to go to the Fifty-seventh Street antique store. She had passed by the day before and seen that Lowestoft platter with the gold and black shield, surrounded by small yellow, purple, blue and red flowers, held up by a bow. It would have completed her set and filled out the shelf, before Michael took the space for his fish collection.

She would return next week. The luncheon with Mummy had exhausted her.

She lay down on their bed, depressed about her mother and, in a way, depressed about herself. She really had been a fool charging off to luncheon full of herself, full of challenging her mother. I should have left poor Mummy alone, she suffers enough, she thought.

Fiona slipped the cord holding back the curtain to the bedpost. The four red tassels dropped with a thump to the side and Fiona was enclosed. Inside, the yellow canopy and side curtains filled her bed full of warming sun colors.

Fiona realized that her situation was the same as her mother's. Michael, after he'd gotten to the top, might treat her just as a wife. That was not enough. She couldn't accept the secondary role. She wanted to be equal, to be part of Michael.

She snuggled up in bed. The quilted, flowered bedspread felt soft and comfortable. Michael had a long way to go before his career could swallow up both of them. She could easily corrupt him and stunt his ambition, or allow him to go on his flabby, fruitless way. She closed her eyes, secure once again in the thought that she would control, not be controlled. Like her mother. Poor Mummy. And Fiona went to sleep, her head turned to the side and her hair trailing behind all over the pink and red cabbage roses with their blue stems and leaves.

Michael rang the bell twice and was about to pull out his gold key chain, a gift of Uncle John. How could he ever forget Uncle John with those keys attached to him? He had just turned the key in the lock when Mary, the maid, opened the heavy mahogany double doors.

"Bon soir," she said. The doors had recently been waxed and Michael ran his hand with pleasure across the smooth, shining wood.

He went down the long blue flocked, wallpapered hall and into his dressing room. He took off his jacket, placed it on the clothes horse, put on his dressing gown which had been laid out and pressed by Pierre. He rearranged his riding boots next to the glass table. He opened the closet and slid out the small black mahogany bar. Mary had placed the ice in the matching mahogany bucket at exactly six forty-five so that Michael would not have to face melting ice. He couldn't stand a watered-down drink. He poured three fingers of Johnny Walker Red, dropped three ice cubes with a musical clink into the crystal glass, and added two fingers of bottled mineral water. He took a long swallow and the drink was gone in the third gulp. Following the same system, he made himself another drink and then pushed the buzzer. Pierre arrived.

"Where is Madame?"

"I believe she is in, sir, in her room. I mean, in your room. I see her door is shut. We did not want to disturb her and, as instructed, have referred all calls to the answering service."

"Fine, Pierre," Michael said curtly and he drank again.

Carrying his glass, he turned to their bedroom and rapped on the door. There was no answer. He banged with his fist.

115

"Yes," said Fiona.

"It's me. May I come into our room, Fiona?"

She rolled over in bed, rubbed her eyes and looked up at the yellow canopy top. "Come in, darling. Here I am," she said softly.

The door opened.

"Where are you?" he asked quickly.

"Snuggled in, darling," and she kicked the bed curtain apart just enough so that Michael caught her wiggling toes and her slender ankle.

"Who are you trying to hide from in there?" he said moving to the bed.

"Not you," Fiona answered.

Michael felt along the curtain for the cord. He caught Fiona's ankle and pulled. She squealed.

"Where is that god damned cord?" he said. He went to the other side of the bed and felt.

Fiona was now laughing. "You *are* clumsy," she said.

Michael slammed his empty glass down on the Louis XVI desk, making sure the wet glass rested in the ash tray.

"Clumsy? That I'm not," and he groped again. He took the curtain and gave a big tug and the hooks jumped out of the curtain rod. He pulled. The curtain opened just wide enough for Michael to see in.

Fiona got up on her hands and knees, stuck her head out of the other side, and said teasingly, "Here I am. Come and get me." Michael pulled at the curtain and one side fell to the floor.

He jumped on the bed, grasping Fiona round the hips, and pulled her toward him.

"My god, you terrified me, coming from that direction," Fiona said. "I thought you would come from the other side."

Michael pulled her closer, holding her hips firmly. His left hand ran up and down her buttocks.

"I'll show you," and Fiona rolled over on her back, pulling Michael down to her. They kissed. She tore at his hair.

Michael licked her ears and nibbled at the lobes.

"The servants, Michael, the servants. The door, close it, you beast, close it," and she pulled his head around again to her lips.

116

"Undress, darling," Michael whispered.

"No, you do that," she answered.

Michael reached around Fiona's back for the zipper. He felt her smooth neck. He wanted to kiss her there. The snap unsnapped, the zipper stuck. Michael ripped the dress down the back and pulled it away from Fiona's body. He lifted the lacy slip over Fiona's head. It fell to the floor. Michael pulled at the one curtain and closed the part around their heads. Then he undressed. Their clothes lay in a pool at the side of the bed.

"More darling, more, please Fiona, Fiona." His words were smothered with his heavy breathing. Fiona went on. She knew she had triumphed. Michael was hers now.

She stopped short, pulled her head up quickly and planted her lips again on his. Then, "Yes, Michael. Go on. Go on."

Finally they fell apart, spent.

"Close the curtain. You see they do have a use," Fiona said.

"I swore I would never sleep under that damn canopy. You always win, Fiona. You always get your way."

"I do? Really, do you think so?" she answered hopefully.

"Oh, I'm exhausted. You're some hussy," Michael sighed.

"That's not a very nice way to describe your wife."

Michael got off the bed and started out of the room. "Hardly what your mother would expect of you," he said, as he went down the hall and into his dressing room. He poured himself another drink.

Fiona got up off the bed and followed. "How about one for me, darling? Now that you're finished with me, you've forgotten I'm still around."

"Oh yes, here you go," and he poured Fiona three fingers too.

"That's too much. I can never take it that strong. You mean you've been drinking those since you've been home?"

"Why not? I had a tough day at the Senator's. That old prune is enough to drive anyone to drink."

"Michael, I'd say you've had a few drinks for yourself. I smelt it on your breath."

"You seemed to enjoy it enough, even though there was a little whiskey mixed in," he snapped back. For the first time Fiona was watching the social veneer peel off Michael. She wasn't shocked, but startled.

"I've never seen you so relaxed in bed," and the last two words trailed away as though Fiona wanted to hide them.

"I wasn't any more relaxed than usual. You asked me in your house," Michael answered defiantly.

"Yes, I suppose I did."

They both stood, drinks in hand, looking at each other. Michael nervously dug his slipper into the beige carpet. He wasn't enjoying Fiona's analysis of him.

Fiona wouldn't let on. Secretly she had triumphed in seducing Michael so easily. She thought of other men. They would fall just the same way. Michael had been right. She had to admit she had been a hussy and enjoyed every minute. The sensuous pleasure was great enough, but Fiona now knew she could play any role—her mother's, the refined, soft young lady, or the savage, strong, sensuous woman. She was satisfied she could choose her way. There were no walls to block her.

But Fiona worried about Michael sitting there in front of her on the couch firmly holding his glass. His face appeared flabby. His mouth drooped, just like his mother's. He was no longer the young, dashing Michael, so sure of himself. The whiskey relaxed him enough to bring out his real character. His controlled sophistication disappeared. Instead, Fiona saw him as soft, sapped of even selfish drive. Suddenly she was frightened. He was perfectly satisfied, smugly secure sitting there on the black leather couch surrounded by the puffy swan's-down cushions in violent shades of red, orange, and purple, a gift of Michael's mother.

"Well, don't stand there, Fiona. Come into my web. Have another drink. Relax. It's been a long day and we still have the night to go."

Fiona passed the globe, spun it around hard with her hand and sat bolt upright on the same couch.

"Don't you think we've had enough to drink?" she asked.

Michael looked straight at her and said, "We aren't children you know. We're over the age. We ought to enjoy ourselves now. You're so critical. I can see you looking at me as though you're disappointed.

I can feel the disappointment all around us right in this room."
Michael took another swallow of his drink.

"I'm not really disappointed. Just worried. We don't seem to be
getting any place," Fiona answered, turning away so that he couldn't
see the sadness in her eyes. She was about to get up and leave, make
some excuse to avoid a discussion.

"Fiona, you're spoiled," Michael continued. "You'll never be
happy. Every day there's something new you want. Think how lucky
we are. I could be in Vietnam. Maybe I would be if I didn't have
this damned high blood pressure. You drive a man into the wall with
your prodding and nagging. Sometimes I want to cover my ears,"
and Michael did, like a little boy.

"I don't mean to nag," Fiona answered, trying to stop the argu-
ment. "Let's forget the whole thing."

"No," he snapped back. "Let's not. You've changed. You nag.
You want to know everything about what I'm doing. You're even telling me what to do."

"That's not true," Fiona answered, pushing her hair back over her
shoulder. "Anyway," she continued, "I thought that now you're in
the Senator's office we would find our life more stimulating. I mean,
get out of the straitjacket of seeing the same people. You never
talk about your job. I never know what's going on. There must be
*some*thing important you're involved in, isn't there?" Why *did* she
have to pry and push so? Was there a wall between them already?

Michael hadn't told Fiona the truth. He was very concerned about
his job with the Senator.

No one should ever know—Michael had decided that—but he really
had no authority in the office. He had ended up making social engagements for the Senator and the Senator's wife. Where they had
trouble getting in, where they hadn't been invited, he arranged
through his contacts. He even fixed up the right tables at the restaurants.

Michael had wanted to do some sort of liaison work between the
Senator's office and Cain's campaign headquarters. He was so far
away from what was going on politically, he didn't even know how
the Senator really felt about Cain.

Fiona decided to be sweet, more tolerant. She so much wanted to talk frankly. If only he understood she was trying to help.

"What are you thinking about, darling? Please tell me. I so much want to know."

"There you go again, Fiona, prodding. I was thinking how politicians who've been with big law firms operate. Let's face it, many of the clients go to these law firms indirectly for political favors."

Fiona didn't know that her father and Uncle John had persuaded the Senator to take Michael on as an administrative assistant.

"We know, don't we, darling, that politics isn't exactly the cleanest game," said Fiona. "But I can't help but admire the Senator, because he started with nothing, no backing, not much money, and he's gotten to the top. He's respected by everyone. I suppose he's one of the last who'll come to power without lots of private money behind him. You remember what Uncle John said the other day. It takes money to rise to the top in politics. He seemed to imply that the young men have to buy their way into power. The idea revolts me. Yes, I know I'm sounding like a hypocrite," Fiona admitted.

"Fiona, it's not that you're a hypocrite. It's that you're just plain silly. The public likes the glamour image of a candidate. For them, the campaigns have turned into a great show—a television show. Only this political show is even better than a play or a movie. It's for real. The people love the fighting, the intrigue, the human drama unfolding right before their eyes. Each man and woman feels important because they can sit snugly at home and decide who they can vote for. The battle and the personalities take them out of their humdrum, boring little lives. The wives like a handsome candidate. The candidate's wife is portrayed as the all American good mother. That's why, when I run, Fiona, you should be pregnant." He meant this last as a joke.

Fiona bumped her arm against the arm of the couch and her drink fell to the carpet. She didn't bother to wipe up the Scotch and the water. The ice melted into the rug.

"Housewives thrill at the idea, I can help get him elected. I'm sharing part of his glory. The masses love their moment of power because they can for once with their vote stand up and make an important decision."

120

Fiona was delighted. She had pricked his interest at last. They were actually excited, alive and together, alone.

Michael was warming up. He felt his former, fiery, ambitious self. He understood how politicians got elected, but could he ever do it? He went to the bar, opened another bottle of Johnny Walker Red, and continued, "Look at the President, the power he has to reach into every home. It's all planned. Every day down in the White House the President is preparing his frozen food package to feed the American public. We are stuffed full, like the Strasbourg geese. We don't have the information. We just have to accept tonight what the President planned for X-day's menu. Did you see the other day in the *Times* the four-column headline, 'U. S. to Step Up Defoliation Missions in Vietnam'? And the story went on to say, 'Pleased with the effectiveness of chemical defoliation and crop destruction missions, the United States military is taking steps to triple the capacity of those efforts.' They call it Operation Ranch Hand. You know, left over from pioneering days. Six planes will spray over a million gallons of nontoxic herbicide over five hundred thousand acres."

Fiona interrupted. "Yes, but will they only kill the crops where the enemy is?"

"Who knows where the enemy is. Thousands of peasants will die because of lack of food. The spray damages the rubber and rice crops, but clears the area of vegetation so our planes can find their targets. There has been discussion about the inhumanity of destroying rice when thirty per cent of the world needs more food. Our enemy casts us in the role of the unmerciful killer. 'Then conquer we must, when our cause it is just, and this be our motto: "In God is our trust." And the star-spangled banner in triumph shall wave o'er the land of the free and the home of the brave.' Yes, how do we explain our mission in Vietnam to the rest of the world and to history?" Michael finished. He had taken his theme from Cain's campaign. Fiona had gone to the rally to hear Paul speak, and the defoliation speech had made headlines.

Fiona did not respond, but asked for another whiskey.

121

13

CHARITY

They were on the roof in the Fifty-seventh Street penthouse gardens
overlooking the cement and glass New York below. The wind was
blowing the soot settling on the white wrought iron furniture and
bamboo bar which had been rolled out for the party. The Italian
houseman, in white jacket with brass buttons embossed with a family
crest, was mixing the drinks. Air whistled through the plumbing
vents just over the flower canvassed bamboo swing. The hostess,
Mrs. Marella Signatelli, was young, pregnant, wearing a free-flowing
black and white tent dress.

It was three weeks since she had called Fiona and lured her to
luncheon by saying Catherine Cain would be there. She kept fixing
her hair, keeping one ear peeled for the telephone. Would Fiona
come? Would they all come? It was important, yes, important for
the charity event, the annual dance, but more important for
the hostess, because she had arranged for months to get the in-
young of this season's most attractive to support her charity. But
would *she* come, that is, Fiona Chase?

The Italian hostess was rich, like her invited guests. Her husband
had the business empire, but she did not have the social position.
At least, not the social position of Fiona. There was no doubt that
Fiona was it right now, right this season.

122

"Mario, did the phone ring? Are you sure Mrs. Chase didn't leave a message?"

Her maître d'hôtel didn't answer. He only shook his head.

She went over to the speaker and pushed it back behind the hibiscus plants which had just arrived that morning. If only just one flower would open in time for luncheon, she thought.

The phone rang. The Italian hostess dashed across the terrace and then back again to the other side. Her maître d'hôtel was holding the red phone out of the window.

"Yes, darling. How wonderful you can come. Oh, tell the decorator to wait just for a few minutes longer. Please, certainly you can hold up the plane. After all, it is your plane, yours alone. Wonderful you are coming," and she hung up the phone and frowned. Still no word from Fiona. Really, she was rude, so rude not to let her know. She supposed Fiona would be checking her mother to see if it was all right.

She walked quickly across the brick terrace and puffed up again the red linen cushions on the white linen couch. She was worried about the cold soup, avocado, creamed with a touch of onion. The color suited the avocado green tablecloths. The seating arrangement had been worked on last night and by now she had it memorized.

"Mario, please make sure the soot doesn't land in the crystal glasses on the bar. You must be able to do something. Cover them with a napkin." The glasses for cocktails were huge, just too big to hold in the hand, but her husband liked the feel of the big round glass filled with whiskey.

Down below Mrs. Wallace F. Renn IV got out of her chauffeur-driven car. She thought to herself, really such a bore, all these charity lunches, especially when I'm so busy, but my Italian friend did say Fiona would be there and the Chases were the makable ones, so I suppose I had to come. I really would not have let them use my name on the list as a sponsor if Fiona's name had not been there. It was right to be there on that list. Very in, Mrs. Renn thought to herself, as she told the elevator man to take her to the penthouse. As the elevator started up, she took her blue glasses from her small straw bag and put them on. It was difficult, because her big brimmed straw hat hung low over her ears. She unbuttoned another button on her purple and yellow snake print mannish shirt and twisted her orange hopsack skirt around so that the belt was right in the middle. The door opened and she was standing in the black and white marble entrance to the penthouse. "My god, that red door certainly looks hellish there. These Italians really have the worst taste."

A short Italian maid, with shiny black hair, black uniform and white lace trimmed apron, let Mrs. Renn in.

"Good afternoon."

"Madame is up on the terrace."

"I'll go up."

Soon she was in their bedroom, the Italian tycoon's bedroom. Double bed, interesting heavy walnut framed mirrors, red silk tassled bed cover, black-brown rug, dreary, and then Mrs. Renn went out on the terrace.

"Darling, how divine," she said exuberantly. "So wonderful to see you. So wonderful. Darling, really, how sweet of you to do this for the museum. I understand the program is going to be a big success."

"So nice of you to be here."

Mrs. Marella Signatelli twiddled with her dyed black hair, which had grown much longer this morning, thanks to Albert's new dyed-to-match piece attached firmly to her real hair.

She stood back, taking in Mrs. Renn—the purple snake print blouse, the Panama straw hat, knitted white stockings, black brass buckled, low-heeled shoes. Mrs. Renn stood back, secure behind her blue, blue glasses.

"A drink?" Mrs. Signatelli asked.

"I will," said Mrs. Renn, placing her hand inside her wide black leather belt. She loved the feel of the smooth, shiny leather. She moved her hand to the big brass buckle and pulled firmly downward. She had lost more weight and that was most satisfying.

"What will you take?" Mrs. Signatelli asked.

"A light gin and tonic," Mrs. Renn answered, and she thought to herself, the Italian lady still has that wonderful neat, slick mannequin look. And the way she walked, talked, turned her head, almost dramatically showed, in spite of her successful marriage, the Italian lady was very much on the runway.

"What big glasses you have," said Mrs. Renn, as she took her drink.

"They hold more, Emilio always says."

"I see," said Mrs. Renn, smiling in that sick, superior way.

"What about the decorating, darling? Extensive?" asked Mrs. Signatelli.

"No, not at all. Lady Eleanor is waiting for me in her car to fly up to Maine. You know we have a fishing shack, as we call it, near the Cove."

"I'm sure it's hardly a shack," said Mrs. Signatelli.

"No, not really—just six cosy bedrooms—all very rough, all chintzes. I'm sure Lady Eleanor will cheer it up with her bright colors. My other decorator did it over two years ago, but it is already looking a little rundown at the heels," Mrs. Renn said methodically.

Mrs. Signatelli continued: "Sorry to hear about Andy. That must have been a dreadful shock," and she sighed sympathetically.

"Andy was a wonderful Lab, so proud, so good and fine with the children. Divine dog. It's just awful he died. I just can't get over it. He got along so well with George. He's our lion—another darling. They never disturbed each other."

"You mean George came in your beautiful house?" the Italian lady said, shocked.

"Oh yes, he even sleeps sometimes on our bed. I love his curly mane, so adorable. I always had toy lions, you know, those cuddly German ones, when I was a child. I was determined to have a real lion when I left Mother and got married," Mrs. Renn said emphatically.

The Italian lady played with her green, red and white enamel snake bracelets, rubbing the three snakes together and twisting them round and round. The snakes' ruby tongues licked her wrist. "To the cause, the museum's benefit," she said and she bumped glasses with Mrs. Renn, who had trouble holding on. The tonic water spilled over the brick terrace.

"Don't worry, it's treated, so much has been spilled here before," said Mrs. Signatelli, who ran for the ringing telephone.

"It's Mrs. Chase," said the maître d'hôtel from inside the bedroom.

"Hello, hello, Fiona, how are you, darling? Of course you're coming, remember, you promised. Oh yes, plenty of time. I expect Catherine Cain will be here later. Good-bye, darling," and she hung up the phone and smiled.

She swept out onto the terrace announcing triumphantly, "She's coming. Yes she is."

"Who?" asked Mrs. Renn.

"Fiona Chase."

"Oh, good. I'll be glad to see her."

Downstairs a photographer stood outside the apartment. He paced back and forth under the canopy, nodding to the doorman.

"When are they coming?" he asked, sliding the strap holding his camera around his neck. He pulled his hat down over his happy face.

"They'll be along. You know the ladies are always late. Who's the big one today? Who are you trying to get, Jacqueline Kennedy?" the doorman asked.

"No, she's not expected. It's Fiona Chase and Cain, the lady whose husband is running for Congress in this district. You've seen him all over the city," the photographer answered.

Fiona was just about to get out of the taxi when she saw Catherine Cain approaching. She felt like telling the cab driver to go around the block. She couldn't face Catherine right that moment.

But Fiona got out of the taxi. Catherine, her long hair falling over her forehead, walked slowly up to the apartment house. Fiona put on her dark glasses. She fumbled nervously in her purse and handed the cabbie two dollars.

"As I was telling you, Miss," the cabbie began, "it's a terrible world—sick, sick. I took my sister ten miles out of the city to the cemetery and all she told me was, 'Bert, you're exhausting me. You will be the cause of my next heart attack.'" Fiona slammed the door. She was ready to face Catherine.

"Darling, how are you? It's been so long," Fiona said cheerily.

Catherine pushed her hair away from her face. "I barely recognized you under those dark glasses. You always are so chic." And they each kissed each other on both cheeks.

126

Fiona pushed her glasses up off her face and into her hair.

The photographer moved in smiling, a leer on his face, like the cat ready to pounce.

The ladies stopped talking and froze to the sidewalk. The doorman moved casually inside the apartment to hold open the door. It had been arranged between the doorman and the photographer to lay the trap.

"Who's he?" asked Catherine, frightened.

"Oh just a photographer shooting the party. He's all right."

"Tony, can't you see Mrs. Cain doesn't want to," Fiona called out to him as he snapped away.

"Never mind, go on, it's great. Both of you together looked sensational," he yelled back from behind his camera.

Fiona smiled. Catherine scowled and moved away from Fiona.

"You know how Paul hates all this social publicity. He'll be furious."

"But Catherine, you're looking wonderful. It will be a great shot," Fiona said, trying to reassure her.

Fiona posed, walked a way out from under the canopy into the sun. The photographer followed her with his lens. Catherine stood isolated from the scene, seemingly uncertain.

"Enough, Tony, may we be excused? We've done our duty," Fiona said, taking Catherine by the arm of her black and white tweed Chanel suit. They passed through the door up the lobby steps, followed by Tony. As the elevator door closed, Fiona heard Tony tell the doorman: "She's a great lady, Mrs. Chase. Just a knockout—perfection."

Fiona and Catherine were closed into the elevator together on their way up. Catherine stood straight, hanging tightly onto the brass rail. Fiona leaned casually against the rail at the other end of the car. Catherine looked through Fiona and after a long pause couldn't resist any longer.

"With the war in Vietnam, all the killing, misery in the world, all these parties and ladies' luncheons seem such a horrible waste, so wrong. I wish I hadn't come." The door opened directly onto the terrace.

Fiona thought Catherine's remark about Vietnam too righteous, almost sickening so.

The bright sun dazzled Catherine and Fiona as they stepped out of the car. All eyes turned on them. Fiona made her entrance, trailed by Catherine. Fiona kept remembering Catherine's words when they were friends painting together in Paris, "I will marry a great man." She hadn't forgotten her reply and she shuddered to think what she had said: "I'll marry for love."

Mrs. Signatelli flew to Fiona and Catherine, just as though she had been released from a bird cage.

"Oh darlings, you have come to us and together. What a happy coincidence, simply wonderful! Come, let's drink and have luncheon," and she threw out her arm to call the maître d'hôtel.

Catherine looked irritated that Marella had come so quickly to Fiona.

The guests split up in groups around the penthouse terrace.

Catherine and Fiona knew all their faces, but Fiona broke away from Catherine and moved to the group on the right, next to the chimney with the air vents rising from the apartments below. Catherine hesitated and finally stayed in one spot near the bamboo swing, which was pushed back and forth by a blond long-haired man, pinched into his double-breasted navy flannel suit. Next to him, an older woman with long, stringy hair cuddled up. They whispered back and forth.

"She is divine, marvelous," said the man as he adjusted his blue and white polka dot tie.

"Who's the lady standing next to us right there?" said the woman pointing directly at Catherine.

"I don't know, but she looks slightly out of sorts," he whispered.

"I suppose you are very busy," the woman continued.

"Yes, so much to do. I've been designing the wardrobe for a movie and you know the White House keeps me running back and forth."

"So unchic, aren't they?" the lady whispered and her hair blew down over her face.

"We try our best," said the designer and he thought the lady needed her hair washed.

Catherine walked away from the swing and straight into the

group gathered around Fiona. When Catherine arrived, they all stopped talking.

"Oh there you are, Catherine. Do you know everyone?" Fiona asked.

"No, I don't."

"This is Janet Smiley. She does so much for the theater. Those park performances, you know." Mrs. Smiley fluttered her eyelashes and gave her hand.

"This is Freddie, my darling friend."

"Oh yes, I admire your clothes," said Catherine.

Freddie stood erect, bowed stiffly, holding himself in in his pinstriped grey suit, white collar and blue and white striped shirt. His hair was flying in the wind and Catherine watched the way he kept putting the windblown strands back over the bare spots.

"And darling, this is Bette Lou Whiting. Of course, you've met before I am sure."

Bette Lou looked puzzled, but managed a smile that Catherine knew so well.

"No, I don't know Bette Lou. How do you do," and Catherine gave her hand.

"I understand your husband is running for Congress," Bette Lou began. She rested her other hand at the waist of her multicolored Pucci dress.

"Yes, he's campaigning very hard," said Catherine.

"Republican, or Democrat?" Bette Lou asked.

"Democrat," Catherine answered, raising her voice.

"I believe he's running in your district, Bette Lou," said Fiona, "and I'm sure it's your district, because you're right around the corner from us."

Catherine looked nervously at Fiona.

"Yes, our town house is on the same block," Bette Lou said.

"Then you must be interested in the campaign," Catherine said.

"Yes, we are, but my husband always votes for that Republican, what's his name? Paul somebody."

"No, you mean Henry Vanderlip. He's a fine man. He's running against my husband," Catherine interrupted.

129

Bette Lou turned to the rest of the group and started her own conversation. Catherine glanced at Fiona, who was smiling.

"The party last night was just divine," Bette Lou rattled on. "We had a small dinner before the opening. Delicious and the company perfect. You know, the Whitmans, just back from Europe. She's giving more of her French signed pieces to the Met. So nice of them," and her words trailed off into New York space. She kept going, "I took Sam home after dinner and we went to the village and danced."

Freddie, the designer, came forward with big steps. He stood stiff and flicked his cigaret ashes from the gold holder casually onto the terrace. "Bette Lou," and he kissed her on both cheeks.

She moved in closer to Freddie.

"Don't tell me, darling," Freddie said, "that you are now becoming political. You never could be that square."

"You're so right, darling. I couldn't possibly take it up. I'm still taking trips on the Madison Avenue bus. They remind me of my old days, but now the buses aren't so much fun. They all run in groups of four and you have to wait so long on the corner."

"You mean they remind you of your young days," Catherine interjected.

Fiona didn't come to Catherine's rescue right away. She decided to let her struggle alone.

Catherine went over to the edge of the terrace and peered out at New York; across the way, Central Park—brown, parched—and to the left, the dirty UN building, so alone, reaching into space, and then the river, sparkling diamonds in the afternoon sun.

Catherine thought of her husband down there, out beating the pavement, shaking wet, hot hands. For a moment she wondered why he shouldn't be up here drinking a gin and tonic. Catherine took a long sip. It tasted good. She realized all that cement and steel stuck into the earth symbolized power and excitement. Paul, her husband, wanted power just as everyone else did, including the people on this terrace. But at least Paul was willing to do something for his. How can they just stand, sit, sleep, play, eat and drink, when there is a war going on? Then Catherine thought of Michael. He was so handsome, but what had he done so far? Not much. He was just like the others, rich, smug, secure and bored.

She was so glad she had married Paul Cain. There was something frantic, disturbing in Fiona. Catherine kept looking at her.

Suddenly Fiona came over to Catherine. Their eyes met. Fiona looked through Catherine severely, with a piercing stare. It was as though Fiona had summarized Catherine's thoughts. And Fiona had.

Fiona moved in closer, forcing Catherine back into the brick corner. Now they both were standing next to the air vents. Catherine felt her tweedy suit scratching against the rough red bricks.

"I know, Catherine, this party is boring you. I'm sorry. But when do we have a chance to meet? You never call," Fiona said, smiling now.

Fiona went on talking, pinning Catherine. "I know you distrust me because Paul used to like me. But I married Michael and it was decided on a weekend I was supposed to have been with Paul."

"Look, Fiona," Catherine spoke in a low, tense tone, "I don't give a damn about what you did or didn't do. But I do get pretty sick of your trying to be the queen bee of this whole silly society racket."

Fiona stared blankly, then thrust her hands in the low pockets of her red jersey dress and said, "For God's sake, Catherine, come off it. Can't you have any fun? Relax and see the good side. You need to swing a little, darling. You're working too hard at being the politician's wife. Haven't you seen politicians after they're elected to office?"

"I'm not a politician's wife. Paul is running for Congress. He's not some party boss. He's doing it on his own without lots of money. He's down there on the pavement working to win. He's not building his career on someone else's money and influence. And he's not riding in on the coat tails of anyone. He is just Paul Cain."

"I see the way it is," Fiona answered and she started to move away, leaving Catherine alone in the corner.

"Oh wait, please wait, Fiona. I'm sorry. I didn't mean to hurt you and . . ." Catherine said pleadingly.

"You didn't hurt me. Only yourself. You're so damn pompous.

Running for office is important, but there are other things too. I'm not sensitive about money, nor ashamed of having money. Maybe you are. After all, Paul's father and your father aren't exactly paupers, especially your mother after her second marriage," said Fiona.

Mrs. Signatelli came quickly across the terrace swinging her big glass back and forth and taking Fiona by the arm said, "Darling, you know all these people want to talk to you. Catherine isn't allowed to keep you to herself."

Catherine was blushing.

"Please, just a minute," Fiona said firmly.

"Oh, I understand. Something personal is going on here," and Mrs. Signatelli planted herself right next to Fiona and Catherine, who remained silent. Finally she moved away.

Catherine continued, "You mentioned Paul's father. He's out of the campaign. Everyone knows that and you also know Paul has publicly disagreed with his father, especially about Vietnam. You must have read the editorial in the *Times*," Catherine said proudly.

"No, I didn't. I really didn't," said Fiona, remembering Michael had taken line for line Cain's speech and given it back to her.

Fiona didn't hear Catherine now. She didn't see the other guests. The party completely blurred before her eyes. Fiona was suddenly lost in her own thoughts. If only Michael could. Could what? And Fiona looked down at the brick terrace.

Catherine put her hand gently on Fiona's shoulder. "Are you all right, darling?" Catherine asked. And Fiona realized for the first time that the word darling meant nothing, absolutely nothing, and she thought, Catherine is no different than the rest of us here this afternoon. Just shrewder, tougher, more determined. Fiona decided she would rather suffer, feel, be sensitive—that was part of the refined life. Mummy had always said so. But Michael . . . She loved him anyway, whether he ever measured up to Cain, or whether he failed. But no, he couldn't fail. He must not fail.

It was time for luncheon. The cold, thick, green avocado soup was on the avocado green tables and the heavy, syrupy rich fresh cream floated on top, waiting to be stirred.

132

14

THE SENATOR

The Senator swung his black box-leather, bowl-shaped chair around quickly and looked through the glass wall. He saw the rivers wrapping their way around Manhattan. The wind was strong and the tiny white caps could be seen moving down river out to sea. *Le France* and the *United States* were both docked and their red and black and white, red and blue stacks stood out clearly against the bright blue fall sky. A few clouds hung up river beyond the George Washington Bridge and the Senator thought to himself his eyes were still good enough to see the cables holding up the double-decker expanse of steel and concrete.

He swung his chair back away from the river and pushed the green plastic button on his telephone box enclosed in a black leather case.

"Good morning, Mrs. Allen."

And Mrs. Allen's voice came back cheerily, "Good morning, Senator, did you have a nice trip up from Washington?"

"Excellent, but the Senate stayed in session much later than we expected. I'm sure my wife was disappointed I missed the dinner and theater. Send in young Chase, will you? He's been here more than three months now and I haven't sat down to talk to him."

"Yes, sir," Mrs. Allen said and the telephone box switched off.

The Senator swung around in his chair again and looked at the river. The Palisades stood out rugged and raw in the cold morning air, but by noon, with the bright sun overhead, the river would sparkle, melded into the land beyond and the sky above.

The telephone switched on and the Senator jumped, because he was thinking about how the Palisades could be used in his speech next week at the Brotherhood dinner at the Waldorf.

"Mrs. Allen again, Senator. He's not in."

"You mean he's out doing some work?" the Senator said.

"No, he hasn't come in yet this morning," she said softly.

The Senator picked up a pear shaped piece of crystal sitting in the left corner of his black leather desk. The pear was encrusted with his birth sign "Leo" and the Senator took the pear and squeezed it firmly in the palm of his hand. His palm was wet with nervous perspiration, as he squeezed even harder.

"Find that boy," he said. "Find that boy. Telephone him at home. I read in this morning's *Daily News* he was out last night at the opening where all the Kennedys went."

"You mean, sir," Mrs. Allen's voice was higher pitched now, as she became nervous, "you mean, Senator, I'm to call Mr. Michael Chase at home?"

"That's what I mean, Mrs. Allen. And tell him to get in here on the double," he shouted back and click, the machine was off again.

Mrs. Allen flicked to off her black button in her plastic telephone box. She pushed her rigid, wheeled secretarial chair back across the beige carpet outside the Senator's office. She got up and went over to the closet, opened the door and ran the water tap. She filled a glass pitcher marked with a line to two-thirds, came out of the closet and watered her plants. Mrs. Allen was a short woman, with long, straight grey-white hair overhanging a long, tired, angular face. Two American Indian silver bird earrings swinging back and forth hung from her sagging ear lobes. Anytime there was a problem with the Senator she always watered her yellowing, rarely blooming African violets, to which she refused to feed plant food because she didn't believe in forcing anything, people or plants.

This morning she wasn't about to force Michael Chase out of bed.

She already knew he was there, because he had phoned in to say he was on his way and Mrs. Allen had no intention of telling the Senator. She just hoped Michael would get to the office now.

The Senator's door opened and there he stood, an imposing, grey-haired, portly and ruddy-faced image of a Senator. His mouth was closed firmly, his jaw set. Mrs. Allen knew there would be trouble.

"Did you get that young Chase yet, Mrs. Allen? Before you answer, I would like to say I haven't seen the lights on your lines appear on my black box. Mrs. Allen, are you listening?" he said, raising his voice.

"Yes I am, Senator." She put down the glass pitcher and returned to her desk and picked up her dictating pad and pencil. The pad was enclosed in a black leather case, the gift of the Senator and his wife for Christmas two years back. She hoped the Senator would want to dictate.

"About Chase, I repeat again, about Chase." He was becoming furious.

"Senator, he's on his way in. I suggest he will be here momentarily."

The Senator started back into his office, but stopped short and dug the heel of his black shoe into the thick carpet. Mrs. Allen saw the mark.

Just as he was about to slam the door, he yelled back, "Mrs. Allen, I wish you would stop trying to mother all the young boys in this office. You really aren't doing them a favor. And don't you forget, you're working for me, not for the boys," and he slammed the door.

At ten thirty-five Michael passed the receptionist, who flashed Mrs. Allen that Chase was finally there.

Michael went to his desk, which was in a nine by fifteen aluminum walled office—pictureless, one chair, a calendar on the oak Danish modern desk with stainless steel legs. Michael hated his office because it was too small and when the skyscraper swayed, the walls creaked and after luncheon he felt seasick if the winds outside were high. He had no window, only the hard metal walls surrounding him and he refused to keep the door open because everyone passing by could see his legs and feet under the desk. Such bad taste the Senator had anyway. Michael had written a memorandum suggesting some

135

other interior decorator, but the Senator had merely penned back in his own writing, "I don't have your money."

Michael picked up his phone and dialed. He was not connected to the private box phone system and was on the ordinary setup, like the other just-out-of-law-school lawyers.

"Mrs. Allen," Michael began, "I'm in. How are you today, Mrs. Allen? And your mother, is she over the cold and feeling better too?" He was about to ask Mrs. Allen about her tabby cat too, but thought that would be exaggerating.

"I'll be right over. Well, when will he see me, Mrs. Allen," Michael said in a worried tone. "Mrs. Allen, I don't intend to be indiscreet, but what was on his mind? You have no idea? Should I wait? Yes, I'll check into the Brotherhood dinner seating arrangement. I'm sure Senator Norton will be there. That should make things complicated."

He hung up the phone. Michael was depressed. He thought to himself he had had it on this job. He never did see the Senator. What was he learning anyway? Just how to make table reservations and check seating arrangements and who is who and who is going to be there. His job had turned into that of a damn table seating agent for the Senator and that pushy wife. God, he couldn't stand that woman, he thought to himself. Maybe I should talk to Uncle John and see if he can talk to the Senator. Anything to get out of this place.

Michael was tired. He had been out late to the opening and then dancing after and until three in the morning. He had drunk too much and his head and the back of his neck ached. He reached into a desk drawer and shook two aspirin out of the bottle and broke two white Gelusil tablets out of their cellophane wrapping. He picked up the phone.

"Please, Miss Alexander, would you mind sending a boy around with a glass and jug of water."

Miss Alexander hung up the phone and turning to the secretary next to her said, "Chase wants his morning water. Yesterday he asked for ginger ale. He's a high, fast liver that one and he wants the service." Miss Alexander didn't need to speak to the clerk stand-

136

ing by. He had heard the conversation and was off for the water and glass before being asked.

The clerk placed the water jug on Michael's desk and waited.

Michael didn't look up. He was reading papers. He just waved his hand, signaling to the clerk, who retreated out of the door, worried he had offended Mr. Chase.

Michael knew he should have at least said thank you, or good morning. He worried about his intolerance toward people, but the worry was only momentary, because Michael was too concerned with himself to take the time for someone else.

When he was frustrated as he was now, he took his frustrations out on the object, or person nearest him. People were objects to him anyway.

Michael for the first time feared he might not succeed. He was worrying this morning. It must be his hangover. Then he told himself, be patient. You've only been working since August. If only the job wasn't so boring. He thought at that moment of Fiona. She cheered him. Beads of sweat ran in between the wrinkles on his brow. He wiped the trickles away quickly with the handkerchief he pulled out from his inside jacket pocket. Fiona was so busy with her social life and her possessions and at the same time deliriously happy with him that she couldn't really be worried. After all, she had many times deplored politics and admitted she really did not understand politics or business and wasn't even really interested. Like many women, Michael thought, Fiona only prodded, but didn't really think too much about anything.

He had to make sure Uncle John would see to it that his situation improved in the law firm. But he knew that was naïve. Uncle John would tell him to work harder.

Michael decided at that moment that he would insist on seeing the Senator. But how?

He got up from his desk and swallowed another glass of water. Bad taste, that New York water. If I had this office I'd buy the big green bottled mineral water, he thought to himself.

Michael was out of his cubicle and heading down the strawberry red carpeted hall. The skyscraper swayed. He could feel each move

137

and the grey metal walls creaked. Soon he was standing in front of Mrs. Allen's desk.

"Your African violets are looking better," he said softly and with gentle charm.

"Oh, I do hope so," said Mrs. Allen, looking up from her black electric typewriter.

Michael fixed his eyes on Mrs. Allen. He had a way of fixing on the little people, staring through them and sometimes appearing to be keenly interested, but really not listening at all.

"Mrs. Allen, thank you for this morning," and Michael smiled.

"I knew you and Mrs. Chase were out. I read about you in the paper this morning. It must have been a smashing party. Were the Kennedys really there? How did Mrs. Kennedy look?"

"Oh yes, I had a talk with Robert. You know we're quite friendly," he said in a blasé tone, knowing full well he had tried to approach Robert Kennedy, but had been given a casual nod only. Michael had a definite passion for anything Kennedy. Kennedy-mania, as Fiona called it.

Mrs. Allen looked warmly into Michael's eyes. She didn't speak, only enjoyed the few moments alone with this attractive young man, as she identified Michael around the office.

"Mrs. Allen, could you please do me a favor? I hope you don't mind me asking. Please get me into the Senator this morning," he said almost pleadingly.

"Mr. Chase, it is almost lunch time now and he will be leaving soon."

The Senator's door opened. He stood tall, framed in the door-way with his dark overcoat and Homburg, looking just as a Senator should look—a tower of self-content and outward calm. He pulled his black pigskin gloves out of his pocket. The gloves reminded Michael of Uncle John. He always carried them, but of better quality, Michael was thinking.

"Mrs. Allen, I'm off for luncheon. I'm hungry and grumpy. Pre-pare yourself for speech writing. Rough draft on the Palisades and Brotherhood and all that. After I dictate, turn it over to that young Brian, what's his name, that new boy we took from Harvard."

138

Michael stood silent, as though he didn't belong where he was. "Hello, Chase. How are you?" the Senator tossed out.

"Senator, I've been asking to see you. I have been—" Michael started to repeat the same phrase again.

"Yes, my boy. I'm always available. I've been meaning to see you. Set up an appointment with Mrs. Allen for eight forty-five tomorrow on the dot, that is if you can make it on time," and the Senator turned his tall, solid frame on his heel and was out of view, just as Mrs. Allen said:

"See how easy it is to arrange things."

"Thanks, Mrs. Allen," and Michael was off down the corridor back to his metal cubicle and this time he left the door open. He felt alone.

Michael got out of the canopy bed at seven-thirty. Fiona had just been warming her feet on Michael's. It felt so warm and safe, feet on feet, in the early morning. She was secretly pleased Michael was getting to work on time for once in two months.

They had been out late and had had a marvelous time at the ball. They had danced until three in the morning. Now Michael was up looking for his breakfast.

Fiona decided to get up too. She slipped out of bed and turned on the light. She shielded her eyes. She hadn't been up that early in a long time, except the day they had been married.

Michael was dressing and he could hear Pierre and Mary rattling the dishes in the kitchen. He smelled the fresh coffee brewing, just after it had come out of the electric coffee grinder. They are late with my breakfast, Michael was thinking, as Pierre, looking sleepy, appeared at the door to the dressing room with the captain's tray, laid with green and white striped doily and napkin. Four small yellow garnette roses sat next to the insulated silver coffee jug.

"What are you doing up?" Michael asked Fiona as she came into the room. Her long white negligee swirled around her body as she moved to the couch. Her hair was tied back with a red bow. Now she didn't look sleepy. Fiona sat down on the couch, tossed off her slippers and tucked her feet under the couch cushions.

"I've come to see you off. To wish you luck," and she smiled. To anyone else her smile was like seeing the sun come up.

"For God's sake, Fiona, what's the big deal?" said Michael, sputtering between a sip of his coffee in the pink rose cup. He went on talking, "I'm only going to see the Senator and who the hell is he anyway? Just a Senator and there are ninety-six, or ninety-eight. I can never remember the exact number."

Michael opened the door to the full-length mirror in his closet. He checked his navy blue and white polka dot tie, placing the knot in the middle and then turned sideways to look again. He was out of the door to the dressing room and left behind a cold "good-bye."

Fiona sat alone, waiting for her breakfast, which Mary set on the glass table with the flowers and the folded New York *Times*.

She picked up the newspaper and flipped through the second section and stopped at a picture of Cain with his Republican opponent. She thought Cain looked handsome and hadn't changed a bit from the days when she knew him well. What a strong face and those penetrating eyes, so secure and warm, so kind, she thought to herself. His Republican rival looked tired, weak and doomed, Fiona realized, as she sipped her fresh orange juice.

Fiona couldn't face the comparison between Michael and Paul Cain. She was realistic enough, though, to know that the comparison was always in her mind. Poor Michael just didn't seem to be getting there. He was not much of a fighter. She read the article. Cain's Vietnam theme was paying off. All the private polls and the experts picked him as a sure winner. If only Michael were there on that page, running. Fiona closed her eyes. She imagined Michael on the same page looking slick, elegant, handsome, but the picture still couldn't hide his weak brow, those thick sensuous lips and his almost effeminate beauty. She dreamed on. What would the article say, what could the article say, what had Michael done? These thoughts chilled her.

Mary came into the room. "Madame is feeling all right, I hope. You're looking so pale." Mary was always hoping that Fiona was going to have a baby.

Fiona looked up quickly and, recovering, said, "Oh Mary, really

140

I'm fine. Really I am," and she dropped the newspaper to the floor and clasped one hand to the other.

Michael wasn't taking any chances today on being late. He was in the subway and at the turnstile. He had only a ten-dollar bill, so he had to run up the subway stairs to get change in the tobacco shop.

"It's too early, Mister, I can't change that for you now. I haven't enough cash to go through the day," said the fat man puffing on a smelly cigar behind the sales counter.

"I need some cigars," Michael said quickly. "What's the best you've got?"

The man took another long puff. "In the back I've got some Havana cigars brought in by a friend at the UN. They're expensive."

"Fine, I'll take them," and Michael handed over the ten-dollar bill.

The man put his wet cigar down on the counter. It burned away and the stench was awful. He brought out the box and wrapped it quickly in ordinary brown paper. Michael was ashamed to carry the box, it looked so gross.

He left the store without counting the change. He went down the stairs into the subway, past the walls wet with water. The smell of urine permeated the stale subway air. He handed a woman sitting in a high wooden chair a dollar.

"How many do you want?" she said impatiently.

"One," answered Michael.

He fumbled the change and a nickel fell to the floor. He didn't bother to pick it up. The floor was too dirty.

The subway stopped and Michael had to push his way into the crowded car. He reached out for the shiny steel pole, grabbed it and he felt that slimy sweat of human hands. He let go, repulsed, and the subway started up. He lurched backward, stepping full force on a burly Negro with black polished shoes. The Negro smiled politely. Michael scowled.

The Senator was just out of the door of his duplex when his wife, Julie, stuck her head out.

"Now remember, don't be too hard on that boy. They give the

most divine parties," she said and the door opened wide. She stood clutching her bathrobe, spotted with coffee stains, as the Senator disappeared into the elevator. She slammed the door.

At the office, the Senator passed by Mrs. Allen.

"Good morning," he said.

"Good morning, Senator."

"Is Chase in? Get him please, right away," and he went into his office.

Michael came down the hall, his coat over his arm and the cigar box hidden underneath.

"Go right in, he's waiting. Good luck," and Mrs. Allen got up to run the water for her plants.

"Here, Mrs. Allen, I thought you might like these for friends," Michael said abruptly and handed her the cigar box.

Mrs. Allen didn't have a chance to say no, because Michael was already in the Senator's office and he closed the door behind him.

Inside, the Senator took his seat in the leather bowl chair. He turned quickly to the left to look north, up at the Palisades and then turned back again and fixed on Michael, who had never been in the private office alone with the Senator.

The Senator sat on a raised platform and big bowl-shaped, non-swiveling leather armchairs were placed below him in a half circle. Michael had first sat in the middle chair, but to escape the Senator's penetrating stare, moved to the end. The Senator swiveled around to keep his fix on Michael.

"Now, my boy, I can guess why you're here," the Senator began. He paused momentarily because he kept remembering his wife standing in the doorway. Her full-length portrait was on the wall looking down at him. Mrs. Borden was painted in a red velvet dress trimmed in ermine, and she stood with her hands on a pale blue Louis XVI bergère, her blond head turned out, her blue eyes a-sparkle.

"Yes, as I was saying, I imagine you want to see me about your job." The Senator now spoke in a Senate-resounding voice.

"Yes, Senator," answered Michael as he clasped his hands to the arm of the chair and sat up straighter.

"You're young and inexperienced. You haven't learned the funda-

142

mental rules of a law office. First rule: be on time. Now I know you might think being on time is passé, but I am a stickler for that. I don't have the time to be late. I know you're keenly interested in politics. That's good. I have been in touch with your uncle and your father. Uncle John agrees wholeheartedly with me. You're young and inexperienced and have lots to learn before we could even consider floating you for office.

"You've got to get out and beat the pavements. You boys with money think the grassroots, the people, are enticed with a name, good looks, publicity, all the phonies as I call them. Still the old way to the people is the winning way. Your image, Chase, is that of a playboy and I know your uncle is concerned. Correct it. Stay home and stay out of the social and fashion columns. Don't let your wife be photographed wearing the latest this and doing the latest that at the newest place. Have babies."

Michael's hands were wet. The Senator paused, swinging his chair back toward the Palisades. They look so strong, majestic in the early morning, he thought.

Michael couldn't speak. He waited and finally began, "Senator, I agree about my image, but, you see, my wife comes from a family used to being in the social eye."

The Senator was shocked to think that this rich young man sitting below him could blame his own weakness on his wife. He didn't respond, but waited for Michael.

"I know, Senator, what you mean about getting to the people, but I'm not permitted to here with my work," and Michael hesitated.

The Senator pushed the red button on his black box. "Mrs. Allen, take a memorandum. Transfer Chase to working down at the court with Burns and Cahill. Give him some of the detail work on real estate closings. I want him to be with the people who do a job."

"Yes, sir," Mrs. Allen's voice came back, almost sadly.

As Michael went out the door, the Senator, remembering what his wife had said that morning, trailed after him. "Don't be too discouraged. We'll give it a year and see how it goes. I know your Uncle John will be pleased and so will your father. Give my regards to your beautiful wife," and he shut the door, picked up the phone, and asked for John Chase.

143

15

CAIN

Cain's election day victory was, as predicted, a 3–1 plurality. A complete triumph. Now Catherine and Paul Cain were on their way.

Michael and Fiona watched Catherine flower. She went out more often to the right parties. She became chic. Paul's popularity increased to the point where he was compared to a Kennedy. The aura of stardom, the good looks and vigor, so popular today, were all theirs and together the Cains started to dominate the New York social scene, where the influence was.

It was only after Catherine overnight made the Best Dressed List that Fiona was stung badly. She had made the list at the same time, but Catherine was singled out for her impeccable taste, grace, and charm. What's more, Catherine was cited not only as a fashion leader, but for her role as "active and creative" in the arts, in civic and charity affairs.

When Michael read the civic affairs part of the citation, he was quick to criticize Fiona.

"You're too busy buying clothes, wining and dining, and going to parties and openings. Look at Catherine, she's risen above all this social bit," he told Fiona.

They were sitting in the dressing room. As usual, thought Fiona, always here together, bored most of the time, unable to communicate reasonably.

Michael's words stuck in Fiona's mind. He wanted the social part, she thought bitterly. I wanted more. What more, she asked herself then? But that was treacherous, because it was Michael on whom she'd counted for the "more."

"She's clever. Yes, she's clever," Michael went on, "about doing the right thing."

So is Mummy, Fiona thought to herself. They *are* clever; the whole phony world traps them and us. Yes, I'm trapped, she conceded.

"And you know, Fiona, they talk about us—spoiled, high living, wining, dining, but nothing about decadence. You know, all the bit Uncle John told me at luncheon. We've got to be careful," he urged.

"Careful of what?" Fiona said. She sat silent, composed. Michael's lecture didn't disturb her, only made her think of what she might have done wrong. Let him go on, she thought.

"Are you listening?" Michael finally asked.

"Yes, oh yes," Fiona answered immediately and added, "I want a drink." She wanted to say she needed it badly.

Michael looked at Fiona. He could see the sadness and anxiety in her eyes.

Fiona knew now that Michael was frustrated in his work, but she didn't dare sympathize. Sympathy was something Michael couldn't stand.

Fiona decided now was the moment to face the problem. She held her drink while Michael mixed his, but he was facing the mirrored bar wall.

"He's won. A great victory." She suffered in bringing it up. The idea that Cain really had it made, all the fame and fortune that were only Michael's dreams, tormented them both.

Michael dropped two pieces of ice into his glass. "A great victory. Bravo," and the bravo was weak, Fiona realized. Michael quickly added, "He won't last. Cain will burn out before he's forty. He's started too soon and got there too quickly."

"It's wonderful for them, especially for Catherine. She's so ambitious. She's fought to get there. She wouldn't leave a stone unturned," Fiona said and just as she finished, added her final thought.

"I'm intrigued how they will handle their success. I can't wait to see Catherine—good old independent, intellectual, opinionated Catherine—I can't wait to see her becoming public property." Fiona put down her glass and folded her arms.

Michael came away from the bar and sat down next to Fiona. He still couldn't say what really was on his mind, that he suffered so much because Cain, his friend, who had always won all the success, had now won his greatest triumph. If there was only some sure success in his own future. And then to think that he would be beholden to Paul Cain if he pursued a political career . . . That thought was unbearable.

Michael looked up. "It's going to be all right. Isn't it, Fiona?" he asked.

"What do you mean?" Fiona countered.

"I mean, one day we will win as they did."

Fiona took Michael's hand. She didn't know what to say. She was stunned. It was like talking to a child. "Oh darling, darling, I love you. Yes, our day is coming," she said.

Michael took his hand away. He realized how wrong it had been to confide in Fiona. "You know," he said, his whole tune changing, "we've got to face facts. He's won. He's going to be important in New York politics. He's our friend. We like them both. We can't fight them, can we? Can we?"

"No. Why should we? They used to be fond of us," Fiona said.

"I think we should make it our business to see them often. We should celebrate the victory of our friends."

"How?" Fiona asked. She unfolded her arms and looked at Michael in amazement. He had come full circle from hate and envy of the Cains to friendship. How weird, she thought, that feelings, real feelings never do come through.

"Simple, darling. We've got to give a party. A fabulous one. Let's honor the Cains," Michael said. "But will they come? They're busy, and I understand she's having a baby."

"How wonderful. How lucky they're having a child," and Fiona turned her head away from Michael's eyes and put her face into the corner of the couch.

"What's wrong?" Michael asked, sensing Fiona was disturbed.

146

"Nothing, nothing really at all," she answered and Fiona thought of Thursday morning, her visit to Dr. Saunders' office. "Of course, you're fine. You can have children." She remembered his warm, friendly eyes, so consoling and his words. "The next step is for your husband to have an examination." Fiona shuddered at her response: "I couldn't ask him to do that. He's too proud. He's opposed to having children now."

"Fiona, are you with me, or miles away?" Michael asked.

"With you, darling," she answered. "I was only thinking of having a baby."

"I've told you, Fiona, that will come later, when we're settled. There's too much going on. Now, about the party, make it the best. Call Catherine right away." He left to go to the bar.

Later, when we're settled, too much going on—all his words—Fiona thought meaningless. What would happen later? When would they be settled? What was going on? Nothing, really. Nothing. Fiona felt bored, emptied of life already.

Fiona picked up the Cain party list, neatly typed out with the names categorized into three groups: social, government, arts, and a listing for "just friends." Michael, with great enthusiasm, had made up the list, and Fiona had sat quietly by suggesting a few names. Finally the list had become so large that Fiona insisted it was impossible to seat so many people. Michael suggested they stick to the original two hundred, but invite fifty of the most important for dinner first, and "let in the crowd around eleven." They had decided the listing on Monday and already it was Thursday, and Fiona hadn't contacted Catherine Cain to see if they would agree to the party. Fiona couldn't face Michael's wrath if Cain refused.

She picked up the telephone to dial Catherine and stopped in the middle and redialed her mother.

"Mummy, how are you, darling?" Fiona said, raising her voice to sound happier than she was.

Mrs. Stephenson could tell Fiona was not herself.

"Mummy, I'm working up the list for the party, you know, for the Cains."

Mrs. Stephenson wasn't a bit surprised. She assumed Fiona would be gracious enough to give the party. She sensed disappointment and lack of enthusiasm in Fiona's conversation.

"Yes, Mummy, I'm glad you thought it such a good idea. The old guard, yes, I do think we should add a few more. You're a darling to come. I know how Daddy doesn't like the late evenings."

Mrs. Stephenson knew Fiona was worried when she had invited her family to the party. Mrs. Stephenson asked about Michael.

"He's fine, working hard. The Senator says maybe in a year there will be a new job. But you know Michael, he's always hoping for a miracle. He always says something could happen."

Mrs. Stephenson sat down on the yellow silk Louis XVI armchair next to her writing desk and frowned. She put her hand to her head. She felt a migraine coming on. She knew Michael was floundering, and her first thought was to send her husband to his rescue.

Fiona continued: "That magazine reporter has been after us for days. They're doing a profile on us." If they only knew, Fiona thought. "The reporter has interviewed our friends and enemies. Now he wants to see *us*. We've refused to talk to him. We've had enough publicity, for now anyway."

Mrs. Stephenson didn't like the sound of the magazine interview. She would see what her husband could do. She remembered he was very friendly with the publisher.

"Darling," Mrs. Stephenson broke in, "what about the flowers? Luigi is available. So are the girls who serve so well. I can see we might dress them up in Tyrolean costume. Divine, don't you think?"

"Mummy, how sweet of you. But you know Michael wants the party to be one hundred per cent our party. Our flowers. You know, my arrangements."

"How silly," Mrs. Stephenson said, "we've the most beautiful flowers, rows and rows. So many white and yellow freesia. They smell divine. You must have the whole greenhouse filling the living room."

"Yes, Mummy, fine, but Michael must never know," and Fiona could smell the freesia while she talked on the telephone. "You're so sweet, Mummy. Thank you. Good-bye, darling," and Fiona hung up. Somehow, this morning, she felt closer to Mummy.

148

Catherine Cain sat in the large bedroom overlooking the East River. Two months after their victory and Catherine referred to it as "theirs," the Cains had moved into an eight-bedroom duplex apartment next to Paul's club. They had waited until after the victory to take over the duplex. Actually, Paul's father and Catherine's stepfather had provided the funds—about $300,000—for the duplex. They finally decided to move in before the decorator, Lady Eleanor, approved. Catherine and Paul had tired of traveling every morning to inspect the redecorating work, even though Lady Eleanor had sent her chauffeur-driven Cadillac to fetch them.

The Cains' new, real life made them, in Catherine's words, "blissfully happy." They relished their glamour and their power. They gained added strength through their outward humility and kindness toward everyone. They really knew how to charm. They worked hard at the job of being perfect politicians. They even spent time together touring the Bedford-Stuyvesant area, to meet people and to check on party headquarters. Cain had his sights on being Mayor of New York, or perhaps a Senator at the next go-round. He was building steadily toward one of these goals. Catherine had her sights on being the first lady of New York and she had frankly admitted to herself that she had little or no competition, except possibly from Fiona Chase. Paul had said, "The Chases have no base to operate from."

The new duplex would be a show place and now that they were finally living there, they would entertain, Catherine vowed, "to perfection."

Catherine was pregnant and the child was expected in six months. They hoped for a boy.

When Catherine picked up the phone to speak to Fiona, Catherine couldn't have been happier, and being on top made it easier to do everything to please. She was willing and ready for any important party because she was ready to step out as first lady. Paul would approve, because he had said the Chases attracted important and interesting people.

"Darling, how nice to hear from you," Catherine answered Fiona. "It's coming, the duplex, and it should be beautiful. The plaster from knocking down the walls is all over the place, but we like being

149

in our new house in spite of the mess. We're told there're three months more of work."

Fiona was startled at Catherine's friendliness. It was so easy. She even talked to Catherine about Michael.

"Well, you know Paul went through that working summers in a Senator's office and for a Supreme Court Justice. No, it wasn't too pleasant, but he learned every day. They had him running around touring the depressed areas, but we're still doing that. God, it's awful, and Paul doesn't like me to refer to them as depressed areas. He calls them underprivileged areas and he's going to change all that."

Catherine stood up and looked at herself in the mirror. Her hair was down over her face, hanging thick, shiny, over her dark eyebrows. She turned sideways and saw her profile. If only she wasn't pregnant now at the height of their glory. But there would be more glorious times ahead, she hoped.

Fiona then asked about the party.

"Darling, how sweet. Paul and I had talked about giving one ourselves, but with the duplex in shambles . . . We'd love to come. I only have to check the date and see if I can have a new dress designed in time. It takes so long getting anything through customs and they charge the duty in gold when the dresses are beaded. I'm mad for beads. They're worth their weight in gold. En principe, darling, we would love the party. Of course, Paul might like to take a peek at the list. He and Michael can have lunch together at the Club. Till soon, darling, and thank you, darling. Good-bye."

Fiona was elated and could hardly wait to tell Michael the good news. But how pretentious, all the darlings and en principes. It was interesting to see how Catherine would handle her rise to prominence. In a way, Fiona was disappointed. Fiona had always seen Catherine as so intelligent, so basic, impervious except to success. Fiona was secretly pleased to find Catherine was actually just like anyone else.

Michael arrived home earlier than usual, and went straight to his dressing room. Mary had just brought in the ice.

"Sorry, sir, you arrived a little early," she said.

"That's just fine, Mary, please don't worry."

150

Fiona went to the dressing room and rapped on the door frame. The rap hurt her knuckles.

"May I come in, Sir Michael?" She began to laugh. Michael hadn't seen Fiona looking so gay and peppy in many months. Her happiness must have something to do with him, he thought. He felt better.

She was now in the room and her arms were wrapped around his neck. Her fingers stretching out from his starched collar were all a-wiggle. She stood on her tiptoes kissing him gently on both cheeks. Her lips were warm, wet and soft.

"Well, what's prompted all this bubbly stuff?" Michael said, secretly pleased and flattered that Fiona was paying some attention to him again.

"They're coming. Yes they are, without any fuss. They're just coming," and Fiona dropped her arms and twirled around the dressing room. Her short skirt went so high Michael could see her long lace bloomers.

"I knew they would," said Michael. "I was sure. After all, why shouldn't they? We give fine parties and they know we'll have everyone." Michael spoke casually and Fiona was hurt by his blasé attitude. She longed for him to praise her. If only he could give her some credit. She felt so inadequate and then she realized how stupid they both were. To think that she was dancing around the room because the Cains had agreed to come to their party. My values are shot—shot to hell, she thought.

"Now that list, Fiona," Michael began as though he were still at the office. "I thought about it and I feel certain guests just don't fit in. You know we've invited people we just know as friends. People who don't mean much—" and Michael stopped short, realizing what he had said.

Color came into Fiona's pale cheeks. She threw back her head.

"You mean," she said, "those people who are just nice people who are invited to our party. And they just happen to be our friends. I suppose your friends, if we have any, don't mean much to you—unless," and she raised her voice, "unless they are great-something-or-others. Well, I'll tell you some of those greats you've been seeing lately might be great in print, but as people, as ordinary, living, breathing human beings, they're a bust, and worse than that, some of them are perfect bastards." And Fiona was out of the room.

Michael was shaking. He felt his legs go numb, his eyes ache. He made his drink. He walked over to the closet, opened the door and looked into the full-length mirror. He could hardly smile that smile when he looked at his teeth. He saw his eyes; they looked tired and his eyelids twitched. Fiona had never spoken to him that way before and his pride wouldn't let him forgive her emotional, stupid outburst. It didn't matter that she was right. It only mattered that she had crossed his bow and that he couldn't forgive. He downed the Scotch, pulled in his stomach, and brushed back some wayward strands of hair from his reddening ear.

He turned away from the mirror and was about to start down the hall after Fiona. There would be trouble if he put Fiona in a bad mood before the party, that Michael knew. She could upset the whole thing.

Fiona came out of their room. She went to Michael, tears in her eyes.

"Michael," she began calmly, "I have decided that our friends, my friends, should be included in this party. Our life is becoming a sham. We act all the time. We don't know what fun is. I'm tired of it, fed up and bored. Either you let me have something to say about this party, or I won't be there."

"Calm yourself, my dear girl. Let's look at this logically. We are giving the party for the Cains, right?"

"No, we are not," Fiona interrupted. "We're giving the party to show that we are in with the right people, including the Cains."

"You can see your real friends other times, at luncheon—that is, if you can remember who your real friends are," Michael said.

"That's the cruelest remark you've ever made," and Fiona began to sob. "Give me your handkerchief, Michael."

Fiona held her stomach and crumbled onto the couch as though she had been broken into pieces. "Don't you see, Michael, don't you see how unhappy I am, how alone I am?" she cried.

Michael closed the dressing room door so the servants wouldn't hear. "How can you be unhappy? We have a wonderful life, we never have any worries. Everything is ours," and Michael smiled his nervous, insecure smile.

Fiona saw the cover-up. She knew Michael was faking. She knew Michael knew that their life was really a sham. She pitied him and now hated him. She sat silently wiping her red eyes and twisting his wet handkerchief around her fingers.

"Michael, has it ever dawned on you that I could be unhappy because you are not a success?"

Michael turned pale.

"I don't mean a success so much in politics, or any career. I mean that maybe you aren't a success as my husband," Fiona said firmly.

"Well, I don't know what you mean. For God's sake, we have everything. I love you and we have the whole world to enjoy. You *are* satisfied," he said, sure of himself.

"No, there's lots lacking in our life. We have no children, there is no natural link between the two of us except sometimes maybe sex and that's less and less important. There is no communication. We can't just sit at home, or out in the country and talk about the sky, the flowers, or just about some everyday things. You don't know when I'm unhappy. I wonder if you ever feel anything about someone else. If you took off your shoes on a bright, warm spring day, you'd wish you had your shoes on so that your feet wouldn't get dirty. Or you'd be frightened that you would step on a hornet and get stung."

"Fiona, you haven't a clue about life. Not a clue. As a matter of fact, I think you're stupid, really stupid. You rant and rave like some spoiled child. A little brat who has everything, but who doesn't understand the import of it all," Michael answered defiantly.

"What import? What import, Michael?" she screamed back. "What have we done well? Just nothing, except spent our family's money to buy the best, the best in taste. We've bought and bought objects and bought for our collections, and now we're collecting and buying people, the best people. But are they really the best? Do we know them? I think *you* are the spoiled brat, the big shot without having done a thing except graduate from school. What have you done? Please do tell your stupid wife. Tell me. Tell me," and she fled the room slamming the door hard.

Michael heard the slam over and over again ringing in his ears. He stared blankly at the smoothly polished door, closing him off from everywhere and from everyone. He turned around quickly and ran toward the glass table. He kicked it hard so it broke into pieces and his drink went with the broken glass. He threw his mother's down cushions to the floor and stamped on them. The pillows lay scattered across the room. He mixed another drink and slammed the door to the bar. The glasses rattled and a shelf fell shattering into the sink.

Fiona heard the shattering glass from her room. She didn't care any more. Her husband was a little boy, throwing a temper tantrum because his wife had told him the truth. As she thought of the truth, as she thought of what had become of them, as she realized their life was confined to a four-walled room—money, power, objects, Michael and Fiona—she became hysterical. Nothing was real to either of them anymore. Their friends didn't exist unless they were useful. Michael treated Fiona as another convenient object in his life and their relationship was nonexistent. If only Michael could be taught his shortcomings, if only she could change him. Fiona went on incoherently. Her lips moved as she remembered the past, lived the present, and feared the future. They had fought before many times, but now for the first time Fiona saw how barren and boring their lives had really become. It was as though she was drying up as a person and she remembered the doctor again. "I'm certainly barren as a woman," and she was talking to herself.

Fiona got up off the chair and kicked aside the white mink rug at the foot of their bed. She grasped the bedpost, raised her arms high up and rested her head.

She knew Michael was in the next room, probably drinking and with each sip hating her even more. She assumed Michael hated her because Michael hated any person who defied him.

Fiona had lost her fear. She took her head away from the bedpost. "If he strikes me physically, I can stand it very well." She smiled at the thought. She was ready for anything from Michael. She knew that really she was the stronger person. She could play on his fears and if she wanted to make their pretty little life a nightmare for him and for herself, it was easy. She relished the idea that Michael for once

154

could be made to suffer. She was delighted that she could bring him down to the level of the real and destroy his self-deceptions, his so-called dreams.

She thought suddenly, unexpectedly, of her weekend in England with Richard Talbott Ross. Had she loved him in his country house, cold, somber, covered with clinging ivy? She remembered the ride in his black Rolls-Royce station wagon to the London Airport. His eyes had been warm, inviting. And Fiona had returned the look. Yes, she could have loved him, and she fell onto the canopy bed thrilled with the thought there could be someone else.

She thought too of Cain. It might not be too late. Catherine was pregnant. Both were vulnerable. As for Michael—well, Michael really didn't matter anymore, did he?

Fiona jumped off the bed, flung open the door and it banged hard against the iron bulldog doorstop. She flung open the door to Michael's dressing room and stood there leaning against the frame, with her hand on her hip and her right leg out in front.

"Well, is my little, darling boy over his temper tantrum? Has he stopped breaking the glass?"

Michael just stared blankly at her. He was stunned by her defiance. He didn't know what to do. He lay sprawled over the couch. One foot rested squarely in the middle of a red cushion. The sight of Michael now repulsed Fiona and her face showed disgust. He hesitated, then took his drink off the table and flung it straight at her. The glass hit her in the chest and she bent over with pain.

She straightened up and took the same defiant position. "Try again, my darling, maybe you would like to kill me. Break all the glass in the room, break up the damn place and me with it."

Michael continued to stare. His eyes flooded with tears. Fiona saw the tears coming down his cheeks. Her chest hurt and she saw that her dress was wet and felt the water running down her side. Michael suddenly got up and put his arms around her and held her tight.

"Oh my darling, what have I done? Will you ever forgive me? Let me call the doctor. Please forgive me. I must have had too much to drink."

He guided Fiona down the hall and they stopped in front of their

155

bedroom. Fiona removed his arm from her body, stepped in front of Michael, and closed the door gently on him. He stood there just looking, not knowing what to do.

After two weeks, there still hadn't been a word said about that evening. Fiona had withdrawn into her own shell. She had decided to carry on at least for a while. Michael was stupid enough to think the whole unfortunate incident would be forgotten. He was certain Fiona loved their way of life too much to break it up. He was horrified that he had thrown a glass and blamed it on the drinking. He cut down and started to play squash at the club.

Fiona was concerned only about her future. She saw herself following Mummy right down the line, ending up fixing flowers, running the house, entertaining, society, more society. Where was the living that she heard others talking about, or had she dreamed too much? Then she thought of the big difference in her life compared to Mummy's.

Mummy had said she admired her husband because of what he created; he was the big mover of men. What had Michael moved so far? But it was a fraud to live only for success. Mummy's values were wrong. Success won't save us, will it, Fiona wondered.

What she really wanted, she decided, was for Michael to love her, just to love her for what she was, nothing more. She suddenly pitied him. She realized he had problems, serious problems. She would rise to the party for his sake, not for the Cains. Or was that true? Wasn't she honestly anxious to be with Paul again? Paul Cain represented a big challenge. She could visualize him all too well— tall, husky, with heavy red eyebrows and red hair. His brown eyes looked almost black, they were so acute, so penetrating. His voice was gentle. Fiona stopped, was she imagining too much? For the moment she had found new stimulation.

She rode horseback every day. When Miss Howard at the club saw her coming so often, she realized the change in Fiona. It was as though Fiona had broken away from her stereotyped world. Miss Howard didn't want to believe marriage could mature a woman, but Fiona rode with zest and, looking out the window of the club office, Miss Howard saw that Fiona was getting the most out of Terence. When she returned to the stable, Fiona stopped off to talk to Miss Howard, who could see the color high in her cheeks. Fiona's eyes were alive, almost wild. She talked freely, removed her hat and let down her long hair with abandon, as though some great burden had been lifted. She was no longer just a beautiful, spoiled girl.

Albert, the hairdresser, had never been so busy. The ladies had been in days before the Chase party to order new hairpieces and to look over sketches of what might be done for them. And then there had been the usual business of the ladies trying to find out from Albert what others would be wearing on their bodies and on their heads. The talk of the Chase party was all over town, in the gossip columns, in the editorial offices of the newspapers, where plans were set to photograph the guests as they arrived. One newspaper had succeeded in getting the ladies to pose in their dresses three days before.

For Fiona, arranging the party had been a nightmare. She decided she would never go through such a thing again, and she could never have done the job without her mother's help. Michael stood by, suggesting and criticizing. He had planned that about two in the morning, when the guests would be hungry, a second staff of twelve would come in to set up a large oyster bar and prepare omelettes.

The old guard of New York had earlier decided not to attend the party because they felt the younger crowd should be alone. Secretly they resented the younger crowd and their ostentatious showmanship. Finally, many of the old guard, out of snobbish curiosity, decided to come. They had read so much about the Chases and the Cains and their high living that they couldn't resist the party. They were coming prepared to pan the performance, the food, the drink, the guests and the hosts. There was still enough old reserve left around Manhattan to stand off from the new guard. But with the advance publicity and all the talk about the two most beautiful couples—the Cains and the Chases—it was hard to stay away and as for those who had not been invited that had been for some a real tragedy. The noninvited included at first the Senator and his wife, but, at the last minute, Michael realized his blunder and had Fiona call the Senator's wife, who was so overwhelmed and delighted that she had been now invited, that she quoted the Senator to Fiona as full of praise for Michael's work in the last few months. Of course, the Senator had never said any such thing and it was too late for Fiona to be impressed.

16

THE PARTY

Catherine and Paul Cain were dressing for the party high up above the East River in their duplex, which had a commanding view of the New York skyline and part of Long Island.

From his bathroom, Paul Cain watched a tug push three coal barges up river against the heavy swelling tide. He was concerned that he didn't see very clearly tonight. The tug coughed black smoke and sounded a throaty whistle. Cain saw the whistle's white smoke disappear into the night sky off the port side. Another barge filled with railroad cars was coming cross river.

He turned back to the mirror. He felt hot, feverish, as he went on shaving. The smell of the shaving soap was clean and medicated. It soothed him after a tiring day. Cain wasn't thinking about his work; he was only dreading tonight at the Chases. Normally he liked such a party, but tonight was a real effort, because he didn't feel well. He shrugged his shoulders and decided it was probably just the flu. But his legs didn't ache.

Catherine stuck her head into the bathroom. "And how's my famous husband doing tonight?" She came in dressed in a heavy yellow silk evening dress with a pink and white lace bolero jacket. She looked very young and beautiful, Paul decided as he saw her in

159

the mirror. She put her arms around his waist and hugged. He was wrapped only in a towel and, as she hugged, the towel fell to the floor. She liked the scent of his body and kissed his shoulders.

"Darling," he began, "do you think I have a fever?"

"Why no, you feel as cool as ever," and she continued to hold onto him. She was taken aback by his question about the fever, because Paul was never one to complain about anything or worry about his health.

Paul was relieved Catherine didn't find him feverish, but his image in the mirror was blurry. He turned toward Catherine and bent down to kiss her. "Now, darling, you had better sit down and get off your feet like the doctor said. It's going to be a long night." He led her to their bed.

"Oh I can't really lie down. I'll muss my dress," she protested.

"Who cares about the dress? Now put your feet up and wait until I'm ready."

He went back to his shaving. Catherine came back to watch.

"Aren't we lucky?" she said impetuously. "This apartment, your election, the baby . . . I'm just in the mood to celebrate. It will be wonderful seeing the Chases again. I've missed Michael."

"You have, darling, really?" he asked. "And I've missed Fiona. She's so beautiful—sensitive too." Paul was more than half teasing.

"I know you've always had a passion for her. But you're mine now. And don't forget the weekend she left you high and dry and went off with Michael," Catherine said.

"And what were you doing in Paris?"

"That was a bad show, I admit now. André and all that. My intellectual period. Now I'm in my social period. I love it, Paul darling," and Catherine had her arms around his waist.

"I'll never get dressed for this damn thing if you don't let go."

Catherine still held on and moved in even closer, running her hands up and down his chest.

He turned to look back in the mirror. He didn't look himself. He was thinking about Michael, how he really wasn't anxious to see him again. Somehow, they resented each other. Some sort of deep-rooted jealousy that had started at Princeton still existed. It's easy for me to forget my prejudices, he thought, but for Michael it must be more

160

difficult now that I'm ahead. And Paul decided he would try to make it easier for all of them because of Fiona. Still, he had no confidence in Michael's ability. Michael was a spoiled brat, he couldn't help reflecting.

"What are you thinking about?" Catherine asked and she was disturbed to see Paul just standing there looking into the mirror.

"Nothing. Just us, darling," and he took her arms away, turned around, and held her tightly, not wanting to let go.

"Hurry now, or we'll be late," Catherine said, and left him.

Congressman Cain got into the shower and turned on the water. He felt better with the spray beating down on him.

Fiona was sitting in a French armchair covered in a white chintz printed with roses. She had her feet up on a dark blue petit-point stool, and behind her, Albert fixed her hair. He had just attached the large false hairpiece, which fell way below her shoulders. He then took the false piece and intertwined it precisely with her own to create a soft, curving round ball at the top of her head. He then placed a diamond necklace at the top of the ball and let the large pendant ruby fall down Fiona's neck.

"Marvelous, Albert. Just marvelous. It's amazing what you can do," and Fiona picked up the mirror to examine herself. She was pleased as she moved the ruby to the middle of her neck. Albert quickly darted around to the front and touched her hair gently with the comb and then brushed the last strands into place. He stood back and put his hands into the pockets of his grey, pinstriped flannel suit. He admired his creation and couldn't take his eyes off Fiona. She looked up at him and smiling sweetly said, "Are you pleased?"

"So pleased, Mrs. Chase. You look beautiful and my hair is just right for that black velvet dress. Be careful when you get into it not to catch the beads in your hair."

Albert slipped out of the room and just as he was about to leave, Fiona told him to ask her husband for some champagne.

Albert found Michael standing in front of the fire in the dark blue burlapped library. He was looking at his fish collection to the right of the fireplace.

"Your fire smells so good. I love the cosy feeling of a fire," Albert said, trying to strike up a conversation.

Michael wore a navy velvet dinner jacket and his monogrammed slippers. He had debated about the velvet jacket. Maybe it was "too-too-too," but he decided that after all he was the host, so he should wear something different than the rest. He liked to stand out. He had seen Fiona's velvet dress and they had put the dress and the dinner jacket together on the canopy bed.

"So sorry, Albert," Michael began, "it's so bare in here, but we've had to remove the furniture and put it in storage for the night, because we're going to dance here after dinner." Michael saw Albert didn't have a glass. He pressed the white ivory servants' buzzer.

Pierre, in full, long tails, quickly entered the room. "Yes, sir," he said solemnly.

"Champagne, please, Pierre. Before you go, is everything all right with the others who are assisting?"

"Yes, sir," said Pierre, looking carefully at himself in the gold Louis XV mirror over the mantel. As he went out of the door, he adjusted his white tie to the left.

"Well, this is going to be a splendid party. So nice of you to do this for the Congressman and Mrs. Cain," Albert said, realizing his remark was innocuous enough.

Michael paced in front of the fireplace. Albert saw that he was nervous. Michael finished his glass of champagne.

"Excuse me, please, Albert, we'll wait all night here for your champagne. Let me go and get the bottle." Before Albert could say don't bother, Michael was off down the hall toward the kitchen.

As he headed for the kitchen, he heard Fiona open the door of their room. She stood in her black velvet dress, her hair severely in place, her eyes heavily made up, her lips dark, dark red, every feature exaggerated. She had aged in her transformation just for that evening. Michael paused. His wife had indeed changed. She looked superior, defiant, even savage.

"Well, do you like me, Michael darling?" and she moved toward him, her eyes bearing down. He stopped short. He kept thinking of a scene in Macbeth. There they were, both in velvet, staring at each other like two total strangers down the long hallway. How somber the blue flocked paper looked—almost like tropical leaves dripping in the rain—and the highly polished dark woodwork reflected their images. As Fiona moved toward Michael, he stepped backward with the champagne glass empty in his hand.

Michael didn't answer Fiona's question. He remained silent and then managed to say in a quiet voice, "I'm on my way to get some champagne. May I, for you?"

"Of course," Fiona said, in a sure voice, no longer soft, but harsh and loud.

Then she called sweetly, softly, "Albert, Albert. Here I come, give me the final inspection. Please be a darling and make sure I look my best." She went into the library and twirled around twice and stopped short right in front of Albert and looked into his eyes.

"You're divine. Just divine," he answered. Then they both turned side to side and looked into the roaring fire, at the flames dancing and licking away at the logs. The big white birch log fell off the top, the red and blue ashes sparked and the smoke curled up toward the flue. They dreamed their own dreams as they looked into the fire. Michael came into the room followed by Pierre with the silver tray with the champagne bottle and he poured the champagne. They drank and the bubbles tickled their noses.

The bell rang. The door was opened. Paul and Catherine Cain were there. Fiona was in the hallway to meet them. Michael stood next to her. Paul Cain kissed Fiona on both cheeks and again on the right cheek. Fiona held her face to his and pressed her cheek closer. Michael took Catherine's hand and pulled her close. He kissed her gently.

Fiona saw that Catherine was pregnant. She felt a pang and dropped her eyelids. She said to Catherine, "Oh, how nice! When?" Michael frowned that unhappy frown he displayed when Fiona said something he didn't like.

"Let's have a drink before the party. Pierre, the champagne, or whiskey."

Paul Cain put his hand to his head. Catherine watched him closely. She moved away from Michael to her husband. "Darling, do you have a headache? Poor darling," and she put her arm around him.

163

"Nothing really, Catherine, just a miserable pain in my head," he answered. "It will go away."

Fiona turned to Paul. "Let me get an aspirin," she said. She went off to the bathroom followed by Paul, who still held his hand to his head.

He walked closely behind Fiona, following the red glow of the large ruby hanging down at the nape of her neck. He took in the beauty of her shiny black hair a-sparkle with diamonds, her white skin, the black beauty mark on the side of her neck. He heard the quiet swish, swish of her black velvet dress as she led him to Michael's couch. She rearranged the cushions and without her saying a word, he sat down holding his head.

"I'll fetch the aspirin. I hope you feel better," and she turned to Cain and bent down to him, brushing her cool, soft hand across his brow. "I don't think you have a fever."

Paul loved her touch. He felt her body so close and had a desire to put his arms around her narrow waist and bury his aching head in her velvety body.

She turned away and went toward Michael's black and white marble bathroom, but stopped to take another look at Paul. Fiona was concerned. Her eyes examined him with great care. She smiled. He returned the smile. He saw Fiona blurred, the white skin, the black hair, the black velvet and her comforting eyes.

She went to the bathroom and opened the medicine cabinet. She saw herself in the mirror. Her face was relaxed, her eyes gentle and the color was back in her cheeks. Fiona shook the bottle and tossed the cotton aside and let out three aspirin. She filled a glass from the green mineral water bottle and started back to Paul.

As she went out of the bathroom into the dressing room, Fiona saw Paul sitting erect, trying his best to keep his composure in spite of the pain. She looked at him again. She remembered Michael slumped on the couch a month before and now there was Paul. Oh God, she thought to herself, how could I have? It's awful. Paul, Michael. Paul, Michael.

Suddenly Paul's body started to tremble. His face turned ashen. Fiona rushed to him and handed over the glass. He reached for it with his right hand, which rose trembling. He took the glass and

164

put the aspirin in his mouth and drank. The water went down quickly and he choked, forcing the color back into his face.

"Please Fiona, go before the guests arrive. I'll be fine. I'm sleepy."

Fiona didn't ask. She just took Paul by the hand and led him back down the hall to their bedroom. Paul trailed behind, his hot shaking hand clutching Fiona's.

She guided him gently to the bed. He lay down without a word before Fiona could remove the bedspread of roses. She lifted his head off the pillow and then let it down. She felt his strong, thick red hair. He closed his eyes and Fiona caressed his brow. She tiptoed out of the room and shut the door quietly behind her.

Catherine was standing there, right in front of the bedroom. She glared at Fiona and brushed her hair back out of her eyes.

"How is he?" she said severely. "I see he is in your good hands."

"He'll sleep," Fiona answered calmly. "He will sleep well after the three aspirin."

"I guess I had better not disturb him," and Catherine turned the brass ball knob, to open the door. She looked at Paul on Fiona's bed. He slept, breathing heavily. She closed the door and returned to Michael, who was in the living room, sitting with his champagne glass on an ice-blue silk Louis XVI chauffeuse. He sat slumped, with his outstretched legs crossed.

Fiona went back to Michael's bathroom. She closed the door, turned the lock, and sat on the red lacquered bamboo chair next to the sink. She dropped her head to the cold basin, thankful to be alone for just a few seconds.

Michael uncrossed his legs as Catherine came back into the room. She waved her hand, "Oh, please don't get up. You look so relaxed and comfortable there by the fire," Catherine said.

Michael made an effort to rise, but didn't. Catherine put her hands on Michael's shoulders as she came to him. Her dress and her legs brushed against his cheek. She sat down on the floor in front of him and rested her left arm on his outstretched legs. She looked up at him.

"How is he?" Michael asked.

"Paul is sleeping soundly," Catherine answered. Pierre bent down and held out the tray with a filled champagne glass.

"To you, just to you, Michael," Catherine said and the glasses clinked. Michael ran his fingers up and down the stem. The guests would be arriving soon. He was pleased they had asked the Cains half an hour before the others. Michael knew that he had succeeded in charming Catherine, and Catherine was perfectly satisfied to pursue the game, especially after she had seen Fiona with Paul.

"I suppose Fiona is fixing herself," Michael said.

"She is. And she put Paul on your bed to sleep. I saw her taking care of him."

"I hope she's ready before the guests arrive," Michael said imperiously. He was about to get up off the chauffeuse to go look for Fiona.

"Please don't go. Stay here by the fire with me," Catherine said, putting her hand on his legs and sliding her fingers just once up and down. Michael hesitated and then put his hand next to Catherine's hand. He touched her diamond ring.

Catherine sensed that there was tension between Michael and Fiona, that Michael was seeking comfort, reassurance from her. It gave her a feeling of power, along with her awareness that Paul would now have a good deal of control over Michael's future.

Fiona came into the room and saw them together on the floor. Michael heard the swish, swish of the velvet as Fiona approached. She passed quickly by them, as though they didn't exist and took her place on the quilted blue and white couch. She folded her arms and looked into the fire. Her legs were crossed and her right foot swung back and forth.

They didn't speak. The fire held them spellbound. Catherine felt proud, so proud that she and Paul were on top. She would be charming, humble. Her new role called for all that. Michael was flattered at Catherine's response to him. He was stimulated by the idea that Catherine, who had Paul, still found Michael attractive. Michael even wanted Paul to know that Catherine felt Michael irresistible —that was the word he applied to himself. As for Fiona, it wouldn't do her any harm to see another woman interested in him.

Fiona saw only the flames burning away at the white birch log. She smelled the perfume of the birch—strong, real, as though the logs were still lying on the earth, in the warming sun, smothered in red, green, orange, and brown fallen leaves.

She didn't remember when her senses had been as acute as right now, but she felt confined, imprisoned. Fiona imagined the years from this moment, alone with herself, but still with Michael by the same fire in a different room, probably bigger and better, waiting for a greater party. We will improve as we go on, she thought. What next? Paul? It was too late now, but what if we had been together just once? It might have been different . . . My fault, all my fault. I saw Michael and . . . Tortured thoughts, greener grass across the room.

So what. I'm in, and I can't get out and there's no place to go, except out. Out of this world to where? Way down below to the everyday, the humdrum, the ordinary, the mediocre . . . She couldn't go out, not even for a minute. The outside was so much worse, Fiona thought.

She watched Catherine sitting on the floor next to Michael, resting her elbow on his leg as though they belonged together.

The large birch log fell tumbling to the hearth and the sparks flew out hitting the folding brass screen, except for one, which shot out of the side and onto the rug. Catherine, Fiona, and Michael saw the spark burn a small black hole into the rug.

The buzzer buzzed, and the sound startled the three, as though it signaled a new beginning and an end for Catherine, Michael, and Fiona. Paul Cain slept on while the party got under way.

Pierre opened the door. The first guests were the chairman of the board of one of the largest radio and television networks, Mr. and Mrs. John S. Sargent. Mrs. Sargent was coolly beautiful, her neck long and as thin as her pendant ruby and diamond earrings, her eyes as soft and warm as her full length sable coat. Her husband, bald on top, greying at the sides, with piercing brown eyes, shrugged his shoulders and clasped his hands behind his back, a sign for them to make their entrance. Catherine rose, assisted by Michael. Fiona quickly moved out past Catherine and Michael, as though they weren't there. She held out her bared arms, took Mrs. Sargent's hands, kissed her, dropped her hands and took Mr. Sargent's. Mr. Sargent drew her in and kissed her with pleasure and smelt her flowering jasmin perfume. He didn't know that his wife had been wearing the same perfume for years. After the kiss, his nose twitched.

The Stephensons arrived and seeing the fuss being made over the Sargents, discreetly went to the back of the apartment. Mrs. Stephenson wanted to see the flowers. "They're divine," she said to her husband. "Smell the hall, full of fresh freesia. I adore it." If only the apartment could stay as it is now, so beautiful and uncrowded, she thought. "I'm happy for them. Aren't you, Walter? They've done a magnificent job."

"Yes, they have," he said, taking Mrs. Stephenson into the living room where she sat near the fire.

They came. They poured in. The coats were checked at the door by two handsome maids dressed in red Tyrolean dresses. The ladies hesitated about their coats—to keep them, or leave them. When they were spectacular furs they usually did not leave them until after they made their entrance. As the room warmed their fur-covered bodies, they removed the coats and left them to the maids, or to Pierre.

"Darling," said Mrs. Sargent, who had worn her sable into the living room, "would you mind giving my coat to the maids at the door?" Sargent obediently held out his arm for his wife's coat. He casually grasped the sable collar and his arm dropped with the weight. He pulled up the coat and left to deposit it.

For years Mrs. Sargent had been a social rival to Mrs. Stephenson. Not that they had ever disliked each other, but when there was conflict about parties, there had been talk, bitter undercurrents started by others, especially Homer Breadcraft. But Mrs. Sargent and Mrs. Stephenson were too reasonable and secure in their top social positions to dispute. Instead they had agreed without saying so, to each her own, and outwardly appeared to be close friends.

From where she had taken a seat, Mrs. Stephenson could see the whole room.

The black, highly lacquered grand piano was decked with hyacinths—blue, purple, pink, red, and the whites all together in front and nestling in a large wicker straw basket, big enough to cover almost the entire top of the piano.

168

Mrs. Stephenson could see the orange and blue flames burning, up the side of the piano, the blue chauffeuse chair—all reflected— but soon there were too many people in the room and they blocked her view. She felt closed in.

Mrs. Stephenson worried about the fingers on the piano, that ashes would drop on the rug, that wet glasses would leave rings, that the cigaret smoke would discolor the room. She worried that the hyacinths which now smelt so sweet, even from across the room, would be stifled by the human heat and smoke.

Flower bouquets were scattered around the room in small, fine objets. The garnette roses—all white—the cornflowers, the daisies, the mums, the cut-down snapdragons, the sweet peas and the white and yellow freesia everywhere the guests looked.

By now the room was filled with people. The Kennedys—Robert and Ethel—had come. The drone of voices dropped off as they made their entrance, but the guests quickly went back to their conversations. Michael rushed to them and kissed Mrs. Kennedy. She responded warmly.

Mrs. Sargent went over and sat down next to Mrs. Stephenson on the couch in front of the fire. Mr. Stephenson approached. "Good evening," he said brusquely and took his place on the low chauffeuse and, looking up at the two women, folded his arms.

"The room is lovely," Mrs. Sargent said to the Stephensons.

Mrs. Sargent didn't take her eyes off Fiona, who led Mr. Sargent to a corner. They sat together on a Louis XVI sofa. Fiona leaned against the yellow bolsters and played with the big button at the end. Mr. Sargent sat back looking at Fiona. The black velvet dress, the white swan neck against the yellow—she was radiant. With her eyes on Fiona and her husband, Mrs. Sargent said to Mrs. Stephenson, "Really, Martha, your daughter is a picture over there on the yellow sofa with John. You can see that youth always wins out," and she turned away to gaze into the fire.

Mr. Stephenson watched Fiona and Mr. Sargent. He didn't like what he saw. His daughter was too made up, her eyes looked hard, that strict sophistication didn't suit her. He was saddened to see she was going the way of the rest of the social herd. He preferred remembering Fiona in Paris, standing on her tiptoes, looking up at him.

"Yes, she is beautiful," Mr. Stephenson answered rather gruffly. "But we worry, don't we, Martha, about what will happen to them later on."

Mrs. Stephenson was embarrassed. She pulled her shoulder strap up and fixed her emerald and diamond frog. "I suppose we've been through it the same way and we've all survived the boredom and the disappointments."

"What disappointments?" said Mr. Stephenson.

"You see the disappointments right over there on the yellow sofa, don't you, darling?" said Mrs. Stephenson, raising her hand to point, then stopping.

"Oh, I see," said Mr. Stephenson.

"Do you?" asked Mrs. Sargent. "Martha and I see it well. We mean that our husbands turn to youth so quickly and we are left to find our way."

They laughed, because they now understood.

Mr. Stephenson left the two ladies alone and went over to Fiona.

"Daddy, I thought you would never talk to me. You had better before the others arrive," and she took her father's hand and he squeezed her long, fine fingers.

Mr. Sargent shifted on the couch. "How are you, Walter?" Mr. Sargent said in a voice that really didn't expect an answer and that didn't care.

Fiona quickly jumped up from the couch and the two men were left alone, not knowing what to say.

Mr. Stephenson was dismayed that his daughter had left so quickly. To meet the other guests, he figured, but no, there was more than that going on in her mind. She was cold, her eyes no longer were happy, they had that distant look. She must be thinking of something else.

Fiona was now with Homer Breadcraft across the room. His entrance was showy. He threw open his cape, letting it fall on a chair. The red lining lay spread out, half on the white silk brocade chair and half on the blue rug. He kissed Fiona's hand, then her cheek, and then gently put his arm around her velvet waist.

170

"Darling, you look divine, ravishing, sensational. The beauty of New York. Catherine doesn't stand a chance. Where is she? Ah there, across the room in that yellow robe. I see her now," said Breadcraft. Fiona removed his arm from her waist.

"Now, Homer, just try and be nice," Fiona said. And he was off to Mrs. Stephenson and Mrs. Sargent. He just had to be there with the two most important ladies. He soon was sitting on the floor at their feet, telling them what was the latest, and what wasn't true he made up anyway. They loved his little gossips. The party had just now started, because Homer was there to amuse and titillate.

"She's divorcing, I know," Homer said. "My masseur does him, so he knows. I get tidbits about them, from him, as he rubs. Such a handsome masseur, Swedish, big, muscular and those blue, blue eyes. You know the Swedes, they love everything, the contrasts, the cold, the hot."

"You're so wicked, Homer," Mrs. Stephenson said, urging him on.

Homer didn't intend to stop. "The masseur is handsome like your son-in-law." Mrs. Sargent looked at Mrs. Stephenson. They didn't answer. They just stared into each other's eyes and Homer's message came across.

Homer had been drinking before. He realized the gaff. But why shouldn't he say what he wanted? He rose from their feet. He saw that Mrs. Sargent had a run in her stocking. He went looking for Michael.

He found Michael talking to Senator Borden. They were in heated conversation. Homer listened, then interrupted in his deep, grating voice, "Good evening, Michael," and he took Michael's hand gently and held it. Senator Borden stopped talking. "Your velvet dinner jacket is divine," and Homer ran his hands up and down the jacket. Senator Borden stepped back and Michael followed.

The Senator said, "I enjoyed your book, Mr. Breadcraft."

"I'm glad," answered Homer.

"Some called it a masterpiece," said the Senator in a solemn tone.

"Yes, I know. I intended it to be. Such a success." Homer didn't continue. He ignored the Senator. "And Michael, what have you been doing? You promised a lunch. Just the two of us alone."

Michael turned away and continued to talk with the Senator. If only Homer would go away, he prayed.

"Just don't get discouraged. It takes time. You have to be patient," said the Senator to Michael, as they sipped from their glasses.

"Let me get you another one, please, Senator," Michael said.

"Fine, only if you do too," the Senator answered.

Michael raised his arm to call Pierre. Another waiter came.

"Please," said Michael and he pointed to the empty glasses. "Two more."

"Now, Senator, may I be frank? Fiona and I were talking the other night. Don't you think it was rather hypocritical after the election for the Cains to come out in society? So strongly, you know what I mean. Remember, you criticized me for our spoiled image."

The Senator was shocked at the snide remark. Michael knew that he had said the wrong thing.

"I mean," Michael went on, "to the general public it must look strange moving into a three-hundred-thousand-dollar apartment, with all the trimmings."

"But isn't it even stranger that you live here among all these treasures and work in my office?" said the Senator.

"You're right," said Michael, trying to look depressed, humble enough to receive the Senator's sympathy.

"Where is Cain anyway?" the Senator asked.

"Oh, he's not feeling too well. I guess tired and he decided to lie down for a while because it's going to be a long evening. He felt dizzy and his head ached. I guess too much partying after the victory."

"That's not possible, Chase. The victory was weeks ago," the Senator said.

"That's true, but there have been lots of parties," Michael said in a suggestive tone.

"Did I hear someone say parties?" and Mrs. Borden was at their side with both of her arms locked around her husband.

"Now, darling," the Senator began.

"Yes, darling. Let's be frank. I love parties," and she dropped her arms and stepped back with two dancing steps. "To parties,

172

parties, more parties, tra la la." And away she went across the room, the gold lamé train of her low-bosomed dress swinging from side to side.

Georgette Jordan had been looking for Michael. She finally spotted him across the room with the Senator. She went to him. "Brother, there you are. I've found you at last," she said bombastically and threw her arms around his neck and kissed him on the lips. Georgette hugged Michael and kissed him again until Michael gently removed her arms. Senator Borden stood there, unintroduced, his hands clasped together. Georgette kept rustling her dress, entwined all around with a large blue and yellow hand-painted snake. Michael thought the dress crackled like tissue paper.

"Senator, this is Georgette Jordan, my sister," Michael said feebly, as if to hide the fact.

"Delighted to see you, Mrs. Jordan," and the Senator extended his hand.

Georgette looked at Michael and pulled her hand away from the Senator's. "Oh don't go, please, Michael," she pleaded as Michael started to move away.

"Georgette, I have to take care of our guests," and he patted her hand reassuringly.

"Where's your husband?" asked Senator Borden.

"He's over there with Fiona, you see, in the corner," and they watched Peter standing with a bored expression, holding a glass, while Fiona talked to Mr. and Mrs. Laurence F. Perkins.

Laurence Perkins had longish black hair hanging over his collar, but he was short of hair on top. His wife wore her piles of hair twisted and formed into two balls at either side. Her black cape was velvet, with hundreds of multicolored velvet balls, all jiggling. From her ears hung Ubangi trapeze diamond earrings, swinging back and forth, almost to her shoulders.

"I love your earrings, Peggy," Fiona said to Mrs. Perkins, who was too busy sizing up the crowd to give an answer.

"It's one of your small, intimate, little affairs, isn't it, Fiona?" said Laurence Perkins with a leer.

"Now come, Laurence, stop being bitchy. All your friends are here," Fiona answered.

173

"Friends and enemies too," he said, laughing. He loved to torment Fiona, who didn't really mind.

"They say, Fiona, you're giving this little party for the Cains. I want to say it's the most charming idea you've had in months. I understand Cain's here, but sick. The maids said he's in the bedroom sleeping. What a pity he's all alone."

"Now stop. Laurence, don't be so miserable," and Peggy Perkins twittered, delighted her husband had dared say what he thought. She figured someone in the group had to speak up before they all became so overly impressed with themselves.

Peter Jordan shifted his weight to his other foot and thought to himself he might as well be standing in Grand Central at the rush hour. He kept his eyes on Fiona.

Uncle John appeared. He was one of the last to arrive. He had been playing backgammon at the club and hadn't wanted to leave. He walked up to Peter Jordan, shook hands and said, "I'm glad to find you, Peter. What a mob."

He thought to himself, how could they? Bad, so bad for them, opening their house to all these people.

"Oh, where are my gloves?" said the lady with the ruffly Balenciaga dress. The ruffles tickled her nose. "Oh, where are my red gloves? I just bought them," and she was all over the room and in and out of everyone trying to find them.

"Fiona, darling, I didn't see you," said the gloveless Mrs. Annabel Ashbourne. "How are you, darling? We've just come back from the season in London. Simply divine. You know Paris is a dead city. Oh, where are my gloves?" and she took a long sip of her drink and then another sip. "My gloves. We took the dogs, Mabel and Abel. They loved it. Opened the house. Now we're back getting ready for our New Year's thing. I know you and Michael will come." The ruffles went up and down as she talked and breathed heavily. "Another drink. No ice," she said and went on in a heavy fake English accent. "We saw the Duchess and him, I mean His Royal Highness. Spent the weekend at the mill. The water wasn't running. They need rain in Paris too. But we had water in the house. Perfect weekend. So perfect. The Duke, rather gay in a black and white checked suit, with a jazzy tie and shirt. He really is extraordinary."

174

"And how is Bert?" asked Laurence Perkins.

"Oh, Bert's fine. He's a little slower this year, but still holding up."

Bert was over in the corner alone, except for his cane, which he kept tapping up and down on the floor.

"My gloves are still missing," and she lifted the skirt of the blue and white flowered chintz chair to look underneath. Fiona looked under the chair too for the red gloves.

"Well, Fiona, I see you have the whole cast. Where's the Chinese Empress?" Laurence Perkins said, curling up the side of his face.

"Now come on, Laurence, let's not be too mean," his wife cautioned.

"Ah, there she is, in the corner, all done up with her high, silk-embroidered Chinese collar and the Maltese cross around her neck. You must say she's unique. Does she still speak in that throaty voice, hesitating before each word, then coming out with nothing of substance?"

The Chinese Empress was in fact Mrs. James D. Robertson. She stood with her short husband in the corner. Her black, very black hair was tied back severely. She dramatized each word, each expression. From across the room, it was as though the Chinese theater, complete with the screeching, piercing music, was performing.

"I hear she's having a thing with that art magazine editor who poses nude on the side for his painter friends," Laurence continued.

A young fashion magazine editor, Mrs. Lallie Pentcheck, had just started saying, "My darling, it's simply, simply marvelous. I'm pushing the Southwest. That rugged, craggy, dry air is simply marvelous. No doubt it's the coming place. We all should go there. The radioactive rays are much more penetrating. They dig deep into you, warm the old bones. And you know how I feel about bones, darling. They are everything to us. Besides holding us together, they form us. Beauty starts right in the bones. The way they are shaped— marvelous," and she went on, holding her head high, twisting her neck, flicking out her fingers. She sucked the cigaret and curled the ends of her polished blond hair. She stood firmly planted on the rug, her legs apart, her left hip turned out.

175

"No," said the politician's wife in the four-inches-above-the-knee black leather dress with the rhinestone straps. "No, no, no," she said again. "The Senator is for freedom in sex. He believes in the pill, definitely."

"I think he could lose the election, darling, if he doesn't change his stand," the young man answered. "You see, marriage is a thing of the past. They all know it. The women pursue their mates today in the jungle."

"How wonderful," she answered, pushing the strap off her shoulder.

The young man wore a tuxedo with a diagonal zipper across the jacket. "I'm dying of heat. Now, marriage is passé. So are LSD, poppers, as out as alcohol."

"What's in?" she asked frantically.

"Vitamin E. Sensational. Absolutely sensational. Makes you relax, a de-depressant and you feel so sexy."

"How marvelous. I must tell everyone. Evelyn, have you heard of Vitamin E?" she said, turning to a lady in a velvet "smoking" with velvet pants and ruffly blouse.

"No, darling, I haven't. In London, it's implantation. They open your thigh and inject asses' milk. Firms you up. You know, at our age, after thirty."

They laughed, "Who's the doctor?"

"I'll give you both his name tomorrow. Phone me," he said, looking around for a drink, and he thought, this party isn't groovy. It's really down.

Fiona was determined to find Catherine, but as she pushed her way through the crowd in her living room, she saw only faces, legs, arms, feet—all over their home.

Terence Gateway, the artist, and his wife were standing in the doorway. The artist was bald and wore a leather dinner jacket and a red Texas string tie. His wife, with long hair, stood, bony, in a black witch-doctor-feathery evening dress, with a belt made of animal teeth. "Who are they anyway, the Chases? What do they do?" the wife asked.

"They're rich. They bought a painting from me once. They give to the Museum for American Art," her husband answered.

"Yes, but I don't get it. Why ask us? We don't mix with this squareville crowd. They aren't our types. I dread the dinner. All that formal serving. Let's take off before we get stuck."

"If you insist. Anything for business. We artists are businessmen too," he said as Fiona passed.

"Oh, I don't read the *Times* anymore. It's just too passé for me and too detailed. And they do tend to lean to the left, so my husband says," said the lady whose husband had made a fortune in frozen foods.

"The way the war is going in Vietnam we are going to have to face those higher taxes, whether it's Bobby or Lyndon in the White House," said the tall, husky Harvard economics professor, who nodded to Fiona, not quite sure who it was, as she still pushed her way.

Mr. Stephenson went after his daughter. He touched her arm gently, asking, "Darling, where are you going so fast?"

Fiona stopped and looked up at her father. "Daddy, please leave me. I've got to take care of my guests."

"But you're in such a rush. What's on your mind?" he said, as Fiona pulled away from him.

"At last I've found you, Catherine," Fiona said.

She was in the corner with Homer Breadcraft and Fiona didn't want him around at this moment. "May I talk to you—alone?" she said, looking straight at Homer. He moved away just far enough so he could still hear her.

"Don't you think we had better take a look at Paul? He's been sleeping at least for an hour," Fiona said.

"No, I think we had better leave him alone. He's just worn out. You know he didn't want to come because he was so tired. I really made him come because I thought the change would do him some good. He's been working so hard, you know," Catherine said, looking around the room and away from Fiona.

"I still think we had better look at him," said Fiona strongly. A tall, dark-haired man, George Hampton, editor of a weekly news magazine, bumped into Fiona.

177

"Oh, I'm sorry," he said and he touched Fiona's hip with his hand.

Catherine wanted to talk to George, but Fiona was determined to keep Catherine with her.

"You know, Catherine, I think you're rather calm about Paul," Fiona said.

"Calm? What can I do? Leave the party and spoil it for you and for all of us? I could take him home, but I don't think we should wake him up," and Catherine looked around the room for Michael.

Michael was sitting on the floor with Mrs. Stephenson, who kept trying to find out about Michael's work. He evaded the subject and finally Mrs. Stephenson asked, "What do you really want to do? You know, there is always a big opportunity in publishing with your father-in-law."

"No, Martha, I don't think I'm cut out for that. I'm more for the public life. I want to help the country in some way. Publishing would be too limited for me," Michael said.

Mrs. Stephenson was shocked at Michael blatantly declaring to her that the publishing business was limited.

"You know, Michael, Fiona told me about that magazine article to be published about you both. I understand it's been killed and you know that your father-in-law took care of that. As a matter of fact he became so interested in the whole affair, he's negotiating to buy the magazine. He's such a brilliant man. He never misses an opportunity," Mrs. Stephenson said enthusiastically.

"Really, are you sure it is killed? What a relief. I must thank him. I wasn't too concerned, but you know Uncle John and my family when it comes to publicity about me. I think they're all a little bit old-fashioned," Michael said.

Fiona threaded her way through the room to Michael. She finally reached him.

"We've got to look at Paul, darling. He's been down for more than an hour," Fiona said.

"He's asleep. Leave him alone. We don't want to disrupt the party," Michael said casually, looking at Mrs. Stephenson as though he expected her to agree with him.

"I'm going to see if he needs anything," and Fiona left Michael with her mother.

"I think Fiona's right. You just can't leave him lying there," Mrs. Stephenson said.

"Fiona likes Paul. You know she used to be very friendly with him. In fact, you realize, Martha, it was Paul she used to date and I interrupted Fiona one weekend on the train going up to Boston. That was the beginning for us," Michael told her proudly.

Mrs. Stephenson nodded and coolly said, "I never knew. How interesting." He sounds just like my Walter, she thought.

Fiona headed down the hall to the bedroom. She saw a man dropping ashes on the rug, and signs of spilled drink. The smoke was everywhere. The apartment smelled of stale perfume on hot bodies. She opened the door and closed it quickly. The air in the bedroom was fresh. There Paul lay, curled up on the bed. She sat down next to him and took his hand, which was hanging over the bed, and put it at his side. She felt his brow. He seemed cool, almost cold. Just for a second he trembled and the color went out of his cheeks. He turned white, yellowish white, and she saw his mouth was wet and the saliva had soiled the bedspread. She put her head down next to his. She listened for his faint breathing. His throat made a dry, gargling noise.

She realized Paul wasn't breathing normally. She wanted to run out of the room, out into the crowd, out into her party to get Catherine and Michael. But she didn't. She hesitated, then quickly got off the bed and picked up the telephone. She dialed.

"Dr. Saunders. I've got to speak to him quickly, it's an emergency. I can't wait. Please, please," and there was panic in her voice. "Have him call me, please. Any doctor, please."

She put down the phone and went back again to Paul. She propped him up on the pillow. His head was so heavy. She pulled his limp body up and uncurled his legs to make him more comfortable. He didn't open his eyes. He just slept. Fiona realized that he couldn't wake up. She spoke to him softly, "Paul, darling Paul. Paul, Paul, please wake up." Now she shouted, "Paul, Paul." He didn't respond.

"Oh my God," she said. The telephone rang. Fiona rushed over. "Thank God. Come quickly. No, no it's not Mr. Chase. No, not my husband, but Paul Cain."

179

She went back to Paul and listened to his breathing. She put her head to his chest and tried to listen. "Thank God, I can hear his heart," she said aloud.

She went to the closet and pulled out a deep burgundy red wool blanket, but changed her mind and put it back and instead took out an ivory white blanket. She put the blanket down, folded, on the end of the bed. Fiona gently lifted Paul's heavy, limp feet. She undid his laces and tugged hard to remove his black patent leather dinner shoes. She untied his bow tie and slipped it through his collar. She reached into his collar with two fingers and felt his warm skin and the soft hair on his chest. She undid the button and loosened the collar. She took the blanket and shrouded his trembling body. Fiona was sure he was cold. He must be so tired, she thought, as she put her face to his lips to catch his uneven breathing.

Doctor Saunders ran to the elevator and waited impatiently for it to come down. He heard the voices up above. He started up the stairs taking two at a time. He reached the fifth floor and stopped in front of the barrier of coats. He squeezed in between the coat racks, banging his worn leather bag as he went. At the door, which was half open, he paused. The smoke and smell of animated bodies crammed together in one room came through the door. The doctor adjusted his glasses and pushed the door open.

Mrs. Wallace F. Renn IV was just coming down the hall and she saw the doctor. Mrs. Renn was alone and looking for someone to attach herself to for the rest of the evening. She had just fixed her face and had decided her husband was really miserable because he always deserted her at parties. But the doctor, he must be a doctor, she thought, was hardly expected. She liked his looks, his long, bushy eyebrows, his thin, ruddy face and his intelligent eyes and the wry smile lines at the side of his mouth and that big, unshaven dimple hole.

"Well, doctor, are you sure you have the right place?" and she took a long sip. "Come in and join our little party; fifty of New York's busiest, boring best," and she threw back her head and roared with laughter. The doctor thought he was in the wrong apartment. He looked at Mrs. Renn—her short, short dress a hand above her knees,

180

the miniest of minis, he thought, and black silk bloomers, blooming out below the skirt slit up the side.

"Excuse me, but I'm here for Mrs. Chase. Where is she?" he said curtly, looking down the hall at the guests circling each other, with their arms moving as they talked and fed themselves more drinks.

Pierre approached, fixing his unwieldy tails on the way. He looked right through Doctor Saunders, who dropped his heavy bag on the black Chinese Chippendale chair, squishing the orange-red cushions.

"Sir, Madame is entertaining. Is she expecting you?" he said as the doctor stood in front of him.

Mrs. Renn saw the concern on the doctor's face. "Pierre, get Mrs. Chase immediately. Something has gone wrong."

Pierre continued on his way into the living room. He looked everywhere for Mrs. Chase.

Mrs. Stephenson was all alone, and wished her husband had come back. He was across the room with the magazine publisher he was about to buy out.

"Excuse me, Madame. Where is Mrs. Chase?" Pierre said methodically.

"I'm not sure, but I know she was concerned about Congressman Cain," Mrs. Stephenson answered.

"Madame, there's a doctor here looking for her."

"A doctor? What's wrong, Pierre? What's happened?" and Mrs. Stephenson was off the couch and down the hallway followed by Pierre.

She stopped in front of the doctor.

"I'm Mrs. Stephenson, Fiona's mother. May I help you, doctor? Who phoned you? What seems to be the matter?" she said, pulling her hand back quickly from the doctor's.

"Mrs. Chase called me, said it was an emergency."

"Come right with me. They must be in the bedroom."

Mrs. Stephenson knocked, and then she realized how stupid. She flung open the door hurriedly, followed by the doctor, Pierre, and Mrs. Renn.

Fiona was sitting in her black velvet dress on the ivory white blanket and leaning forward. She adjusted the blanket high up around Paul's neck. He was now lying straight out on the bed, flat on his back, his head way back on the flowered pillow. Fiona looked up slowly. "I know, doctor, there is something wrong. His breathing doesn't seem normal."

The doctor moved toward the bed. He removed the blanket and took Paul Cain's arm and stared steadily into his face.

"His pulse is weak. You were right to call me."

"Is he going to be all right, doctor?" Fiona asked and her eyes were swimming with tears.

The doctor didn't answer, his stethoscope was already listening to the heart beat and his eyes were now on the sweep second hand of his gold watch. Fiona thought how cold the stethoscope must feel on Paul's chest. She remembered dreading that moment when the doctor put the stethoscope to her chest.

Mrs. Stephenson moved next to Fiona. She put a restraining hand on Fiona's shoulder. Mrs. Renn stood at the foot of the bed. Pierre stood at the other side.

"I think it would be better if we all left the doctor alone," said Mrs. Stephenson, and she added, "Pierre, you'd better summon Mrs. Cain and Mr. Chase immediately. I saw them in the salon in the far corner."

Mrs. Renn didn't leave. She went up to Fiona, as though to shield her.

The doctor was silent. He looked up from Cain, and turning to Fiona said, "It doesn't look very good. I think he may be in a coma. We must get him to the hospital immediately. There may be a hemorrhage."

Pierre found Catherine and Michael.

"Oh, you're too much, Michael. You're just too wicked to talk about the Senator that way. You mean, really, his wife had to be invited?"

"She did insist," said Michael, crossing his legs and moving closer to Catherine. She didn't move away. He dropped his leg and pressed his buttocks into Catherine. She still didn't move. She felt the warmth of his body. The champagne, bubbling, satisfying, freed their minds, whetted their appetites. Michael thought the sport of teasing was half the fun and Catherine knew she could afford now to loosen up at last. She was ready to play just for a short moment. Catherine moved closer. Michael's leg and thigh felt firm. Her foot twisted and turned up into his cuffless trousers. Michael felt the sole of her shoe against his skin.

Pierre was standing above them. "Pardon me, sir, Madame, but Mrs. Stephenson and Mrs. Chase are anxious to have you in the bedroom. The doctor is attending Congressman Cain and they're waiting."

Catherine looked at Michael and he turned his head away. She went pale and her eyes froze into a panicky stare. Then she turned back to Michael and took his hand.

"Catherine, I'm sure everything is all right. Let's go quietly and not disrupt the guests," and he followed Pierre, who cut through the people. Catherine elbowed her way after him. Her shoe wasn't on over the heel and it rubbed her. She dropped the shoe at the hallway door and ran to the bedroom. Michael started running too and they burst into the room.

Catherine threw herself at the doctor. Fiona didn't stand back. She stayed next to Paul. Her mother was behind her, with her hand still on Fiona's shoulder.

"Doctor, tell me. I'm Mrs. Cain. Is he all right? Oh, my God. How could this happen? Why didn't we know? Why didn't we get the doctor sooner?"

"Mrs. Chase phoned me soon enough. It wouldn't have made any difference."

"How can you say that?" Catherine snapped back.

Catherine moved around the bed and near to Fiona. "Why didn't you come and get me? How could you let me stay out there with Michael while this was going on?" Catherine said, and grasping the fluted bedpost she dug her nails into the hard mahogany and slipped to the floor.

No one moved. Michael stood above Catherine, who sat curled up at his feet. He held out his hand. Catherine didn't take hold. She sat on the floor. "Paul, what's going to happen to Paul?" and she sobbed.

The guests filled the hallway now. "Cain is dying," Breadcraft had told someone and someone had told someone and the hallway was jammed. They were pushing and shoving to see a dying man.

They drank their champagne, filled their glasses to ease the shock. Doctor Saunders calmly asked everyone to move back from the bed. He went and telephoned for an ambulance. He spoke to the doctor on duty. "Yes, I think so. Yes, aneurysm. We will try. Phone Doctor Graham. I'll be there in twenty minutes."

The doctor looked up from the phone and saw the guests pushing and shoving to get in the room. The ladies with their braids of hair teased and tricked in all directions, their silk and lace long evening dresses covering their warm, alive bodies—the men, their eyes red and tired from the push, the parties, surviving, all dressed in black tuxedos with shining silk lapels, and the jewels, so many glittering jewels—the smell of stale perfume and eau de cologne on their bare necks and many faces. The smoke came into the room and the air was soon as stale inside the room as outside.

They didn't talk as loudly now. Suddenly the din of busy, busy voices, the laughter from drink, all the party noises had passed away. It was more like the rustling noise heard on Sunday at 11 A.M., when people entered the pews at church.

Mr. Stephenson moved to the front of the crowd. "I'm Fiona's father, please let me through. Please."

Uncle John was jammed in the hallway with the others. He tried to break through, following Senator Borden. They both got to the bedroom door. It was locked. Mr. Stephenson had been the last to enter.

Mr. Stephenson was now in the room next to Fiona. She fell into his arms and her head rested against his chest. Michael still stood with Catherine at his feet. She refused to rise. Should he go down to her, or stand there, stiff, unknowing, confused and lost? The party couldn't go on, or maybe when the doctor took Paul they would have to eat.

Michael told Pierre to wait. "Let's see," he said.

"But the meat will be overdone," Pierre whispered to Michael, "and the chef doesn't know. He's already half an hour late."

"Pierre," Michael answered, "tell him that he will have to wait. The Congressman will be taken to the hospital."

"Darling, he's going to be all right," Mr. Stephenson tried to reassure Fiona. Her head stayed buried in his chest and he stroked the back of her neck and rested his chin on her black hair. He could feel Fiona shaking. If only he could shield her from the shock. But what had she been doing in the room, he wondered?

Fiona looked up, her eyes full of tears. "It was as though he were dying while I did nothing, while he was . . ." and no one heard except Mr. Stephenson, who pressed her head into his chest.

"Please clear the room. Everyone out," said Doctor Saunders with authority. And he put his hand to Mrs. Renn, to Mrs. Stephenson, to Pierre, and started to lead Mr. Stephenson from the room but saw Fiona buried against his chest. He hesitated. Should she leave or not? Better not, he decided.

He shut the door and went to Mrs. Cain, lifted her from the floor, and sat her in Fiona's pink and green print chair.

The guests still clung to the outside of the door. They waited, hoping to have the news. They chatted quietly.

"He was brilliant. Such a fine man."

"Don't say that. He will pull through," said the Senator, who waved his hands as though he were pushing the herd back.

"What a tragedy, so somber, so sudden," Homer Breadcraft said, his voice funereal. "At the height of his greatness. It was as though fate had decreed," and as they moved back into the living room, some listened to the author who was writing his next book.

The ambulance attendants stood at the door and had trouble squeezing the adjustable cot through the coat racks and around the people. They unfolded the cot and rolled it down the hall. The ladies stood aside, fearful the stainless steel cot, with the grey blanket and the dirty white rubber wheels, might stain their dresses. Michael saw the wheels scrape the door frame as they went through to the bedroom.

"We got here quickly," the attendant said and he handed a small yellow paper pad to anyone. "Who's going to sign?"

Doctor Saunders snatched the pad out of his hand and motioned to the bed. "Let's remove Congressman Cain and hurry."

They lifted Paul Cain off the bed and Fiona moved away from Mr. Stephenson. She wrapped the white blanket around Cain's legs and then around his shoulders. The white blanket, his pale white face, and then the bright red hair glowed on the white pillow, as

Cain was wheeled through the door. The guests stood back, not far, because they wanted to see.

Catherine got up from the chair. She followed the cot out of the room. Fiona went right behind the attendants, her head bowed down, her arms folded. She went with them to the elevator.

Michael stayed for a moment with Catherine. Then, as if making a decision, took her hand and together they walked quickly out of the apartment and into the elevator, followed by Mr. and Mrs. Stephenson. Downstairs they passed through the dimly lit lobby. The three doormen stood by in a line and one held the door.

Fiona was outside. The first snow had just fallen. Big flakes were coming down. The snow hushed the city noises. Paul Cain, covered in the white blanket, was lifted into the ambulance and the snowflakes fell on his pale face and red hair. Catherine and Doctor Saunders sat together, silent, on the side seats of the ambulance. Fiona stood alone, outside, the snow drifting gently onto her black velvet dress. Then Michael and her father and mother surrounded her. Michael removed his velvet coat and covered Fiona's bare shoulders. He saw the red ruby still shining, with one big snowflake which clung to the stone. Then the flake slipped down off the ruby and onto Michael's velvet jacket and melted away.

They all turned back as the ambulance rounded the corner. Fiona saw the tracks from the cot still in the snow. And she watched the snow drift slowly and fill up the tracks. She turned and went upstairs to the party with the others, with Michael's arm around her shoulders. He held her tighter than he had in a long time.

The door to the apartment was wide open. The guests were still drinking and Pierre stood at the entrance. Fiona went in first, then Mrs. Stephenson, Mr. Stephenson, and, last, Michael.

Michael stopped: "Pierre, serve the dinner." Fiona turned to Michael, "How could you, Michael? How can we go on with the party?" Mr. and Mrs. Stephenson didn't speak. Michael answered, "It's snowing outside and the guests have no place to go. It's late. We must feed them. Life goes on anyway."

186

17

THE FUNERAL

Fiona came out of St. Bartholomew's after Paul Cain's funeral. She was alone, that is, alone within herself, but surrounded by people and strange faces. There was a big crowd, the grey police barriers were up on the snow-lined sidewalk. Michael had stayed behind inside the church with Catherine.

Fiona had seen during the service that Catherine, from underneath her black lace veil, had stared out at Michael.

There had been no recriminations about who called the doctor. Did they wait too long? Doctor Saunders cleared away any reasonable doubt. Paul Cain had died of an aneurysm and it could have happened at any time in his life. Just at the moment of Michael and Fiona's party, the aneurysm burst forth, hemorrhaging and paralyzing Cain's right side. He remained in a coma for five hours, his brain destroyed, his body numbed. He died in the morning.

As she stood on the church steps, breathing in the cold, crisp air, Fiona wondered if with Paul's death that she was dying inside. His death was so futile, so undeserved, so unjust, so everything that was wrong with life, Fiona thought. And yet for those brief hours with Paul, Fiona had cared for this fine man whom she might have married and now the man, Michael's rival, was out of the way. Fiona thought she had loved Paul. She still saw him lying asleep on the flowered bedspread, his strong, wiry red hair, his pale face, his heavy breathing suddenly growing fainter, then smothered. He is gone and soon to be forgotten, even by me, Fiona thought to herself. To live, to be alive every second, as she had been on the bed with Paul Cain, to cheat on death, to live, to live. Fiona had never wanted life more than at this moment.

Soon Michael was at Fiona's side and so was Catherine, with her arm firmly grasping Michael's. Fiona really didn't care that they were standing next to her. They might as well not have been there and she realized that possibly Michael and Catherine had wished she wasn't there. The black lacquered coffin smothered in red roses came down the steps and soon was placed in the glistening black limousine. Death must always appear to be clean. Men spruced up for the splendid way to heaven. Did men feel guilty, evil, unclean, when death took away? Fiona thought she shared that guilt.

Fiona looked at Catherine, who had lifted her veil off her face. She was dazzled by the sun, just as on the day Fiona and she had stepped out onto the penthouse terrace together. Catherine watched the hearse door close on her husband, and now they beckoned her to follow.

"Darling," Michael said softly.

"Yes," answered Catherine and she dropped the veil back down over her face. She was glad to hide her face. Catherine found it hard to weep in public. Paul would not have expected it, but the crowd would have.

The camera was on Michael and Catherine. The flash went off and Fiona stepped aside. Catherine just took Michael's arm more firmly.

"Michael, I'm not feeling well. I think I had better go home," said Fiona, as the photographer disappeared down the steps. The chauffeurs in the cortege switched on their motors at the same time. The exhaust hitting the cold air swirled around and then upward.

"Yes, I think you'd better go home. I'll get someone to take you," Michael said to Fiona, who stared at the hearse with the coffin.

"Michael, you cannot leave me now. You must go with us the rest of the way to the cemetery. Please, darling," Catherine begged, holding on to Michael's arm.

188

Fiona at that moment just had to escape. "Oh, please go on. Please forgive me. I don't want to hold up anything. I just couldn't go. I want to remember Paul the way he was that last night," and Fiona put her hand to Michael's shoulder, urging him to go.

Arm in arm, Catherine and Michael went down the steps, followed by Catherine's mother and stepfather. Senator Cain stood alone at the top of the steps, his hand firmly holding a black cane. He turned to take one last look at the church. Then he started down the steps, quickly for an older man. He stopped next to Fiona.

"You are Fiona Chase, aren't you?" he said gently, touching Fiona's wrist.

His hand felt warm and she looked up into his eyes. "Yes, I am. I'm so sorry, Senator. I'm so so sorry," and she turned her head away.

"The doctor tells me you were with Paul while he was dying," Senator Cain began. "And he told me you called and stayed with him until they left for the hospital. I want to thank you," and he dropped his warm hand from Fiona's wrist and taking his cane went down the steps and into the second limousine. Fiona saw Michael move over and onto the jump seat. She saw Michael take the Senator's hand and she watched Catherine looking all the time at Michael. Soon they drove off and Fiona was glad to be alone.

Michael hadn't bothered to find someone to take Fiona home. She was about to hail a cab and then decided it was such a beautiful day, why not walk. She started up Park Avenue. The cars moved by, three abreast uptown, three abreast downtown—they traveled uniformly, colors different, shapes different, but all the same, machines heading uptown, downtown, crosstown, and all around the island. Death couldn't stop the monotonous movement of machines and people.

Fiona was about to start uptown, when Uncle John, his glasses almost off his nose, with black chesterfield over his arm, came running after her. He doffed his black Homburg. "Fiona, what are you doing so alone? I see you don't like funerals—macabre affairs, they really are. We should all be thrown to the fishes," and he smiled. Fiona was delighted to see Uncle John.

He took her by the arm. Soon she was sitting comfortably in

his warm Mercedes. He twiddled with his gloves and asked, "Where to? Let's have some luncheon together."

Fiona had always feared Uncle John. But today, across the table, with the bourbon old-fashioned warming her, Fiona thought Uncle John was really just like a nice, friendly Teddy bear. His black hair was obviously touched up; his complexion was ruddy from the wines. His friendly eyes, with those fallen-down thin-rimmed glasses, Fiona calculated, set Uncle John apart from the usual, wealthy, hard-driving, Wall Street tycoon. Fiona was glad to be with him at the table. They were both hungry. She faced the muraled wall—a scene of the Tuileries Garden in Paris. A little girl in a red coat on a red tricycle rode through the park. It was a Paris spring, Fiona thought and she wanted to be there.

"I suppose it's been a big shock, Cain's death. So sudden," Uncle John began. "Another bourbon old-fashioned, two more, waiter," and he turned to face Fiona.

"Yes, his death was terrible. Not so much a shock for me, because I was there when he was stricken on our bed. You know, during the party."

"I know," said Uncle John, "because I was standing in the hallway when we heard he was dying. And I know Michael and Catherine were together in your living room."

"I went to them. I called the doctor. But you see, it didn't make any difference. He was dying and no one could save him. I thought I could help. I thought I was helping, but I couldn't do anything. It was too late."

"But at least you were there at hand and you called the doctor," said Uncle John, trying to reassure.

"But what good is trying? Uncle John, all we do is try. I try with Michael. I try, but we never seem to get there," and Fiona was sorry she had mentioned Michael.

"If you don't help Michael, no one can. He needs you, Fiona. I've watched you. You are kind, intelligent, but spoiled. We are all spoiled. We are surrounded by this enormous wealth. I include myself in this spoiled category. You know I have no interest in money anymore. It bores me, because I have so much and it seems to make more and still more.

190

"Damn it, waiter, where are those old-fashioneds? Get Jean over here," he said gruffly and the women at the next banquette whispered.

Uncle John continued, "Money piled up in stacks higher and higher leaves you so alone. You build barriers, layers around you, so that you lose touch with the real, breathing things of life. Money doesn't give life, or stop death. When you no longer struggle, you turn to others ways for amusement, like drink, sex, even drugs. I've seen it happen. We're always looking for something that will stimulate and money doesn't provide stimulation. After a while money is a routine happening. So like Michael and our friend Cain, bless him, they turn to power, to be do-gooders for the common man; they say the common man. I suppose they all try to do good for the common man, but they really are doing good for themselves. They must build up their own egos. After making so much money, their egos want power in the name of the common man. Thank God, there is no such thing as the common man who thinks and does exactly the same as his neighbor next door. The common man is a figment of the politician's imagination. The human mind, the human body—everyone is different. Look at Cain who comes into the world born with a pin-size clot on his brain. The clot is silent, dormant, unknown to the best doctors, and then breaks forth on the night of your party, at the height of his success, and he's gone, almost forgotten, as they quickly bury him. That one, fine man is unlike any other man," and Uncle John, expended, exhausted, finished talking. His face was red and his eyes watering.

Fiona didn't answer. She thought of Michael. What was Michael doing? They both were seeking security and shoring up their own egos. She couldn't help thinking that one of them, she, or Michael, one day would have to break out, express themselves, make themselves known, if not to the world, at least to each other. She wanted to tell Uncle John. But he was busy devouring two lamb chops encrusted in potatoes and onions. He told the waiter, "The wine is superior."

He turned to Fiona, "You see, eating and drinking are part of living. There's something real about cutting into the flesh of these succulent chops and then consuming them. What pleasure. No one told us we had to eat them, but we followed our instinct and with gusto. Yes, that's what I believe in: following instincts. Our instincts let us know how to fight, to kill, and to die. That is real. The body lives, draws life from all that is around us. We all should live and forget those artificial barriers we have constructed to protect our egos."

The women at the next banquette moved closer together. Uncle John looked straight at them and poured his own wine. Fiona wasn't shocked. She loved his raucous, unrefined, man-to-man talk. She smiled as Uncle John took her hand and squeezed it. "If only I had been ten years younger," and he laughed so the whole restaurant could hear. "Ten years younger. My goodness," he said, squeezing Fiona's hand so the blood seemed to stop.

Fiona's smile gave way to a frown. She looked warmly into his eyes above the glasses which were never up where they should be. "Now, Uncle John, you know that you aren't that old."

Uncle John was happy and thought Michael had selected a fine wife, but he also was sure Michael wasn't up to her.

"I hate to be serious, Fiona. But I really wanted to talk to you about Michael. You know, of course, his work at the law firm, I mean, the Senator's, hasn't been exactly satisfactory. He doesn't seem to enjoy it. I told him, stop the partying. The Senator told him, get in on time, settle down and have some babies. You know, for a young man, coming from a good, rich, really middle-class family—just like mine—we have got to be realistic. We aren't trying to be the Vanderbilts, the Astors, or like any of them, because times have changed. We all saw in Michael the chance to take our family out of the money class and into politics. I know his father wants to see his son big in public life. But so far, Fiona, and I hate to be serious about this, I don't think Michael is suited for politics or public life. But he's still young and there's still time."

After Uncle John had mentioned "having babies," Fiona stopped eating. The brief, happy episode with Uncle John was now gone. The truth about Michael was out again. Michael had never told Fiona the Senator had urged settling down with a family. Fiona knew Uncle John was right about everyone following their basic instincts and Fiona with Michael had failed to do just that. They had never once

192

crossed the phony barriers that separated them from each other and the rest of the world. I'm just like Mummy. Our life is just the same, she realized.

Fiona felt warm all over, that sick warm feeling that comes with a fever.

"Are you all right, Fiona?" Uncle John asked. "You look so pale. Have I said something to upset you?"

"No. Really nothing, Uncle John. You're a dear," and she took his hand.

"What is it? Please tell me," he pleaded.

"It's really nothing much. It's that you've hit on the truth, without knowing it. The truth about Michael and me," and now Fiona was looking at Uncle John hoping for help.

"It's all happened rather quickly. So much coming our way and now all the wonderful part of our life has disappeared almost overnight. We're total strangers, Michael and I, living in our beautiful surroundings with our friends, the friends we have selected because we think they are important."

Uncle John was confused, because Fiona hadn't revealed to him the real facts. He was wise enough to see Fiona couldn't tell him all and, besides, he wasn't sure he wanted to know. Along with Michael's father, he had banked so much on Michael, and to have a failure would be totally unacceptable. Uncle John had never been able to accept failure, in spite of all his talk about following one's own instincts.

He had failed too, badly, with his own wife, Anna, who, driven by the frenzy of her ambitious husband, had ended up in an institution and as far as Uncle John was concerned it was better that she stayed there. True, he had followed his own instincts and Uncle John knew that they were selfish. Now he wanted to forget Anna, the past. His own mistakes could never be admitted and as for Michael, he just couldn't accept failure. Uncle John was longing for someone else in the family to go beyond the money that was already theirs. Money was within the grasp of everyone.

And what of this beautiful young girl sitting next to him on the red velvet banquette, in her black mourning suit? Couldn't he at least for once break down and help her? Uncle John was about to, but he was afraid. He might find out what he already knew, but what he couldn't accept. Michael might fail.

"The check please, waiter," and then he stopped. "I'm sorry. I just don't have time for coffee, I've got to get back to the office before the market closes."

But how could he leave Fiona without at least one bit of hope? He looked at her again and he felt that pang of sadness going through him, like the pang when you leave someone behind and alone forever, like the spring day he put Anna away. He told himself it was for the best. Maybe they could help her. But he didn't have the humility to stay to help his wife when he had failed her as a husband.

Fiona wrapped her mink coat around her shoulders and was about to get up from the table. She knew Uncle John had something more to say, but he didn't have the guts to follow his natural instincts and say what was on his mind. Uncle John had panicked in front of a young girl. He hasn't grown up much either, she thought. He's just like the rest of us, rich, barricaded inside, secure in his collection of people and objects, just like me—more like Michael.

Uncle John put his arm on the soft mink and rubbed his hand up and down. Fiona slipped into the coat. The mink felt warm, secure.

"It will take time—this thing between you and Michael. It always works out. And don't worry about his career. I have taken care of that. We are behind him, his father and I, all the way. Why, this morning before the funeral Michael called me at home. I was just shaving and couldn't believe he was up at seven. I bet it was the first time in his life he had shaken a leg at that hour," and Uncle John gave a big, raucous laugh that was utterly false. "Well, he was on the telephone to me and like a true Chase was thinking ahead. Michael wanted to know how to go about taking over Cain's Congressional seat in the Seventeenth. He's following his instincts. I told him, 'Michael, you'll have to stand for election, go to the people if you want his seat.'"

Fiona got up and beckoned the waiter to move out the table. She walked rapidly through the restaurant, through the revolving door,

194

followed by Uncle John. She gave him her hand and said, "Well, Uncle John. Thank you for the nice luncheon."

She turned around and ran down Fifty-second Street toward Fifth Avenue, her coat unfastened, blowing out from her in the wind. Fiona reached Fifth Avenue. She dashed out across the street, against the light, in between the one-way traffic. On the other side she waved frantically for a taxi. Fiona jumped in and slammed the door hard and she couldn't help herself any longer. She wept.

But even as she wept, she wondered why she was so upset. It was crass of Uncle John, of Michael, to be planning that way even before Paul Cain was buried. But hadn't she wanted Michael to be ambitious? Hadn't they both envied Paul and Catherine's head start? So what was the fuss? She didn't really know the answer except that she felt frightened, deserted, and, facing the actual possibility of Michael's achieving success—or, even worse, of encountering failure—she wanted only to retreat, to be safe again.

The driver just headed downtown, not knowing where to go. He didn't dare ask his passenger. She's in bad shape, he thought to himself, as they passed Forty-second Street.

A month after the funeral, Fiona was still haunted by that death day. She saw again the limousine door closing on Cain in his black lacquered wooden box—the same black lacquered wood as the piano in Michael and Fiona's living room and now that piano became to Fiona a symbol of death. The piano, once so beautiful and admired when decked with hyacinths, was never played. It stood lifeless in the living room, just like all their other objects.

On those lonely days, when she felt more and more alone, Fiona wandered through the apartment. She ran her fingers across the tables and the objects. Back and forth she paced, throughout their rooms. All she saw was their collections gathering dust and then she was after Mary to clean.

The luncheon with Uncle John left a bitter mark on Fiona. For all his instincts, which Fiona reduced to getting ahead at all costs, Uncle John was cruel, insensitive to the world around him, to people. She still found it difficult to face the fact that Michael somehow planned to take dead Paul Cain's Congressional seat. Michael

195

was no better than Uncle John in his unscrupulous drive. Michael had never once mentioned his plans to Fiona. But she suspected now that he was even brash enough to think that he could achieve his end through Catherine.

Catherine was everywhere with Michael and Fiona. The triangle was drawn on the night of Cain's death and now that Cain was gone, Michael cast himself in the role of Catherine's protector.

Fiona, naturally sympathetic and kind, had accepted the presence of Catherine everywhere they went. Cain's death had left Catherine really alone and she played up the fact that now Michael and Fiona were her closest friends. She talked, but not seriously, of returning to her family in Virginia. She hesitated, because she really did not get along with her mother and had more than a passing fancy for her stepfather, who had been, ever since the marriage to Catherine's mother, strongly attracted to the daughter. Catherine's mother was determined to keep her daughter, now a widow, out of the Virginia estate.

To Fiona, Catherine had confided almost proudly about her stepfather, had openly discussed her desire to take her stepfather away from her own mother, and she admitted it was because she not only detested her mother, but loved her stepfather and meant to have him. Fiona wasn't suspicious enough to believe Catherine really had her eye on Michael.

Secretly Catherine resented anyone else's happiness and she would never forgive Fiona for her possessiveness toward Paul the night he died. In her pregnant state, Catherine was embittered and more determined to protect herself and her child, even if it meant destroying others. As Uncle John had said, those who made their mark had to follow their instincts with verve.

Catherine had said she would marry a great man. She had never mentioned love, or happiness. From the first night after she returned home with Michael, her only thought now was to secure her position, and with Michael, his money and potential power, the two could make an unbeatable combination.

At first Catherine expected Fiona would not interfere. Fiona, to Catherine, had always been such a sweet, easy-going friend and Catherine assumed Fiona could be brought under her thumb. Cath-

196

erine didn't accept that without Paul her brief moment of glory was gone. Fiona still had Michael, but Catherine had no idea what Michael really was. She only knew Michael wanted what Paul had gained through hard work and Catherine was determined to dangle the bait of potential power in front of him.

The triangle agreed the mourning period should last for a month. During the period, Catherine regularly dined with Michael and Fiona at their apartment.

Michael was working harder. The idea that he now had a specific if secret goal in his sights spurred him on. Mrs. Allen, at the office, saw the difference and even the Senator noticed the change. Michael was happy. He assumed the responsibility of Catherine and her affairs. Word-of-mouth praise went to the right ears of the right New York groups. Michael was for a brief moment a knight in shining armor, but only Uncle John knew why Michael had suddenly changed. He added his encouragement and Michael's father commended Michael for his fine interest in assisting the Congressman's widow, even though both father and uncle knew Michael's ulterior motives. The Chases were interested only in the end results.

18

TRIANGLE

Pierre let Mrs. Cain into the apartment.

"Don't disturb them. I know where to find them. In the dressing room. They are always there at this hour having cocktails," Catherine said in her assured tone.

She dropped her black and white plaid coat on a chair before Pierre could take it from her, and unwound the black lace veil wrapped around her head and neck.

Catherine went down the hall, past the room with the canopy bed, and into the dressing room. She stopped at the globe. Michael got up and broke into a warm smile.

"Here she is, our daily dinner companion," and he adjusted his bow tie. Michael went toward Catherine and kissed her on both cheeks and held both of her hands. He then pushed her out in front of him. "My, you're looking better every day," and he paused to admire Catherine, who twirled the globe around and around, all the time eyeing Fiona. That globe had been mine, that had been my pose, almost my line, Fiona thought to herself.

"How are you, darling?" Fiona asked. Fiona sat on the couch, her feet curled up and her shoes scattered under the glass table, which Michael had replaced the day after he had destroyed the original. No one knew the difference.

"I've lit the fire in here, Catherine, in your honor. It's so cold and raw tonight, I thought the fire would keep us warm," Michael said.

"Your fire isn't doing too well, darling," Fiona said. "I suggest you put the big log in the back and that small birch underneath to make some heat."

"I've made more fires than you. So please let me do it my way," said Michael, banging away with the poker. Smoke started to come back in the room.

Catherine twirled the globe around and then placed her hand on the back of her hip. "I've the worst backache. I guess it's being pregnant," she said.

Fiona got up off the couch and went to Catherine. "Poor darling, I'm sure you're in agony. But think how lucky you are to be having a child," said Fiona and she touched Catherine's hand atop the globe, as if to express a small amount of sympathy.

The smoke continued to pour out the chimney. "Damn it. I told you, Fiona, we should never have widened this chimney. I told you so," said Michael, turning away from the smoldering fire and waving the poker at Fiona.

"Lucky to be having a child now, Fiona? Lucky? You really think so? Without Paul—alone to face everyone? To bring the child up alone? I'm not so happy, I assure you," Catherine answered and she removed her hand from Fiona's and walked over to the couch and sat down, still holding her hand to her hip.

Fiona was left standing alone.

Michael put the poker back in the large brass bucket by the chimney and followed Catherine to the couch. He knocked against the side of the glass table as he moved next to Catherine, who sat with arms folded over her stomach. Just then a puff of black smoke poured out of the fireplace, another puff, and then the room was filled with smoke. Catherine started to cough. Michael sat on the couch banging his foot against the table.

Fiona still stood at the globe. Her hand rested on the top, her eyes fixed on both Catherine and Michael. She turned toward the fireplace and watched the smoke pouring out. She didn't care, let the smoke come out, let more smoke come, no, she really didn't care.

There was really nothing Michael could do about the smoke. He had tried and failed. He had insisted the fireplace be made large, because it would be more impressive. Fiona dropped her hand from the globe and went toward the fireplace. She picked up the brass tongs and, leaning against the mantel, opened the firescreen, balancing it on her hip, and, putting both hands into the smoke-filled chimney, lifted the top log to the back. The smoke went up. Fiona put the tongs back in the bucket and turning to Michael and Catherine, who sat silently, said, "See, it isn't so difficult. I learned in England how to lay a fire. Always keep the biggest log in the back, not in the front." Fiona smiled, knowing she was right. "Now, don't you think it's time for a drink? A good, strong one for me," Fiona added. Catherine nodded in agreement.

Michael got up off the couch and started for the bar. He twisted his foot on Fiona's shoes. "Damn those shoes," he yelled, kicking them aside.

He opened the bar. The glasses shone. Very thirties, Catherine thought, as she surveyed the room. She felt she was almost a part of it. All the bottles were filled, untouched, but Pierre had unsealed all tops ahead of time.

Fiona looked into the bar. She imagined the glass scattered into a thousand pieces, like the night when Michael had slammed the door shut. She saw the glass wall cracked right down the middle. All those shining glasses lined up, reflecting back into more glass, over and over again, their reflections on the sides, in the back, on the ceiling, all dazzling, so dazzling, so clean.

Michael started to pour three fingers of Scotch. "Ice, Catherine, darling?" he asked in a gentle tone. "I don't take any now. I like the taste of the whiskey neat. Fiona always crams her glass full of ice."

"I'll go along with you, Michael. No ice," said Catherine and her eyes examined him. As he turned away from the bar, their eyes met. He hesitated at first, embarrassed by Catherine's stare. Then he looked back at Fiona. She was looking at him too. He took the drink to Catherine.

"Here, darling." Then he returned Catherine's stare. He felt his own eyes brightening. He rolled them back and forth, the way he had at Mrs. Allen.

Fiona stood silent, just waiting for her drink. Catherine wasn't flattered or excited by Michael's stare. She had known that he would do it.

Michael turned away and went to Fiona, who was still standing by the fire. The warmth and the slow hiss of the sap dripping into the ashes and the crackle of the log she had just put to the back somehow gave her confidence and security. The logs burning at her feet made Fiona think about the men who had planted the seedling for the tree, the men who had chopped the tree, the men who had brought the logs to the city to sell, the handyman who had delivered the logs to their apartment. What were these men like?

Fiona looked back into the bar and she saw the glasses again lining the shelf, one right after the other, clean, crystal, glistening, reflecting a thousand images. Those are our friends. Yes, they are. That's our life right in that bar, image on image, shining, beautiful, monotonous, enclosed and only glass, ready to be easily broken, shattered into a thousand pieces to be picked up by the maid. In spite of her determination not to be, Fiona knew that after her luncheon with Uncle John she was shattered into a thousand pieces, but she would never let anyone else pick up those pieces. She was ready to put herself together again. No Humpty Dumpty am I, she thought, and Fiona downed the drink and asked for another.

"I feel so wonderful tonight. And you two sit like old folks, rocking on the porch, looking out at the stately elms. Of course, you know those beautiful elms are fighting off elm disease and no one can prevent it. That's right, you're looking out at diseased elms," and Fiona threw back her head and with bitterness in her eyes laughed in Michael's face. He looked away and then to Catherine, hoping she would say something to cut off Fiona. Catherine couldn't. She was too surprised at Fiona's sudden change.

"Come, Michael. Come, my darling Michael. I want another drink. Let's have another one before Pierre and Mary feed us. Feed the animals in their zoo, so everyone can watch us. Let's eat in here by the fire, so our friends, all those shining glasses, can reflect down on us. Let them watch us. Here's my glass," Fiona said, her voice fading away as though she was passing on to another phase.

Catherine regained her composure, and Fiona knew she had, because Catherine brushed her hair away from her brow. As Catherine lifted up her hair, Fiona saw the streaks of grey already coming through. Months ago that would have given a few moments of pleasure to think that someone else, young and beautiful, was grey and she was not, but now grey or not meant nothing. Albert the hairdresser would fix the grey tomorrow.

Fiona blurted out, "And Albert can fix it tomorrow. We can get anything fixed. Oh yes, we can," and she smiled that satisfied smile that was not real, the smile that was frightening, because it was so forced.

"And you know my mother has her hair fixed every day. Every day at the same hour. Imagine, every day. In New York, when she's finished with her social secretary and after five minutes of reading the paper and then in Antigua it's twice a day. The hairdresser arrives at the house before she swims if there are guests and then he arrives after she swims. As I said, everything is fixed for us. All the way, no problems, everything can be arranged."

Catherine shifted on the couch. "Fiona, aren't you carrying this a little far? Why don't you settle down, sit instead of standing there, giving us a lecture?"

Fiona remembered the day of the charity party on the roof with Catherine, almost shy, so noble, and tonight she wasn't going to let her escape. Fiona felt like a tigress about to destroy the prey. The pleasure of pouncing and capturing was so much better than the sweet, tender, bloody flesh.

"Imagine all that trouble," Fiona went on, "the hairdressers coming and going. Imagine the time it takes for Henry, that's mother's butler, going back and forth to the door to let in the hairdressers and then to announce them and then to take them out again. Think how much Mummy must sit looking at herself in the mirror, fixed here, pulled there, fitted, worked over, admired, and still she's just another woman. Oh, I forgot, she really isn't just another woman, because everyone says she's the most beautiful, the most—take any most you want—she's the most in New York and yet she still worries when she goes to luncheon that she doesn't look right. There's always going to be that one hair out of place." Fiona stopped talking and turned back to the fire. She looked into the fire. She couldn't care less that Catherine and Michael were staring at her shocked, dismayed, horrified at her boldness.

Fiona rested one elbow on the mantel and dropped her hand limply holding the whiskey at her side. Fiona turned her hip out to Catherine and Michael.

To change the subject, Catherine said, "About the masked ball, Fiona, have you decided what to wear? It sounds so amusing and you know everyone in New York is clamoring for an invitation. Paul and I received ours yesterday. It's a month off, so I should be able to go, that is, if I don't get any bigger and can't get into my dress."

Fiona lifted her arm from her side and lowered her head as she drank. Paul, there had been a Paul only weeks ago and still Catherine was saying she and Paul had received the invitation. Fiona turned around to watch Catherine, to see if she really had been struck by the mention of Paul. Catherine was looking at Michael.

"Michael and I wouldn't miss the ball for the world. I think they had a stroke of genius wanting to mask the ball. That's the way it should be, all of us masked from each other and masked from the people who can't make it. But at midnight we will all have a chance to look at each other and what a disappointment. We are just the same, ordinary people as before. I have decided what to wear. Masses of bird feathers, black and white feathers. Those poor little creatures are going to cover my entire head. But Mummy has changed her mask six times. First jeweled, then a complete covering, then a fur mask, but now she has decided her eyes are her best feature, so she is going with a mask to show off her eyes. Imagine, we are supposed to hide from each other, and Mummy wants to show off her eyes, knowing she will be immediately spotted.

"Why is it that we all want to be spotted? But when we take off those masks, what a disappointment. At least to me. All those same, tired faces. All those people Michael and I have cultivated, because Mummy and Daddy did too. And look at you, Catherine, you are now one of us. At last you have joined the party, late, but you're in the club now. Remember the day you were so opposed to parties, 'All the chichi,' I believe you used those words. Now, Catherine, what do you think of chichi? Just remember the day on the roof. You're just like the rest of us, no different. Not that I'm criticizing you, nor you, darling," Fiona said, turning to Michael, who wanted to stop Fiona. She went on, "Now let me finish. I've got to get this out of my system. Please listen."

Catherine and Michael shifted on the couch and Fiona, knowing full well they were uncomfortable, proceeded. She was going to cleanse herself of all her thoughts, even though some might be considered impure. If she didn't speak up now, Fiona knew it would be never.

"Michael," she began, "fill my glass, please, darling." She reached out, glass in hand, but Michael didn't get up. He just waited. "So you won't. I will fix my own," Fiona said and she went to the bar. She had trouble removing the cork from the Scotch bottle and when it did come off, the noise disturbed her. So cheap, so cheap, and the smell of whiskey, she thought and poured without measuring. She picked up two ice cubes and let them drop with a clink into the glass. "May I serve one of you?" Fiona asked.

Michael got up off the couch and took Catherine's glass without asking. He mixed the whiskey and the water. This time he forgot, and put two ice cubes into his own glass.

Fiona talked away: "You see I've thought for a long time about our way of life. The whole damn thing is coming down on me, shattering like the glass could in the bar if I plunged my fist hard into the wall. There's something about all this money, this pile of money. I have grown to detest it. The curse of all the money, all the little nice people who bow and scrape. All the lust for power. Yes, power, Catherine, like the power Michael wants. His whole family have the money, all the money. They can go on clipping coupons the rest of their life, but after money, there has to be something else—public life—that's the only place people like Michael and Paul can go. It's not a calling, like the calling to the church. I thought maybe it was. I know now it isn't. It's just their only way to turn, politics, the public eye. The do-gooders today all must come from people with money. You see, Michael and I have everything taken care of—I mean our house, our lives even. We really don't have enough to do. Why, I wander through the apartment early in the morning and sometimes at night when I can't sleep and I see all these dead objects surrounding me. All my collections, all Michael's collections.

Have you ever felt furniture at night, your glassware? Have you ever really looked at a room when you are alone in there with all your worldly possessions? Have you ever stood by and watched a guest burn a cigaret in your rug? All these objects are replaceable. But people aren't. You can't buy them, or bring them back. They're gone forever, Catherine—like Paul, gone forever."

Catherine slammed her glass down on the table. "How could you, Fiona? You're a beast, really horribly bitchy. You stand there like the lady in her castle, smug, secure, criticizing everyone, including your own mother and now me. You're after me. And you haven't even got the decency to leave the dead alone. You criticize Paul and now Michael because they adore politics. There's nothing more noble, no higher profession than politics." Catherine stopped talking, hesitated, and went on. "You just don't understand, Fiona, the meaning of politics, the intellectual thought that makes a great leader. I remember Paul telling me government is the ultimate in power today and it rests supremely in the hands of too few, like the Kennedys."

"You are so right, Catherine," said Michael and he looked at Fiona with hate in his eyes.

Fiona still stood at the fireplace. She ran her hand up and down the mantel and looked down at the heavily grained wood. She didn't reply. She was waiting—waiting to tell them both. She could barely contain herself and she felt her body trembling and the heat of her body turning to perspiration. She only needed Michael to aggravate her.

"Fiona, we had better see to dinner. We cannot go on arguing like this all evening. Let's try and be pleasant to each other. After all, we're all tired and have been through a lot. Never mind politics. You don't understand politics. The money you detest, the life it makes possible, you couldn't do without. You seem to consider it smart, clever to criticize our own kind, our friends. This life we have, the comfort, the ins and the outs, the wines, the food, those objects you talk so much about, you didn't have to take any of them. But you did and they were given without obligation by our families, because they loved us and hoped we would one day understand the beauty and the fineness of living in a civilized way, as I hope we do," and now Michael was up at the side of the couch looking down at Catherine when he finished talking.

Fiona stood, her head bowed and then she sipped her drink and she felt the cold glass hard on her lips. She wanted to bite the glass until her lips ran red.

Catherine got up off the couch and went to Fiona and put her arm on Fiona's shoulders. Her hand felt like ice. Fiona wanted to turn away. Michael was now next to her. She was surrounded by the two of them. They didn't understand her savage attack, her bitterness. They were sincerely puzzled. She would have to tell them, Fiona knew.

She waited and then turned away from the fireplace and faced them both. She was now crying.

"You see," she began, "I just lost my temper, just for a minute. Catherine, I'm sorry, so sorry to hurt you. But the strain of the three of us together all the time. No, that's not it at all." And she turned back to the fireplace and looked down into the dying fire. She wanted to put on another log to keep that fire alive.

She moved over to the large straw basket and with both hands lifted a large log. Catherine held back the fire screen and Fiona tossed the wood onto the hogbacks. The sparks flew up, the fire hissed, and the log caught and soon was burning bright.

Fiona still had tears in her eyes. "You see, Catherine, I want to have a baby. I do. I do. I'm lost without a child. There is nothing to hold us together, nothing at all. I've got to have a child," she sobbed.

Michael didn't move. He didn't speak. He looked into the fire. Catherine put her arm all the way around Fiona's shoulders, pulling her in tightly.

"But you can, darling," said Catherine. "And I'm sure you will."

"I'm not so sure, Catherine," Fiona said. "You see we've been trying. I've been trying now for six months. I've been to the doctor. I'm fine. Nothing happens." Fiona was about to mention Michael, but she didn't have to.

Michael blushed. He went to the bar and mixed himself another drink. "You see, it's not the right time. It's not right. We aren't settled. My career, and Fiona . . . you can see, she's unsettled

206

emotionally. We have our whole life ahead of us. No, not now," Michael said and he looked at Fiona and she chilled at the look in his eyes.

"Oh, Michael," Fiona said, going to him and leaving Catherine alone. "I'm sorry, darling. I'm sorry."

She put her head on his shoulder. His arms hung limply at his side and the full glass tilted, pouring the whiskey to the floor. Fiona held him tightly, but she could feel there was no feeling in his body. He didn't move. He just stood there while she embraced him.

"Dinner is served, Mrs. Chase," Pierre said. They hadn't even seen Pierre come into the room. Fiona dropped away from Michael. Catherine turned to look at the fire. She was satisfied now. The tension Catherine knew existed was now an open secret to the three of them and Catherine was an important part.

Fiona with tears in her eyes said, "Thank you, Pierre."

Michael sat at the head of the honey mahogany English Hepplewhite table, Fiona on his left and Catherine to the right. The door to the kitchen swung open and Pierre served the first course, prosciutto and melon. Michael saw right away the melon wasn't ripe and he looked at Fiona. She knew the unripe melon was bothering him.

Catherine leaned back in her chair and for support placed her palms flat down on the edge to relieve the pressure on her back. The black leather felt smooth and warm.

Fiona cut a small piece of her prosciutto, wrapping it around the dry melon.

"Will Mr. Chase have the wine now, or after the melon?" asked Pierre, coming forward with the Bordeaux bottle.

"After, please. You know melon gives wine a very bad taste," Michael answered.

Fiona looked up from her plate, first at Michael and then at Catherine. Michael ate on. Catherine was uncomfortable and tired.

They were alone in their dining room. So alone. Fiona knew now that all communication had been cut. She might as well have been talking to the two Staffordshire roosters on the Louis XVI commode filled with all the beautiful silver. She remembered the day in Paris

207

when she and Michael had passed by the Boulevard Haussmann and had gone in to the silversmith's. She recalled what Michael had said, "French silver is heavier in weight." Fiona had answered, "But it is more beautiful, except for maybe the English. Wouldn't it be marvelous to have beautiful French silver back in New York?"

Catherine wasn't hungry. She knew now her one hope was to hang onto anyone. She just couldn't let herself be alone. In their trouble she could forget about her own. She delighted in the idea that Michael still hadn't gone as far as Paul and that Fiona suffered so much without a child. She enjoyed the friction between Michael and Fiona. That silence that means unhappiness, bitterness, it was all there with the three.

Pierre was back with the second course and the door squeaked.

"Pierre, how many times have I asked you to put some oil in those hinges, or have them changed if they need it," said Michael.

"Yes, sir," he answered, as he put the warm plate down. Fiona put her cold hands on the plate and the tips of her fingers burned. Michael touched his plate just to see if it was warm.

Catherine wasn't thinking ahead to her future. She was enjoying just that moment the pleasure of coming between two unsettled people. Somehow she thought it was her job to help them, even if it meant she might destroy their relationship and even the relationship between the three.

Catherine possessed, she thought, the power to control those around her. From her early days at Vassar, Catherine led the girls around her. One of those typical, big-girl-on-the-campus types, super in everything, and in every activity, dating, extracurricular, student council, and den mother to many in the class. Just popular all the way around and being a popular political animal, Catherine had no intention of letting her influence die where her influence was, whether with her mother and stepfather—and she delighted at being in the middle between them—or being in the middle between Michael and Fiona.

The roast chicken perfectly sliced, the skin browned, the potatoes cut oblong, crisp, the purée of broccoli sat on Fiona's white plate. Pierre passed the dark brown estragon sauce. Fiona took one small ladle full, another and another. Her plate was swimming with sauce. She took a small piece of the breast and the estragon tasted medici-

208

nal. She looked up at Catherine. She remembered Catherine, so important and big in their college life.

As a freshman, Fiona arrived at Main, that big, lumbering brick building built around the tower where Catherine had lived. Everyone knew and liked Catherine. Fiona was just another student and a bad one. She couldn't take the discipline, the little jobs like waiting on table in the morning and carrying those heavy trays. She would rather not eat breakfast, but lie in bed and sleep. She was too young and immature to be at college, she remembered her advisor telling her. Fiona had learned eventually that she just couldn't make the grade and, as always, her family came to the rescue and took her away for a long vacation. She gained weight, the pressure was off, and she shuddered at the thought of returning to Vassar for another year.

Catherine sitting across the table from her now, framed so well between two six-candle crystal candelabras burning so brightly, still had that self-contained assured pose that Fiona always envied. They hadn't changed since Vassar. Fiona knew she was the weaker and she really didn't care because she was beginning to find her way through the twisted maze. She refused to be bored. She was satisfied that she could feel, feel every feeling. Was it wrong to enjoy the sensation of a feeling and to feel like no one else? Not everyone could be like Catherine in the daisy chain running through the grass. Fiona was a different girl than the rest and she would never be ashamed again of that.

Michael poured the fresh, thick cream onto his fruit salad. The apple, the orange, the pineapple were all covered. The cold fruit in his warm mouth tasted sweet and tender. He looked up from his salad, first at Fiona on one side; pale, her hair short now, cut away the other day, black bow nestled softly on top, brown eyes tired, blank, lifeless, neck aflush—emotion—slender fingers, beautiful, yes, beautiful, as from the first day. She tries, she tries and she loves. She is tender to me, she is fragile, kind, generous, loving. Remember Paul, remember how he died. She stayed on bravely and wrapped him in the blanket. And the baby, the baby. Why have I been such a fool? Of course we want a child. We must have a child.

Michael put his spoon back in the crystal bowl. He pulled up the finger bowl filled with a small amount of water. Two white rose petals torn from the flower floated together. He didn't want to put his hand into the water to disturb the petals.

Michael thought of Catherine, who went on eating. Strong, yes she is defiant, powerful, hard, pregnant—a boy, I'm certain, who will do what Catherine makes sure is absolutely right. Catherine knows my weakness. She could correct me. She could come between us quickly. Fiona had been kind, just a little while ago, when they had stood over drinks at the globe. Fiona had said, "Isn't it wonderful you are having a baby." Michael had seen the love in Fiona's eyes—that brief moment of warm, warm human love and understanding of one person for another. Catherine had rejected the love right away, and after, she must have suffered to think Fiona didn't have a baby. For once, Michael had forgotten about his career, Uncle John, collecting, money, ice in the drink. He wanted to take care of Fiona.

And he looked at Fiona next to him and then back again at Catherine, who sat with her arms folded on her stomach. "I can feel the baby. He's kicking away," Catherine said. Fiona wanted to get up and go over and feel that kick. She sat frozen, not daring to move, for fear Michael and Catherine would not approve. Michael reached across the table to take Fiona's hand. He wanted to hold onto those long, soft, slender fingers. She dropped her hands to her lap, then got up from the table as if to lead the way.

"Shall we have coffee in the library? I think we have another fire there," Fiona said and her voice was hard, almost superior. Michael followed her through the door, forgetting Catherine. He reached out to touch Fiona as though he were blind. Fiona went on. She saw Michael was trying to reach her. The idea of his touching her at that moment repulsed her. She couldn't hate him, that she could never do. She couldn't love him either anymore, that was gone. It was almost too late and yet there was still so much time, Fiona knew that. They were in the library alone, together. Michael went to the fire. Fiona sat down in the yellow wing chair, nestling into the wing and grasping its side. Michael couldn't touch her there. Catherine was left alone, still sitting, until Pierre came in with a long silver candle snuffer on a white Moustiers plate.

"Please go ahead, snuff them. I'm leaving."

210

Catherine got up, leaving the chair out from the table. She turned back and saw Pierre place the snuffer on one candle. He lifted the snuffer off, the flame still lived, and he put the snuffer down all the way and removed it. The smoke rose and Catherine smelled the burning wick. The candles were soon all out and only the twisting trail of smoke remained. She thought of Paul and went down the hall to find Michael and Fiona.

One lamp and the fire gave the only light. So sad and I don't want any more sadness, Catherine thought, as she went in the room. Fiona sat still with her head resting against the wing of the chair, her hand wrapped around the side. She looked into the fire, her eyes hypnotically following the flames. Michael stood in back of the chair looking down at Fiona's head. He moved his hands nervously along the high top of the chair and for a moment Catherine thought he would reach down and stroke Fiona. She could see that he didn't know where to put his hands. Catherine wanted to urge him to touch Fiona, grasp her, take her now at this moment. Don't wait, don't wait, Michael. Catherine sat down next to Fiona's feet on the green and white Spanish rug, its woven design full of charging lions. Fiona turned her head away from the fire and her dreams, to look into Catherine's face. A smile passed between them, and they each knew that certain smile at that moment meant they understood. As Fiona turned back to the fire, she knew there was peace at least between the two of them. Michael had seen the smile and he knew that he was excluded. He suffered when he thought that Catherine and Fiona earlier had been thinking only of him.

Michael put his arms down into the chair and he skimmed Fiona's neck. He felt her skin tighten. She was cold and trembling. Then quickly she shifted to escape his touch. Catherine saw Fiona move and watched Michael's hands following. Catherine wanted Michael to take Fiona's neck and squeeze tightly, and if she had been in back of Michael, she would have applied her hands to his and together they would have been at Fiona's neck.

Michael could only think of being alone with Fiona. He wanted to tell her that he was wrong. Yes, they must have a baby and tonight, yes, tonight, if possible, they would start one. He felt Fiona slipping away from him. That baby could bring her back. She was right.

211

"It was a delicious dinner. I always enjoy being with both of you. Fiona, you will never know how I will remember your kindness at this time after Paul's death," said Catherine looking up at Fiona.

"Thank you, Catherine. You know I love you both. You also know that I am here always as your friend. I'm sorry it's been such an emotional evening. You see, I really have no one to talk to and sometimes I just have to unload my problems."

"What problems?" Michael interrupted and he was trying hard now to be sympathetic.

"I feel so alone," Fiona began. Michael frowned. And she went on, "I feel too much about feelings. I sense so strongly, all of a sudden, emptiness. I don't seem to find you, Michael," and she looked at him sympathetically. "I'm reaching out for you. When you think you love and you lose the person even just for an hour, it's like standing alone in a big railroad station with people rushing around you saying, 'Hello, hello, good-bye' to each other while you wait and wait and no one comes for you. I know, poor Catherine, I shouldn't speak of 'alone' when you are suddenly left without Paul."

Catherine moved against the wing chair, her body resting close to Fiona's legs. Michael stood silent, humiliated at Fiona's brutal self-confession and at the same time terrified that he would be left out and completely alone. But Michael couldn't think of anything to say. He couldn't answer Fiona. Michael knew she was right about their life. But, as with the baby, Michael was going to change all that. He was wrong and was willing to admit his coldness. His hard, calculating mind was prepared to change. Michael realized his whole existence was in danger if Fiona suddenly deserted him. He thought of his political career and as hard as he tried to forget Michael—me— Michael and his future, he could not. He only thought in terms of their life as one life, Michael's, and what would happen to Michael. But he knew all the time he couldn't make that life a success, or what he dreamed was a success, without Fiona. He wanted to grasp her neck and hold her tightly next to him. He had to keep her. He must. He was worried. He didn't understand that Fiona was asking for a little humility, tolerance, and nothing more.

Catherine left early. She went home in the taxi alone, even

212

though Michael had feebly offered to take her the four blocks. She wanted to be alone.

True, she was very much alone, she thought to herself. But wasn't it better to be alone, than living alone like Michael and Fiona? No, she wouldn't want to be in their shoes for anything. She felt her baby kick again and the taxi stopped in front of the canopy. As she got out, she looked up into the clear night. Catherine decided Michael could be useful in helping her find a new life again with someone else. She would carry on and make her life her way. As she passed into the elevator, she was sure she could.

After Catherine left, Michael and Fiona returned to the library. Michael was unsure of himself now that he was alone with Fiona. In a way he wished Catherine were back with them. When she was there, no one could get out of hand, Michael thought to himself as he stood in front of the fire. Fiona went back to the wing chair. She tucked her head back into the corner of the wing and looked at Michael.

"I'm beginning to understand, Fiona," Michael began and he folded his arms together the way he always did when he was slightly nervous. He held on tightly to his own arms as though he were holding himself together.

"What do you understand?" Fiona asked, still looking up at him. Michael decided to remain standing so he could look down on Fiona. He couldn't take her stare, eye to eye on the same level, at least not tonight. Michael didn't answer right away. The fire crackled and sizzled. Fiona wished she could go outside near the chimney to catch the sweet smell of a fire burning away in the cold night. Maybe they should go to the country, desert "the island," all the cement of Manhattan. Maybe far away they might find each other.

"I understand," Michael began slowly, "why you want a baby. I do. You need a child. I need to be a father. We've never had to work together, never had to struggle, it all has come to us—all of this. Now I understand," Michael went on, waving his arms around the room. And he picked up a piece of Fiona's Lowestoft and he looked over at his fish. "Yes, all of this satisfies just for that moment, for one moment when it's not yours, but then you make it yours and the thrill or the feeling is over. I understand, Fiona. I have failed

213

you. But you've got to know now, once and for all, I need you. I want you. I love you. I will do anything to make you happy. I want to give you a baby. I want to make you happy. Please let me, Fiona, please," and Michael was down on his knees, burying his head in Fiona's lap.

She stayed motionless, at first not believing Michael, then froze hard. Michael couldn't move her. She was like ice. He felt her legs stiffen from the shock of having his head on her lap. He put his hands to her hips. He stroked her. Michael expected she would run her fingers through his hair. He longed for her to dig deep into his scalp. He wanted someone, anyone, to hold onto him.

"Do you really understand?" Fiona said, almost whispering. "Do you understand, we're ending up just like our family? We vowed to be different. We're frightened to say and do what we believe in. We're shadow boxing with our friends, with each other. And we never hit or touch the other person. We hit away at the air. I'm so alone, Michael, so alone. I have nothing to work for. I can't admire you and I know this must hurt you badly and I don't mean to, but I have nothing to admire you for. You talk about your career, but there is no career."

"You mean you're disappointed in me?" he asked, terrified of the answer.

"Not really. But Uncle John is. He's told me so."

Michael unfolded his arms and folded them back again. He could barely get his words out. "You mean he thinks I'm a bust."

"I didn't say that," Fiona answered. "You don't understand, Michael. I didn't marry you for your career. I suppose it was for love," and Michael limply clasped her hand. "Now there is no expression of love, no feeling between us, is there really?" she said.

"I love you," he answered promptly.

"What can we share with each other—besides this apartment, all that is in it? The apartment and all the objects are lifeless," Fiona said and she pulled her hand away.

"I know, Fiona. I know I'm wrong. I try so hard, especially now. It came so easily—Princeton, Yale, fun and games, dreams of success. You, the perfect wife. All mine. I thought the doors would always

214

open up. I feel them closing and now you shut me out. I need you so much," and he turned away so Fiona couldn't see his face.

"You see, Michael, life doesn't come that easily. Like the baby. You just don't go out and have a baby. That's the miracle we are missing in our life—the miracle that brings a child into the world. It's as though we aren't deserving, as though we aren't qualified. I have been to the doctor and have been checked. Dr. Saunders says there are no problems," Fiona said.

"What could be the problem?" Michael asked. "I mean, we're young and in good health. There is no reason at all why we can't."

"There must be. I haven't been taking the pills for six months and still no success. I'm resigned to going on this way," she said.

"But why didn't you tell me about stopping the pills? You promised," Michael said firmly.

"Promised what? There you go ahead, planning, calculating. Stop it, Michael, we can't go on this way. I didn't promise you not to have children. You told me we shouldn't until you ran for office. Well, it doesn't look as though you ever are going to run, does it?" and Fiona was sitting straight up in the chair now.

"Fiona, I don't want to argue anymore. I'm exhausted. I will change. I want you to give me a chance. You must."

Before Fiona could answer, Michael scooped her up off the chair and carried her in his arms down the hall to their bedroom. He kicked the door closed and set Fiona down on the bed. She didn't struggle. She just stared at Michael, a frightened stare, not knowing what Michael was about to do to her.

He kissed her. He undressed her. She didn't resist. She didn't stir. Michael removed the clothes from her relaxed, lifeless body. He put his lips to hers. He forced her lips open. He kissed her and kissed her more under her ears and down her slender neck. He felt the mole as he slid his tongue down to her shoulder. She lay on her back naked, her legs together, her body motionless. She didn't respond, but Michael made love to her anyway. She didn't say a word. They were soon asleep under the canopy, the white blanket up to their chins. They were on their backs, their young, innocent, beautiful faces showing contentment and peace in a deep sleep. It was as though they hoped they would never wake up.

19

BLOW-UP

Fiona stood in the library looking out at the bark birdhouse attached to a branch of the dogwood tree. Michael and Fiona were at Georgette's for a weekend away from the city. It was too late now for the dogwood blossoms, which had come and gone after the first of May. Just like us to miss the beautiful blossoms, Fiona thought to herself. Three of Georgette's children sat up on the green bank watching the chickadees flying in and out of the birdhouse. The children had just filled the birdhouse full of sunflower seeds, so Fiona could see the birds come from across the field. A little black and white chickadee flew in fast, high up, then dropping low, lighted on the dogwood branches.

Maybe Michael was right. They should buy a country house and if they did, Fiona would fill the garden full of birdhouses, hoping the chickadees would come to them. Michael was still in bed. They had arrived late last night, after a party. Michael was so tired he hadn't even unpacked his suitcase. He said it was the one time he missed Pierre, who always did the unpacking. The children rolled down the bank, then climbed up again to the top and lay flat on their backs to look up into the sky. Fiona wanted to be out there with them, feeling the warming spring sun on her face. But she'd better wait for Michael. She wouldn't wake him. He needed the sleep.

Fiona rested her head against the dark oak wood of the window frame. She felt the cold, hard glass against her forehead.

"Tanty Fiona, you look so sad," said Veronica, the five-year-old, who had sneaked into the room. She was always coming in unnoticed and surprising people. She stood next to the window at Fiona's waist, looking up at her aunt who now looked down at her.

"You look so pretty, Veronica, in your pink velvet dressing gown," Fiona said, adjusting the lace edging. Veronica pressed her head into Fiona, who stroked the little girl's long, wispy blond hair.

"You forget, Tanty Fiona. You sent it for Christmas last year. Don't you remember now? You remember when you and Uncle Michael were coming out here to visit us and you didn't? Mummy said you were too busy with parties in New York," and Veronica sighed as though she had missed their visit.

"Well, we made up for that. We are here now," Fiona answered, "and we are going to stay the whole weekend." She was now holding Veronica tightly. Fiona wondered if Michael would be getting his breakfast in bed. It wouldn't be too much trouble for Georgette— only freshly squeezed orange juice and a soft-boiled egg, three and one-half minutes. Georgette did all her own cooking, but employed a full staff for the children, cleaning, shopping, and the garden.

The children were up the bank again, waving at Veronica. "I wish Mummy would let me out. Really, my cold is much better today," Veronica said, wiping her nose.

"Tomorrow you will be able to go out and play," Fiona said.

"Yes, but it might not be sunny and nice," Veronica answered and pulled away defiantly from her aunt.

Fiona felt Veronica's thin, warm body leaving her. She wanted to hold on to the little girl, but she couldn't keep her. Veronica was out of the room, running from the library to see her father, who was just coming down the stairs.

Peter Jordan III, looking sleepy, entered the library. He was tall, handsome, and stood straight in his tattersal check bathrobe, droopily knotted to the left side. He wore black leather moccasins with mousy grey fur lining. Fiona looked at Peter carefully. She liked him. She was charmed with his country squire respectability. Michael was still sleeping, Fiona was about to say, but she didn't.

She stood turned away from the window, the garden, the chickadees, and watched her brother-in-law move across the wide, highly polished wide oak floor boards onto the fringed black and white Greek rug.

"Good morning," he said in a deep voice. "Beautiful day. I'm going to work in the garden after breakfast."

Fiona smiled and Peter felt the warmth of the smile. He saw her standing there by his window, in his house, against the dogwood branches, the green grass, the field beyond turning greener in the late spring. Fiona—her black hair, her bright eyes now just for the moment brighter he thought, and happier. She wore no makeup, just a touch of lipstick, and had brushed her hair so it shone. Peter sat down in the rocking chair and spread his legs out full length, crossed his feet, and rocked back and forth. He watched Fiona. She moved toward the deep red leather wing chair and sank into the leather cushions. Her white negligee—strung through with a blue silk ribbon around the bodice and at the cuffs, like a Tom Jones shirt—flowed around her.

"It's nice to be here in the country with you and Georgette," Fiona began. "We should do it more often."

"But you and Michael are so busy with your social life. I know how important it is to you. God knows when we are going to have breakfast. You know Georgette. I'm sure she's out in her studio painting and has completely forgotten she has guests and couldn't care less about breakfast. Are you hungry?"

"Not really. Just relaxed to be sitting here and talking to you. This is a divine room. I love the black and white bird print with the dark oak paneling."

"The paneling is from the pews in an old church, so we were told when we bought the house," Peter answered automatically, as though he had repeated the same story to many others.

"I can't wait to see your vegetable garden. I hear it's outstanding," Fiona said, hoping to stir his interest.

Peter rocked back and forth, shifted the knot on his bathrobe. "I've done the cultivating this year with the new tractor and the automatic watering system should give us a great season. I finally licked the problem of the rabbits and the raccoons. We've electrified the fence."

218

"Oh, how wonderful," Fiona responded and she knew their conversation was at a dead end. Peter rocked, his legs spread out across the floor, almost reaching Fiona's bunny rabbit slippers. He stared down at the slippers.

Veronica ran into the room and stopped short between Fiona and her father. She looked first at Fiona and then back to her father. She wore a blue Batman cape and held her arms out. She was still looking at them in a disapproving way. "Mummy is up and she's in Uncle Michael's room sitting on his bed. I went in. They were talking loudly. They stopped when I frightened them and told me to leave," she said, jumping onto her father's lap. He pulled up his legs and held onto her tiny waist. "And what are you doing now, Daddy, with Tanty Fiona? I'm hungry. It's almost lunch time, isn't it, Daddy?" and she snuggled closer to her father and dropped her head hard onto his chest.

Michael lay back on the flowered Porthault sheets. He stuffed another pillow behind his head so that he could see his sister, who sat close to him on the edge of the sagging bed. The two top buttons of Michael's sleepcoat were open and Georgette looked inside at his bare chest. She had been painting. The colors red, blue, and yellow were smeared all over her torn man's shirt which hung out of her too tight violet corduroy slacks. Her hair was held back by a scarlet ribbon. Michael watched her intently. She was still pretty, though a bit messy. He remembered her the same way as a little girl, when they had grown up together in Grosse Pointe in that big, dreary Tudor lakeside house filled with fake Rembrandts and one real Rubens. Michael had even questioned the authenticity of the Rubens and once had argued with his father about it. Michael and Georgette had always talked together on Sundays, just like now. Only Michael would be snuggled in Georgette's bed while they gossiped and giggled away waiting for breakfast. They had connecting rooms and their pre-adolescent days had been so close. Sunday in bed together had been something special.

"I miss you, you old tiger," Georgette was saying as she adjusted the ribbon in her hair. "It's not the same now. In a way, it's a shame we have grown up and separated. We are separated by so much. We really did run the house, didn't we? I used to love eating those big Hershey bars early Sunday morning. Remember how Anna, the cook, used to get furious when she found chocolate all over the bed sheets?"

Michael shuffled his feet under the covers and moved his leg closer to Georgette. He felt her thigh. "Yes, we did stick together then. Nothing could separate us. We always backed each other up. I felt, together, we had the house under control. It was really incredible when you think what Mummy and Dad let us do. Remember racing in that big Chris-Craft with the family flag blowing, the ink-black night and that rough water and the bright stars? There we were, racing in and out between those big, lumbering ore boats. And the crews, rushing to the decks trying to wave us off and then cheering us on. Fun," and Michael rubbed his foot up and down.

The door banged open and Bat Girl Veronica was back again. "Come on, it's time for lunch. Get out of bed," she yelled and threw herself down on the foot of the bed and sat there staring down at her mother and uncle.

"Veronica, you're a little pest," Michael began, sitting bolt upright in bed. Her entrance had scared him and he felt his heart beating away.

"Come on, get up," she yelled. "Daddy and Aunt Fiona are in the library and they aren't reading. They're just talking, talking. I want to go outside, please Mummy."

Georgette turned around to face her daughter. "Get out and don't come in again. Go see your father. Go watch television, anything, but leave us alone. Children. They really get on my nerves," Georgette said loudly.

"I understand they do. But everyone seems to want to have them, even Fiona," said Michael.

"Why don't you?" Georgette asked.

"We will later on," Michael answered assuredly.

"How's your friend Catherine?" Georgette asked.

"Fine, I guess," he answered.

"I understand you see quite a lot of her. Luncheons and all that," Georgette went on.

"Yes, we do. She's lonely without Paul," Michael said.

"I can imagine she is. But be careful. I heard the ladies talking at

Albert's. Your friend Breadcraft is spreading the word around about you and Catherine."

"That's ridiculous."

"Come now. We know why you're seeing her. You think she can be of help later on. You know she's got a certain amount of influence," Georgette said knowingly.

Michael kicked Georgette in the buttocks. She fell down on him and playfully punched his stomach. They both thought for a moment they were back at Grosse Pointe on a Sunday morning.

"I suppose we had better get some breakfast. It's past noon." And then his voice changed to a whisper, "You're a great girl, Georgette. I love you."

Georgette frowned. She knew Michael so well. He never expressed love, devotion, or let fall a tender remark unless he was in pain and troubled. And she knew why he was suffering. She turned away and felt the tears welling up in her eyes.

"Don't worry, you'll make it. Don't give up," she said, getting up off the bed to switch on the transistor radio.

Michael removed the sheets quickly from his body, turned his back to Georgette, pulled up his yellow and white striped pajamas around his waist and reached out stiffly for his monogrammed burgundy bathrobe. He went into the bathroom and turned on the shower. Georgette didn't want to leave him alone, but did, shutting the door behind her.

She went down the whitewashed hall with the canary yellow thick carpeting, past the children's room, past their room, and stopped under the gold Louis XVI lantern in the entrance hall. Michael is just like me. He can't stand the suffering that goes with life's struggle, she thought to herself as she flung open the paneled doors to the library.

"He's in the shower after a good night's sleep. And what have you been doing? I have gotten my reports from Veronica," Georgette said, flopping into the couch.

"We got ours, too," Fiona answered.

"Are we going to eat?" Peter asked.

"Lunch, or breakfast?" Georgette answered.

"I don't care," Fiona said.

221

"I do. Breakfast," said Peter.

Georgette left and slammed the doors behind her.

"Has she gone to get breakfast, or luncheon?" Fiona asked.

"Probably neither," answered Peter and he started to laugh. "You know she is unpredictable. That's why our life is never dull."

Fiona left the library and followed Georgette into the kitchen.

Georgette sat on a high cherry wood stool, sipping coffee. "Want some?" she asked Fiona.

"Thanks, I'm getting a little hungry." She joined Georgette on the other stool. "How do you find him?" she asked.

"Who?" Georgette countered.

"Your brother," Fiona said, slightly disturbed.

"Like always. Always the same. We Chases just don't change. Maybe a little worried, a little depressed," Georgette added as an afterthought.

"Depressed? What do you mean?" and Fiona's voice was tense.

"You know, darling, depressed. It's not going well. Life isn't going well. Bad moment for Michael. What are you doing to him? Aren't you doing what he wants? You know he doesn't like to be told no," Georgette said in a bored tone, because she had told Fiona before that Michael had to have his way.

"But he does have his way. At least on most things," Fiona said, trying to express confidence.

"Really?" said Georgette, as though she doubted Fiona.

Fiona poured more cream into her coffee and added two sugar lumps.

"I thought you never took sugar, darling," said Georgette.

"This morning I'm taking what I feel like. There is no such thing as never, Georgette. You see, I'm not a Chase."

"Well, you're part of us now, for better, or worse, aren't you, darling?" Georgette said sarcastically.

"I don't look at our marriage that way," Fiona said firmly and she looked at Georgette.

"Well, I didn't really say anything wrong, did I? Come on, get off your high stool," Georgette said.

Fiona was delighted she had embarrassed Georgette. Just like Michael. What happened in that family? They can't express any

222

emotion. They don't even communicate. They are really odd, and Fiona wanted to say it.

Georgette pulled out the frying pan. All the other pots fell down, banging together. I bet Fiona doesn't like the noise of all those pots, Georgette thought. She banged them again. She's so damn chic, she's probably never heard the sound of rattling pots. I shouldn't hold her lack of domesticity against her, though. Let's face it, I hate housework myself, and she slammed a black ironware frying pan down onto the stove. She lit the gas and hoped the puff sound of igniting gas would frighten Fiona out of the kitchen.

"I feel just like eggs," Fiona said hopefully.

"Well, I think Michael asked for bacon," Georgette answered quickly.

"Let's make it eggs and bacon," said Peter, entering the kitchen. He knew right away the two women were not getting along.

Fiona sipped her coffee. Peter sat next to her on the other stool and rested his elbow on the delft blue tile counter. Poor Fiona, if she could only relax. He looked at Fiona tense and strained, high up off the ground on a kitchen stool.

Georgette opened the package of bacon and dropped all of it into the frying pan. Fiona wanted to tell her it would have been better to cook a few pieces at a time. She turned to Peter and they both knew they were resigned to eating the bacon and maybe some eggs Georgette's way. They remained silent. The bacon spluttered away, the grease popping out all over the stainless steel stove.

"For God's sake turn on the fan, Georgette," Peter urged.

"I don't like the noise. I'm cooking without the fan today. Maybe I'll use it tomorrow," she answered her husband.

As the bacon cooked, she flipped the pieces out onto some yellow paper toweling.

Michael, in his double-breasted blazer, Windsor knotted regimental striped tie, arrived in the smoke-filled, bacon-smelling kitchen.

Georgette enjoyed the mess of the bacon and the smoke. Diana would clean it all up tomorrow.

"Georgette is like a little girl making mud pies," said Peter.

"You don't have to eat it. Starve," Georgette yelled back and flipped the eggs over and broke another one and it spluttered in the pan.

"How do you cook your eggs back in New York, Fiona darling?" Georgette asked.

"Not like you," said Michael and he gave his sister a swat in the pants. She didn't respond.

Fiona shifted nervously on the stool. Peter watched her.

"We are going to do some gardening," Fiona said, changing the subject.

"Put the toast down, someone," Georgette said as she prepared the plates. "We have some special jam, so make lots of toast."

Georgette flipped the eggs onto a white plate.

"There's your egg, Fiona darling," Georgette said. Fiona picked up her plate off the counter next to the stove and looked down at the greasy, barely cooked egg swimming in bacon fat and the slimy, transparent embryo covering. She felt sick. She couldn't possibly eat that uncooked egg, but she didn't dare tell Georgette. She just couldn't.

"What's wrong, darling, not cooked enough? Doesn't it suit you, Fiona?" and Georgette started laughing. "I'll put the egg back on the stove." Georgette took the plate out of Fiona's hand. Fiona looked down at the plate and the egg swimming in grease. She felt sick still and the egg, the plate, the smell of bacon, and Georgette reminded her of the days she hated so much at Vassar.

"The trouble with you, Fiona, is you are too delicate for this day and age. You've got to toughen up. Damn this pan, see what's happening now. The egg is sticking." Georgette took the pan off the stove and carried it to the sink and ran some cold water into the hot grease. The pan hissed and steamed.

"Don't put all that grease down the sink," Peter yelled across the room. Fiona stood motionless, embarrassed, not knowing where to put herself. Michael watched his sister and he smiled. He adored her brashness and secretly enjoyed the way Georgette dug into Fiona's delicate senses.

Georgette dropped the pan into the sink and took out another pan. She threw Fiona's egg off the white plate into the garbage bag by the sink. Fiona heard the thump of the egg hitting the side of the bag and she saw the egg sliding down into the bottom of the can, leaving behind streaks of yolk and white.

"It's a jolly breakfast. We still haven't eaten," Peter said, exasperated. "We might as well begin lunch. Let's try peanut butter."

"Come on, Peter, it's fun seeing sister cook. Maybe it will give Fiona ideas. Domesticate her. After all, Fiona darling, we might not always be able to afford our couple."

Fiona hated Michael for that remark. She was embarrassed to think her own husband painted a picture of her as a spoiled child. Fiona knew she was spoiled, that she never doubted. But to flaunt his wife's weakness in public, before his sister and brother-in-law, Fiona thought cruel. Michael was cruel anyway. So was Georgette. Their cruelty must run in the family, Fiona reasoned.

The bacon sat cold, the grease being absorbed by the paper toweling. Cold, greasy bacon, nothing worse, Fiona thought. Georgette handed her the fried egg on the same white plate. The yolk from the first egg had dried up around the edges.

"Take the bacon, it's ready. Oh, just take it with your fingers, Fiona. You can always wash your hands after," Georgette said. Not waiting for Fiona to help herself, Georgette tossed two pieces on top of Fiona's egg. Fiona retreated to the stool and moved closer to Peter, brushing her arm against him as she climbed up. "We are just like the black panthers at the circus, with Georgette the trainer," Fiona said.

Georgette lifted the last pieces onto the toweling. "Here, Michael. Some hot bacon for you. Just like old times when we used to eat the bacon out of the griddle in Grosse Pointe."

Fiona couldn't wait to get out of the kitchen and back to the bedroom. She went into the bathroom and locked the door behind her. She just had to be alone. She turned on the shower hot, then to cold, and stood scrubbing her body all over with one of Albert's massage brushes. She would wear her tight red pants this morning with the straps over her shoulders. Perfect for the garden. She would show Peter that she knew how to dig in the dirt. She didn't mind getting her fingernails full of dirt. That didn't really bother her. It was only the ugly—like that slimy egg, it was really so ugly—that disturbed

Fiona. She must explain to Peter in some way why the egg had repulsed her. She wanted him to think of her as a natural woman. She knew Peter thought her desirable. She turned off the shower and dried herself with a red-tuliped, thick towel. How gaudy, she thought, hanging up the towel on the yellow-flowered rack.

The noonday sun streamed through the long, floor-length window. She sprayed her body all over with a new perfume, then she put on a white cotton turtleneck, long-sleeved shirt. She looked into the mirror and rolled down the collar, then rolled it up again—more sporty that way, she said to herself. Fiona climbed into her red overalls and fastened the brass buckles just above her chest. She put on low white boots and swept out of the room. Georgette was coming down the hall in her man's shirt spattered with paint, egg, and bacon grease. Fiona rushed by, trying to avoid Georgette, like two ladies passing each other in a hotel corridor before a ball.

"My God, but you look so chic. So stupidly chic. Enjoy the gardening and stay clean," said Georgette.

Georgette opened the closet to her full-length mirror. She dreaded the thought, but it was time she took a good look at herself. She stood staring intently. Her violet corduroy pants were too tight. She knew she was too fat, her hair shaggy and stringy. She moved in closely to look at her face—wrinkles, spots, lined tired eyes. "Bags," she said aloud.

"You look fine, Mummy. Don't worry," said Veronica, who had sneaked in the room. Georgette turned around, her face red. She knelt down on her knees and embraced Veronica, who tried to squirm away. She kissed Veronica and the little girl struggled to escape the next wet kiss. "Yes, Veronica, we're all starved for affection," she said.

"I'm just hungry. When are we going to have lunch?" Veronica answered. She finally got away and threw herself on the double bed.

The purple-lilac spread was half off the bed, covering the top part. Just enough to give the impression it was made, Georgette had decided when she and Peter had climbed out. Thank God the maids will be in tomorrow, Georgette thought, staring down at the mess in the room. She went back to the closet, shifting her clothes back and forth. There were four step-in closets filled with clothes. Georgette moved the hangers back and forth, banging them against each other, closing the doors, going to the other closets, then back again. She never found what she wanted. She sat down on the bed exhausted and looked blankly into the closets. What to wear? She could never make up her mind. All these children, the big house, I never have time to take care of myself. I never do think of myself. Veronica jumped up and down on the bed.

"Out, out. Get out. Leave me alone," Georgette said firmly, and fell flat on the bed, burying her head into the pillow. She shifted pillows. She wanted her own, not Peter's. She threw his to the floor.

Georgette couldn't face the problem of dressing. She couldn't face seeing Fiona now, right at that moment when Fiona looked so chic. Why couldn't she look chic? And then she hated herself for being stupid.

She got up and went to the closet and pulled down off a hook a pair of man's blue jeans. She slipped on the pants and took a wide brass-studded Mod belt from the drawer. She buttoned up a pink button-down shirt, opened another closet and took out a false hairpiece. She slipped the hair onto her head, attached the fall to the back, and tied a red ribbon. She opened the closet door and stared into the full-length mirror. I look outrageous, just outrageous enough to make them all look at me. Georgette didn't put on shoes. She went barefoot out on the sunporch and into the grey-pebbled Japanese garden by the pool. She saw Peter and Fiona sitting together on the wide black curved steel seat of a blue tractor, slowly moving toward the vegetable garden. She had ridden the tractor, her birthday present to Peter, the first day and Georgette knew how tight and warm it was for two to ride together. She watched the tractor disappear over the hill and didn't care what Peter and Fiona were doing.

Fiona smelled the smoke from the tractor. She held tightly onto the side, and then they went over a bump. Peter put his hand around Fiona's waist, to hold her in place. She felt his muscular leg and thigh pushing into her. They went over another bump and the garden was just down the hill.

"Let's ride around some more. I've never been on a tractor," Fiona said, grasping the side of the seat firmly. "Take me all around, so I can see everything." Her voice was pleading and excited. The new tools, those dark red ones made in England, were rattling around in the back of the tractor and Peter couldn't wait to dig them into the earth.

"I love this time of year. The sun is so warming," Fiona began and she held her head up into the sun. Peter turned toward her and looked at her long, outstretched neck, with the white turtleneck rolled up. He thought she was too delicate to touch. Surely she would quiver all over. They hit a bump. The tractor came to a stop in the ditch. Fiona held firmly to the seat and her head dropped with force onto Peter's shoulder. He felt her soft hair. He put the tractor in reverse and they backed up out of the ditch. Fiona still rested her head on his shoulder, then removed it slowly, brushing her hair against his cheek. He was insensitive to Fiona's closeness and wasn't at all aware she was trying to be closer to him than she should. His disinterest whetted Fiona's appetite.

The tractor stopped. Peter turned off the ignition and Fiona jumped down. Peter had wanted to help her to the ground, but Fiona wouldn't permit that—too obvious.

She went toward the white picket fence woven through with wire. Peter ran after and quickly took her hand, pulling it away from the top of the fence. "Don't touch it," he said, holding her fingers firmly. "The wire is electrified. It won't hurt you. Only give you a tingle," and he still held onto her hand. Fiona's fingers were soft and long. He remembered Georgette's hands—the working hands, he thought. Hands that worked were much healthier. The gate was open and they were in the garden together. Fiona bent over the earth and reaching down grasped the dirt between her fingers, rubbing them together and then dropping the dirt.

"You're getting your hands dirty," Peter said, moving next to her.

"I don't mind," Fiona answered, moving away. "What's in the garden?" she asked, to change the mood.

"Over there are the fraise des bois plants. I will put some new ones in a little later. Regular strawberries next to them. I have to put cheesecloth over them soon to keep the birds off. You see, we still haven't devised a way to stop the birds from eating the berries. Last summer the kids built a scarecrow and the birds came to sit on him. They ate the berries anyway. We will have string beans, peas, spinach, and my favorite, pumpkins. I can't get over how big the

228

pumpkins grow," Peter said and his eyes were wide open, as though he saw rows and rows of orange pumpkins.

"I love their orange, too," Fiona said. "What about the asparagus patch and endive? I adore both."

Peter didn't answer right away. He thought Fiona loved this, loved that, wanted this, wanted that—asparagus, endive. "They take time and lots of work to grow," he said.

Fiona understood. She felt silly. "Let's get to work and make them grow, make the whole garden come up pretty, green, all of it so good to eat," and she waved the deep-red hoe made like a golf putter. "Where do I start turning over the earth?" Fiona found her spot and was about to dig.

"No, not there, you'll hurt the string beans," Peter told her. Of course, she really isn't going to work long. A few turns and her boots will get dirty and the dust will be all over her. Then she will quit. Already Peter could see the perspiration shining on her brow and strands of hair were blowing around her cheeks. Peter stood looking at Fiona.

"Well, where then? Where do I begin?" she asked, again waving the hoe.

"Right here by the strawberry patch. Turn the dirt over lightly and we can add some bone meal—a good stimulant," he instructed.

Fiona started turning over the dirt. She was determined to stick with it, at least until luncheon. That could be a long time, because they had just finished breakfast and Georgette wasn't inclined to do anything at normal hours.

Peter watched Fiona's slender hands grasping hard at the hoe as she bent down and then came up as she turned over the dirt. She rolled down her white turtleneck, already streaked with dust. Her neck was hot. Fiona didn't stop. Her back ached and her hands were sore. Fiona knew Peter was interested enough now so that he kept looking over at her while he bent up and down weeding around the small string bean shoots. He was getting tired too. He got down on his hands and knees and moved up and down the rows, but still watched Fiona. He hoped she would tire and stop. He wanted to talk to her.

Fiona brushed her arm across her brow. She felt the moisture from her body trickling around her waist and inside her panties. The red overalls were chic enough, but the heavy linen was hot. How creased they looked now. Finally she stopped and let the hoe drop. It fell on the parsley. She realized her mistake and picked up the hoe quickly so that Peter wouldn't see it. He yelled from the other side of the garden where he was checking the wiring on the fence, "That's all right, the parsley is sturdier than you are," and he laughed.

She carried the hoe over to Peter and flopped down exhausted at his feet. She lay on the ground and looked up into the sun and thought of her nephews who had been rolling down the hill in the grass earlier that day. She wanted to roll, roll, roll down the hill, play like a child, play with Peter in the spring sun, with the birds flying to the birdhouse, with the trees swaying in the breeze and the clouds moving across the blue sky. She dreamed and dreamed, always dreaming.

Peter dropped to the ground next to Fiona. She was still on her back, her body stretched out straight, her face absorbing the sun. Her head was on the grass border but the rest of her body in the upturned dirt. Peter rested his shoulders against the white picket fence and looked down at Fiona. She wanted to put her head on his lap, just like in those cigaret ads, showing the young lovers in the spring, she thought, shifting out of his gaze. She moved still farther away, raising her body across the dirt, and then she rolled over and over in the dirt, keeping her head on the soft grass. Her nose fell into a big cluster of dandelions and she looked through the flowers back up at Peter, who sat, embarrassed, with his legs tucked up and held by his arms.

"You really react to the spring weather. It seems to affect you," Peter said. He was going to tease her now. "Your hormones are overworking today, Fiona."

"That was a beastly remark for you, Peter," and she wasn't a bit disturbed.

"Are you trying to seduce me, Fiona?" he asked.

"No. Not at all. I'm only testing you. I want to tempt you. I want to know that I'm still desirable," and her last words sounded sincere. Peter knew the game was over. They both had to be serious.

"You don't have to worry about being desirable. You are. Very

230

much so. You are beautiful. But if I touched you, I'm afraid I would disrupt your face, even your beauty."

She interrupted, "You mean you think I'm put together with a paste box by Albert. The artificial hair and all that?" and Fiona pretended to be insulted.

"No, it's more than that. I wonder if you are real. I see you now rolling in the dirt, but somehow the dirt looks strange all over those red overalls. The overalls just shouldn't be red. You know what I mean. I suppose I'm just a square country bumpkin, children, gardens, you know, the whole framework of the devoted husband and family man," and Peter said it proudly.

"That's why you are so interesting. It's the contrast. You see, I'm never satisfied. I always want to have what I can't have. As you said, I love the endive. I can see it now on my plate, mixed with beet root. What a beautiful salad. I see the green-yellow asparagus, then so very green at the top, with a sauce mousseline over the top. I could eat them both right now. But tomorrow I would want something else. Don't you think really we are all made the same way? We like different food. We always want what we haven't got today but what we might be able to have tomorrow. Looking forward to the next day, to that possibility even so remote, whets our appetites, keeps us going, keeps us from being bored," Fiona said, and she moved close enough to touch if they wanted to.

Peter pushed back hard at the fence and it wobbled.

"No, I don't look forward to something I can't have. It seems for us we have it all now. I'm running out of ideas of new things we don't have. You see, last month it was the tractor. I loved the blue one. Georgette and I went to see the tractor together—a red one. I had to have blue, but they said a blue tractor would take months before delivery. I got the blue tractor by paying an extra hundred dollars. Then we decided maybe the red would be better. Sort of boring when you look back on it, but at that moment the blue tractor was the most important chapter in our life that week. You see it would be much easier for all of us if we couldn't have that blue tractor. Then we could find something else to look forward to. I am disturbed and I mean it that we can have almost everything," Peter said seriously.

"Not people. You can't have them. You can't buy blue people and keep them. I'm interested in people. They are the important ones to possess if you love them, really love them. Or, take Michael. He's interested in people, in helping them through political power." Fiona threw in Michael only to sound out Peter.

"He's interested in politics and people to build his own ego. The whole house of ego is for him and the power that goes with it is just another blue tractor. The grasping of power is never ending. You die anyway soon enough. Such people don't interest me. I don't mean to insult Michael. I know he's your husband, brilliant, charming, but he isn't interested in people like we are. I want to feel their warmth, their beauty, to talk to them, get through to them. Michael will never get through, he is so busy using them to build up himself," and Peter dropped his legs into the dirt next to Fiona's. She didn't move away. She sat up next to Peter and took his hand and turned toward him. She kissed him gently on the cheek. She smelled the dirt, the sun, all the smells of the garden.

"I knew I was right. I knew I was. Thank you for helping me," Fiona said and she squeezed his hand, digging her fingernails into Peter's flesh. He pulled his hand away, got up and walked to the other side of the garden. Fiona picked up the hoe, brushed the strands of hair off her face, and dug into the earth. She turned up a big grey stone; worms crawled from under it. Peter walked to the rows and got down on his knees and did the weeding that had to be done if the vegetable garden was to produce.

Georgette and Michael were sitting by the pool.

"I hear the tractor. They must be coming back to us," Michael said. Georgette was astride a life-size, glazed ceramic leopard, sitting opposite its mate at the far end of the pool. It was still slightly chilly for swimming, but the blue-green pool was filled and the water was being heated. Georgette and Michael held drinks in their hands.

The white pool house was built gracefully into the hill. Low, with a peaked slate roof, eighteenth-century French château in feeling. A complete kitchen with special chimney grills, two dressing rooms, a small gymnasium, and a portico with columns all faced out onto

232

the pool, which was surrounded by grass and then a foot-wide marble pathway. In the distance and below, down the hill, the high oaks were cut away just enough to give a commanding view on a clear day of Long Island Sound. Michael sat under the portico at the base of the white columns thumbing through a large orange and black jacketed book on China.

He couldn't do much reading with Georgette there. She left to check the children who were riding their bicycles on the sand-colored driveway next to the pool house. He wasn't concerned about Fiona. He had calculated she had taken up gardening for the effect and nothing more. She was an adaptable creature, somewhat like the Chinese, he thought to himself. When the climate changed, Fiona changed. He knew that she had wanted to be alone with Peter, just as he had enjoyed the time with his sister.

But listening to Georgette talk about her children and all their problems depressed him. Michael didn't know what he would do if he had to face the problems of bringing up children. He didn't at all feel their emotions. Michael looked down at the picture of the Chinese poling the big junk upstream. He noticed the women were doing most of the work and a man stood at the tiller.

Georgette returned and sat down next to Michael. He felt the rough blue cotton of her tight blue jeans against his soft grey flannels. His shoes needed a shine, but he wasn't going to ask Georgette for polish. Pierre would take care of the shine back in New York.

"Somedays I don't know how I can stand another day with the monsters. All I do is stay behind the wheel driving all over town. Sometimes I forget where I'm going to next," Georgette sighed. She was stitching a needle-point rug.

"Good design," Michael said. "Did you do the design yourself?" he asked, looking away from the book. It was heavy, so he closed the pages and put it down on the marble steps. A yellowish brown unshaven Chinese, with big nose, black dangerous eyes, a towel-textured hood, a black hat and big white buck teeth, looked up from the dust jacket at Michael and Georgette.

"Yes, I do all my own designing. I'm not mad for the colors," Georgette answered in a voice suggesting she was already bored with the sewing. She dropped the needle-point rug over the book. The

Chinese was hidden. Michael still remembered his black eyes staring up at them.

"Another daiquiri, brother darling?" said Georgette, holding out her hand to take his glass. Michael handed over his glass and looked out over the rippling water in the pool and then out over to the Sound. He saw the tractor coming up over the hill. Peter drove with one hand, holding Fiona into his body. Michael stood up to get a better view. The tractor came down the driveway.

He turned away from the pool and followed Georgette into the kitchen. The blender was chopping the ice and throwing up the rum and lemon juice into a white, frothy foam.

"Too fast. It makes too much froth for a frozen daiquiri," Michael said.

"Why don't you make them?" Georgette said and she went ahead and poured into her own frozen glass. She took a big sip.

"Good. Really good. Take your own, or fix another. I'm not a barmaid." And Georgette went back to the pool leaving Michael alone in the small bar, looking out onto the tennis court. He filled his glass to the top and the foaming daiquiri overflowed onto the red brick tiled counter. He pulled the yellow striped bar towel down from the rack and wiped up the pool of rum and lemon juice. He put the stained towel back on the rack and sat down on a stool and finished the daiquiri quickly and poured another one.

He heard Fiona and Peter laughing. They were approaching the pool house. Michael wanted to run away, out of the room, out of the pool house. He didn't want to see them together. He quickly left the kitchen and looked out of the window to the pool. Fiona was there, her shirt full of dust and her hair uncombed, blowing in the breeze. She was sitting sideways on the male leopard and Peter was standing close behind her, touching her head with his legs. Georgette stood in front of Peter and Fiona, arms folded. She was laughing, but Michael couldn't hear what they were saying. Were they talking about him? Michael turned back to the bar and picked up his drink.

He felt so alone in the bar, like an outsider in a club full of important men. A few moments before he had wanted to be alone, or was he always alone anyway, even with people? He couldn't bear

234

the thought of staying closed in there alone, no one to talk to, no one paying the slightest attention to him. He was tired. He needed a nap. A nap, yes, then he would feel better. But what were they doing out there? He looked for a tray and opening the door of the cherry wood cupboard, pulled out a white plastic tray with a red monogram— Peter's family crest he thought—and took two frozen glasses from the yellow striped refrigerator. He poured two more drinks, added some more to his own glass, and started out to join the others.

"We have had a wonderful afternoon. Serious talk about all of us," Peter was saying.

"It looks like you've been rolling in the dirt," said Georgette and she brushed off Fiona's white cotton sleeve.

"We were," Fiona answered quickly. "I was flirting with your attractive husband. You know, tempting him just a little," Fiona said teasingly.

"I'm sure he didn't respond. You know, he doesn't feel, or respond to much, not even seduction."

Michael was standing with the tray. The glasses rattled together. He looked like a waiter, his first day on the job. Michael had heard the word seduction. "Drinks anyone?" he said, his voice cracking.

"Why darling, I never knew you waited so well on table," Fiona said, looking up at him. She turned around to Peter and took his hand.

"Have I missed anything?" Michael asked Georgette.

"No. Not much. I just told them both they looked as though they'd been rolling in the dirt," Georgette answered.

"You have to, isn't that right, Fiona, if you are going to garden? The dirtier the better," Peter said.

Fiona knew Michael was getting upset. She could see the corner of his lip turned up in disgust.

Fiona, realizing she had hurt him, got up off the leopard, stroked its proud head, and went over to Michael. She kissed him gently on the cheek, as she had done Peter earlier, and as she pulled her face away from his, pushed the tip of her nose into his skin. Her nose felt warm. Michael was now again secure for the moment. "We missed you, darling. Come now, not so serious. Let's have one of those drinks," and Fiona was off up the steps under the portico by the trickling fountain. She spread out in the white chaise, with leopard yellow and black dotted cushions. She crossed her legs and sipped her drink and looked out over the pool, knowing she was in control. She decided they would all swim tonight. She went down to the pool and kicked over her dirty white boots and removed a small, white sock. She stuck her big toe into the pool.

"Peter, you'd better turn up the thermostat. The pool isn't quite warm enough for a dip," and Fiona downed her drink and felt like throwing the glass into the pool, but she knew it wouldn't float.

They didn't bother with lunch, evening would soon come.

Peter had cooked the hamburgers in the pool house chimney. Georgette had prepared the salad, opened the wine, made the coffee, and served the ice cream. That was dinner. Michael had expected something more glamorous. No, he couldn't live this way. The children were put to bed, except for John and James, the oldest, who were put to television down in the basement. They would be tired and fall into bed after watching their blood and thunder programs.

"Your coffee is excellent, Georgette," Fiona said. They were gathered around the pool, drawn again to the leopard, who sat sprawled out on the marble under the moon streaked over with a wispy cloud cover.

They had changed for dinner. Fiona, tired of pants, scrubbed of the garden dirt, looked her most romantic and her mood was romantic. Her white cotton full-length lace dress stopped just at the ankles. She was barefoot. Georgette wore a black and white paper evening dress. The idea amused her to think she could afford any dress made but chose to wear paper. Michael had told Georgette he had never seen her looking so wonderful.

"I do, I do," Fiona was telling Peter.

"You cannot accept reality. I know," Peter said severely.

"It depends what you mean about reality," Fiona answered right back.

"No, we are all living this dream existence. We move from one new object to another new object. You forget the people in between," Peter said.

"People. We know all about people. Michael and I have made it a business to collect them, the best ones. At least we are told they are the best ones. It always fascinates me how a certain group becomes the best. Each season the group varies only slightly, but there are always new names added," Fiona observed.

"Oh, we collect them out here too. There are several groups who move in and out. First they join one club, then the next best club. They start young, with a drive to be like the older ones and then by the time they catch up to the older ones who are dying off quickly they are bored with their whole damned existence. You see, they always dream the man on the top is better off than they are," Peter said and poured another brandy.

Georgette and Fiona sat by the pool, dangling their feet, waiting for it to warm.

Georgette stood up and turned to the group and started to speak.

"So we collect objects, climb the social ladder, try for careers, get to the top, and then die off. That's life, isn't it? What more should we strive for? Religion? That's dead today. Religion can't cope with today's living. Religion is a disciplined science without anything scientific—the ritual, the fuss, it's all meaningless. Sex, we can strive for that too. Try all sex—everything, the works. I know some of us have. Sex ends so quickly, just for that hour, minute, or half minute, depending on who you're doing it with. Then poof, all over until the next day, or next week.

"Love, those who have love, strive for love, maybe they're happy. I don't know about you, but I'm too selfish for complete love. I love, I think, my children more than anything. I try and remember how I suffered as a child and what they did wrong to me and then it all gets out of proportion. It's all mixed up. What they did for me might have been right. What we are doing for our children might be right too.

"Times haven't changed really. We just have more comfort, are more materialistic—the collectors, as you say—and we forget all the collecting of objects and people means nothing.

"No, children and my family are the only ones who really show love. Love, that's the Big It of our times. I'm convinced. If only I had the patience to understand the children. If only God gave me the patience," and Georgette's voice was straining now.

237

Michael and Peter went to comfort her.

Fiona couldn't restrain herself any longer. She had to say, "Georgette, we all love you. You must understand. And, and"—Fiona was about to stop—"at least you are striving for your children. I have none. I'm striving for nothing. Nothing at all," and Fiona left the pool. She finished the brandy on the way up the stairs by the fountain. She bent over the trickling water and put the glass under the water spout. The glass filled and she drank the cooling water.

"I'm going to swim now," and she waved her arm with the glass.

Peter ran up the stairs after her. Michael followed. Georgette stayed below at the pool, gently stroking the leopard. She lit a cigaret with a long fireplace match and after taking two puffs, plunged the cigarette into her paper dress. First smoke, then flames, heat, more heat, she couldn't stand the fire. She threw herself into the pool and the paper dress, extinguished, disintegrated.

Peter, Michael, and Fiona ran back down the steps, but Georgette was already swimming to the other end of the pool. She climbed out of the water and onto the diving board and stood there, her hair dripping wet, her nude body shivering in the cold.

"Come, come join me. Let's swim. You see, what counts is just to be alive and be loved, loved, want to be loved," and she dived into the pool and the water drowned her words, "Loved, loved."

The others didn't know what to do. They just waited, looking at each other.

Fiona felt ill. Her head was spinning. She walked down the winding brick path toward the main house and turned around to take one last look at the pool. Georgette was on the diving board and Michael was standing close, right behind her, his hands outstretched. She could hear him yelling, "Georgette, go in. Hurry. It's cold up here. Dive. Dive."

Georgette stood motionless, looking straight ahead out over the blue-green water. A full moon was up overhead in back of them. The lights from the pool lit their nude bodies. Georgette was dripping wet, her hair stringy. Michael was dry, Fiona could see. He stood straight, motionless. She had never looked so closely at him as now, there on the diving board with his sister. He grasped Georgette around the waist, pressed next to her and together they jumped into the water. Peter stayed at the top of the steps next to the fountain. He just watched silently.

Fiona went quickly on to the house. She opened the door to the bedroom. The doorknob was sticky and dirty from the children's hands. She dropped to the bed without bothering to turn down the bedspread. Her head sank into the cool pillow. She turned her head to the side and her long hairpiece fell off. Fiona put her bare foot on the rug to steady herself. She opened one eye. The room was going round and round. She closed her eye quickly and turned the other way and her nose was buried in the hairpiece.

"I'm dying, dying," she groaned.

Michael came into the room. He had left his clothes at the pool and was still wet. Fiona saw him standing next to the door. She looked at his nude body. It's been a long time since I've seen him defrocked like that, she thought. It took his sister to strip him, didn't it? She started to laugh.

"Oh my head," she groaned again. "Why did I drink so much?"

Michael flopped down on the other bed. He stretched out his wet leg to touch Fiona. She moved away as far as she could go, without falling off the bed.

"You're not very friendly," Michael said, in a disgusted tone.

"Why should I be?" she answered back.

"Because I'm your ever-loving husband," he said cynically.

"You're my husband. And I'm tired. That's all. I want to go to sleep. Leave me alone."

Michael withdrew his foot.

He thought of Georgette standing there by the pool, her dress aflame, and then he saw her dive into the water. He remembered how the paper dress had immediately been doused, how she had stood nude on the diving board yelling to all of them, "What counts is to be alive, to be loved, loved, loved . . ." Over and over again the words "alive" and "love" rang in his ears. What a way to get attention. What a way for me, for me. Michael felt sick now. He put his pillow up against the flowered headboard.

"Damn it, why aren't the beds turned down," he said, pulling the pillow out from under the cover. He felt the sheets absorb the moisture from his body. He turned to look at Fiona and right away saw the false hairpiece detached from her head. Michael laughed.

"What's so funny?" Fiona asked.

"You've been scalped. You've been scalped, darling. You look so different," and he laughed again.

Fiona saw his face twisted in laughter. His mouth was screwed up, his hair tangled and standing up on his head. She couldn't look at him anymore. She dropped her head to the pillow and her foot to the floor. The wool rug warmed her toes.

"Please turn out the light, Michael. I've got to sleep. I feel terrible," Fiona said.

"You should. You drank too much," Michael answered.

"Sure I drank. It's not that. I'm depressed," Fiona answered and rolled over to face Michael. "Must you lie there nude? I find it pretty disgusting," she added.

"Since when do you find me disgusting? What's wrong? Are you still thinking of Paul Cain, or is there someone else? He's dead, you know. Cain is dead," Michael said, raising his voice.

Fiona remembered Cain lying on the canopy bed, alone, in her room. She had unbuttoned his shirt and stroked his head. She tortured herself with the thought that Cain had died in her bed, that Cain might have loved her, that she could have spent at least some happy times with him. Now he was gone. She felt the tears come into her eyes. She didn't want to see Michael. Fiona reached out for the light, but Michael grasped her hand firmly.

"Don't. I want to look at you, so sad, so full of liquor, and stripped of your hair. The little married happy Chases tanked up, having a little domestic quarrel. How sweet and normal. The wife is thinking of her past loves. I'm tired of your moods, your noble, gushing sentiments."

"I couldn't care less," Fiona answered.

"I'm sick of you and all that goes with you. All the little dramas. All of it," Michael said and he got off his bed and went over and sat next to Fiona. She wanted to move away as far as possible.

"As a matter of fact," he was talking louder now, "you've spoiled the whole weekend. Running off to the garden with Peter. I saw you on the tractor. Aren't you the little fool. He'd never be interested in you. You forget, he's my brother-in-law. He thinks you're a phony.

240

Don't you see? You were out of place. My family sticks together. They aren't unfaithful to each other," Michael said, pounding the mattress with his fist.

Fiona sat up in bed, placing the pillow in back of her head. The tears disappeared from her eyes. She looked at Michael with cool contempt and examined his nude body.

"You tell me I'm out of place. How about you and all your goings on? Yes, with Catherine, darling, sweet, forlorn little Catherine, the merry widow. She won't be so merry about you when someone tips her off that you're flirting with her because she might be able to help you play Congressman. She's not going to help you, Michael. No one is going to help you. You've never had the guts to do anything on your own. You go through the back door, always the easy way. Don't talk to me about my flirts. At least I've some feeling, some love for someone. I'm not trying to get anywhere. I'm not trying to be some big important person just to flatter my own ego."

Michael's face turned red. He looked away.

Fiona knew she had been cruel.

He pulled her down on the bed. He had never expected Fiona to answer him so harshly.

"Let go of my arms. You're hurting me, Michael. Let go," she screamed.

He held her down on the bed. She screamed again. Michael put his hand over her mouth and smothered her words. Fiona kicked her legs and tried to turn over. She couldn't move.

"Are you going to stop? Are you going to stop?" Michael said.

She bit into his palm. He pulled his hand off her mouth and she screamed out, "No, no. Never. Don't you ever touch me again. Never again. You're not even a man. You're a brute," and Fiona jumped up out of his grasp. Michael went after her and threw her back on the bed. Fiona lay there trembling, terrified Michael would strike her.

"Now calm down. It's all over. We'll be sorry tomorrow. We've been drinking. That's it. It's the drinks, too much," Michael said, out of breath.

"No, it's not. You know it's not that. We've been wanting to get this out for a long time. I've got so much inside of me about you.

I've got to expel it all. I'm full of hate and shame for both of us. I think about leaving you. Yes, leaving you, going with someone else. I can't bear it anymore. I can't," and Fiona started to sob.

Michael couldn't stand to hear anyone cry. He couldn't stand scenes. He always wanted to pick up the pieces, put them all together, so that no one would know the real truth. Now he was afraid Georgette would hear Fiona's screams and then one day she would tell his mother and maybe even Uncle John. He couldn't bear that humiliation. He couldn't bear the thought that the ideal, beautiful couple were, underneath all that rich veneer, seething with hate and distrust. He couldn't bear that somehow they were both immature, unable to cope with life and that their rarified existence was really commonplace, vulgar. He shuddered at the thought that their image would be destroyed, that any hope for his political career would be ruined by scandal if Fiona left him. No, she would not leave him. She had to stay, no matter what, here by his side. She was essential.

Fiona looked up at him. He still held her down, his hands pressing on her waist. Now he moved his hands to her shoulders. He leaned over her and lowered his face to hers. He pursed his lips. She saw he was going to kiss her. Fiona turned her face into the pillow.

"No, I don't want you," she said, trying to rise off the bed. Michael tightened his grip. His face was still close to hers. She could smell the rum on his breath and feel the sweat in his hands rubbing into her skin. His body so close, his touch, repulsed her.

"Leave me. Please leave me alone," Fiona said, looking up at him. She was pleading now in that gentle way that made Michael feel superior. He would kiss her now. She's ready—just like in Paris, when she really wanted me, he thought to himself. He forced her head around and his lips almost touched hers, which stayed firmly closed. Michael smelled her perfume. His hands moved up and down her arms. He loved the softness of her flesh. He put his legs up on the bed, lay down, and turned sideways to face her. Fiona tried to pull away. She freed one arm and started pounding on his back. She felt his lips. He pushed her down again. She bit hard into his lips. He didn't move at first—then he twisted in pain. She tasted the salt

242

of his blood in her mouth. Fiona quickly jumped off the bed and left Michael there alone. He put a hand to his bleeding lip.

"I hate you, Michael. I hate you. You're cheap. I can't love you," she was shouting hysterically.

Michael thought of Uncle John, how he had had to put his wife away. Fiona was going mad, Michael was sure, right there before his eyes. He had to calm her. He could not forgive her violence. His lip was bleeding badly and the blood was trickling down the side of his mouth.

"Calm yourself, Fiona. I was only trying to tell you I love you. I wanted to make love to you," he said and he kept his hand to his lips, to show her she had wounded him.

"I can't, Michael. I can't love you. I feel strange with you. It's not natural. You don't love me," she said, standing next to the bathroom door and looking down at him on the bed.

Michael started to move toward her. He got up off the bed and approached her. She could see his body was wet with perspiration. He took her in his arms. "I want you now. You're my wife," and he pressed into her. Fiona pushed him away. "I can't," she said, "I can't." She turned her back to him and grasped the edge of the Chippendale chest. She saw him in the mirror, his body tensed, his hands out, ready to grasp her again. She swung around to face him and screamed: "I can't love you anymore. Go love your sister. That's all you're good for. You're sick."

Michael started to tremble. He raised his arm and struck Fiona across the face with the palm of his hand. She reeled backward, grasping the chest, and fell to the floor at Michael's feet. He could feel her sliding down his legs. He pulled her off the floor and threw her onto the bed.

"Who's sick?" And he struck her in the face again. She writhed in pain. She scrambled off the bed and he pursued her. She got to the bathroom door and started to close it. He caught her arm and pulled her out and her back hit the glass doorknob. Fiona doubled over. She held her stomach. She was on her knees crying. She could only think she had to escape, get away, before he hurt her even more. She looked up and said, "Please, Michael. Please, you're hurting me," and she sobbed.

243

Michael retreated to the bed. He held out his hands futilely. "I'm sorry. I'm sorry," and he was shaking with fear. He didn't know what he had done. Fiona got up off the floor, took off her pink nightie and hurriedly dressed in a sweater and skirt. She slipped into her shoes.

Michael stood next to her. "Where are you going, where?"

Fiona didn't reply. She quickly left the room, closing the door softly behind her.

Michael scrambled into his clothes. He would go after her. Then he thought, why should I? She accused me of something horrible— too horrible. Of course he loved Georgette. She was his sister. They had grown up together. They understood each other. Fiona was just jealous. She always had been jealous. Catherine and now Georgette. It was Fiona who was sick. He had better leave her alone now for a while. She didn't want him now, but tomorrow she would change her mind. He was tired. They had drunk too much. They must never do that much drinking again. He lay down on the bed. The pillow felt cool on his cheek and he knew it was Fiona's pillow. He could smell her perfume.

He looked at his watch. It was still early, nine-fifteen. From the window he could see that the lights were out in the rest of the house. They were all tired from a long day. He got up, opened the window, and through the bushes could see the pool. Fiona was sitting by the fountain, her legs curled under her, her hand playing with the trickling water.

She tried wiping her bruised face with the water, but it ran through her fingers. Fiona looked up into the sky, as she had so many times before. The moon was cloud-shrouded and she couldn't find a star.

She got up from the steps and went down to the pool. The water was in a large hole going nowhere. She walked around to the diving board, climbed up and out to the tip. She stood there looking out into the night, far away in the direction of Long Island Sound. She could see nothing, just space, endless space. The trees in the distance stood straight and severe against the sky.

Why not jump, jump in, it's not as far as it looks, Fiona thought. And the pool will be quiet, so quiet. When the water covers my face,

I'll go down, down deep, my arms over my head, my body straight, all the way to the bottom. No struggle, the water will carry me where it will. Then I'll float to the top and will lie face down, my hair wet, spread out, and then the leaves will fall all around me and I will be swept back and forth: lifeless, gone, at peace. Fiona looked down again into the hole. Without the pretty lights, the water looked black, cold.

She shivered, turned away, and walked down off the board. She went into the pool house and dialed. Someone had to be home. The phone rang once, twice, and again. She was worried. What if they were away? That was impossible. Someone was always there.

"Hello, hello," Fiona said, trying to be calm. Thank God they are there, thank God, she thought, as the ringing stopped.

"Henry, are they at dinner? Have they sat down? No, no, don't disturb them. Please don't. It's nothing. Please send Jonathan for me. I'm coming home tonight." She hadn't called Brooks Farms "home" in a long while. "I'm at the Jordans. Jonathan knows. Please send him. Good-bye."

Henry was serving dinner. He had put down the silver platter with the cold, pure white halibut, sprinkled with feathery dill. He picked up the platter and opened the door to the dining room. He served Mrs. Stephenson, who was sipping her wine. Mr. Stephenson sat at the end of the table, hidden behind the twelve-candle candelabras. In the middle, Homer Breadcraft inspected the fish, as Mrs. Stephenson lifted a small piece onto her plate.

"We have a movie, darling. Just for you, Homer. *Blow-Up,* by Michelangelo Antonioni—a masterpiece," she said and cut into the fish.

"How sweet, darling. It's just out. How difficult it must have been, Walter, to obtain the first release," Breadcraft answered, screwing up his face as he took the fish.

"It really wasn't at all. We did a big article on the film in the magazine before anyone else. They should be grateful," Mr. Stephenson said.

Henry served Mr. Stephenson and walked back to Mrs. Stephenson.

"I believe . . ." he said, bending over discreetly and Mrs. Stephenson looked at him dismayed. He had never spoken while serving.

"Yes," she said severely, "what is it?"

"I believe Mrs. Chase will be arriving."

"What? She's in New York, Henry. What do you mean?" and there was panic in her voice.

"She called just a moment ago and asked for the car," Henry answered.

"Dispatch it quickly, Henry. Rout out Jonathan. Hurry," said Mr. Stephenson.

"Yes, sir," Henry answered and he went through the door.

"What do you suppose has happened, darling?" said Mrs. Stephenson, dropping her knife and fork to the plate.

Homer Breadcraft finished his wine and twisted his napkin around his fingers.

"Excuse me," Mr. Stephenson said, as he went out of the dining room and into the butler's pantry. Twiggy, the cairn terrier, started to bark. He thought there was a stranger in the kitchen.

"Oh my God, Homer, something's happened, I'm sure," and Mrs. Stephenson placed her arms on the sides of the chair and gripped.

"Now Martha, I'm sure it's nothing. Nothing at all. She probably wants to see you. Is Michael away? He's such a nice boy," Homer said with conviction.

Mr. Stephenson hit the swinging door with his fist and came back quickly into the dining room. He took his place at the end of the table. "Jonathan's already gone. She'll be here in an hour. I don't see calling her there. Henry said Fiona sounded fine. Just wanted the car to bring her home."

"But why didn't you call her back? She might need us. Need something now, don't you see? How foolish," Mrs. Stephenson said excitedly.

"No, Martha, I think you had better let me handle this my way," and he picked up his knife and fork to cut into his fish.

Mrs. Stephenson looked pleadingly toward her husband at the other end of the table. The two candelabras blocked her view and he seemed so far away. "Oh Walter, you must call," she pleaded.

"I know you are going to enjoy the movie, Homer," Mr. Stephenson said, ignoring his wife.

"I hope so. It will be nice to see Fiona again and maybe Michael. I've missed them. They're so different, the young people today. They see the world through different eyes. They have no fears. They face big problems courageously," he said, turning to Mrs. Stephenson, who sat thinking he was so sweet, trying to reassure her.

It must be bad. Bad indeed, he thought to himself and he could hardly wait. He would see *Blow-Up* some other time, even if it meant going to a public movie house.

Michael dozed on the bed. The rum had put him to sleep.

A car coming down the long driveway passed by his window, and as the driver rounded the bend, the headlights lit up the room. Michael woke up and looked over for Fiona. He had forgotten that she had left. He turned over and put his hand to his head. He had a headache and felt sick at his stomach. He slowly got off the bed and went to the bathroom. His throat was dry. He took a long drink of water, and carrying the glass to the window watched the car turn around and speed back down the driveway. He couldn't recognize the car in the dark. Someone made the wrong turn, he supposed.

He lay back down on the bed. He missed Fiona. He didn't like being in the room alone. He wanted her back. He felt cold and pulled the blanket up over him. Then he was warm. He felt beads of sweat trickling down his chest. He sat bolt upright in bed. He tried to forget what he had done to Fiona. He remembered her standing under the mirror pleading with him, and then he had raised his hand and struck her. He saw it all again.

"Oh my God," he said aloud and, dressing hurriedly, left the room, slamming the door after him. He closed the screen door with a bang and was down the steps, running off the path through the stones in the Japanese garden. He fell once, got up quickly and dashed in and out of the low bushes and finally reached the rose-covered gate around the pool. It was locked for the night. He ran around to the other side and into the pool house and down the steps, past the fountain. He rushed to the pool. It was too dark. He couldn't see in the water. He ran back up the steps and into the pool house, where he groped along the wall for a light. He found a white lamp base and, fingering his way to the top, felt for the chain. He pulled too hard and the lamp fell off the table, crashing to the flagstone floor.

He went to the kitchen, remembering the switch near the blender where he and Georgette had mixed the daiquiris that afternoon. He flicked the switch and the lights went on. He saw the rest of the pool house. Now he had to light up the pool. He ran out of the kitchen and into the main room. He found the master switch and flicked all the buttons. The whole garden and the pool were illuminated in a sickly light, like a Hollywood set.

He ran down to the pool screaming all the way, "Fiona, Fiona." He looked into the green-blue water. There was nothing there except for a few floating leaves and a toy sailboat bobbing up against the side. He saw the leopards sitting supremely serene at each end of the pool.

The lights in the main house went on, one after the other. Georgette was the first out, coming down the path in her nightdress, followed by Peter.

"What's wrong? What's happened?" she called while running to Michael. He didn't want to see her, not there, not now with Fiona gone. What was he going to say?

Georgette was standing next to him and so was Peter. He turned away. Georgette could see his body shaking.

Peter put his arm on Michael's shoulder. "Where's Fiona?" he asked calmly.

Georgette looked around and then she turned to look into the pool. Her eyes were fixed on the bottom.

"She's gone. She's gone. I don't know where," Michael answered. He turned around and faced them. "Did you hear her go? Is there a car missing?"

"She couldn't take the car. The keys are inside hanging on a hook in the kitchen," Georgette said.

"I heard a car come down the driveway. Someone has taken her away," Michael said.

"Or she called a taxi and wanted to leave in a hurry," Peter added.

"She'd never do that," Georgette said in a tone suggesting Fiona really didn't have the courage to leave.

Michael nodded. "You're right. She wouldn't leave like that. I'm sure," he said, feeling much better.

"I'm sure she's gone back to New York. She's probably called the limousine service. They work late," Georgette added.

"I remember now. It was a large car. You're right. She's gone back home, back to the apartment. I've got to get there quickly. May I take the car?" Michael asked, already moving toward the garage.

"Go ahead. Good luck. I'll get the keys," said Peter, rushing to the house.

Georgette went after Michael. He was in the white Porsche, waiting. He rolled down the window so Georgette could speak. "I'm sorry," she began, "about tonight. It was unpleasant. You know I was only showing off to get attention. Like I used to. You understand, don't you, Michael?" and she leaned through the window and kissed him. Peter handed Michael the keys.

Michael drove out of the driveway, hesitated at the end, not knowing whether to go right, or left. The dogs across the road barked.

He turned left and soon saw a sign pointing to the Merritt Parkway. He stepped on the gas. He had to find Fiona. He missed the right turn to New York, slammed on the brakes, backed up, and went down the road. Soon he would be in New York and back with her, he was sure. She would forgive him. She was the only one who understood him. He needed her. They needed each other. That was a better way to put it, he thought to himself, as he planned what he was going to say when he saw her again. She'd be in bed asleep, waiting for him, he was sure.

Michael nervously flicked the headlights from low to high beam. He knew he was driving too fast. He had no fear about an accident. Now he was only terrified that for the first time his life had started to crumble. He imagined a scandal if Fiona really was determined to leave him. He must stop her. He wasn't thinking of their happiness. That was for peasants, happiness, not for him. Happiness couldn't exist for people on top, who wanted to do something big.

No, happiness existed only for the nine-to-five men, not for creative people.

Then he thought to himself, he really had been a failure, that is, so far. He had to work harder, that was it. More work, more drive on his part. Somehow, if he succeeded, then their life would arrange itself. After all, they had only been married a year. He was still young. There was time enough.

Michael remembered Cain, how successful he'd been in such a short time. But he died, didn't he? He's gone. There's no point thinking about a dead man. He looked down at the speedometer, the needle approached seventy.

He must feel sorry for Fiona. Yes, he should, but he couldn't. He hated his own selfishness, his lack of sympathy for others, even Fiona. But he did love her, didn't he? Well, yes, he loved her. He loved her as a necessity. He needed her. She didn't thrill or inspire him. She was beautiful, charming to others. Not dynamic, like Georgette, or intellectual like Catherine. Yes, she was a necessary fixture in his life. A flattering accessory. That was a terrible word —fixture.

He turned down the brights as he approached the Greenwich toll booth. He was in the wrong lane; "Exact Change" the red letters said overhead. That's all you want is "exact change, exact change," for everything you do in life. A reward in exchange. A tit-for-tat exchange, that's what he expected and he hated himself for his selfishness. For a moment he pitied Fiona. But she was selfish too. He handed the man at the toll gate a dollar. He sped on, not waiting for the change. He wanted to be home. He needed time to think, time to convince Fiona.

Maybe when she had a child . . . Maybe Fiona was right. A vacation, get away from it all, and he thought of the tropics and that actress. What else could they do? A cruise? That was for old people. Travel around the world by jet, you could see more. They would learn more. Fiona would like that. She loved to travel.

Michael followed the sign around the curve to the Cross County Parkway. How close their houses were to the road. He thought of the people who had once enjoyed the country. Now a wide cement

250

mass cut through their backyards, filled with roaring, fuming cars passing by forever, never stopping.

Fiona could see the lights of Mummy's house in the distance. She tried to fix her hair. Jonathan knew Fiona was suffering. It pained him to see her shifting in the back seat. She kept putting her fingers to her face. Fiona could feel the welts swelling.

"Jonathan, take me to the back. I don't want to disturb them," Fiona said.

"You won't. They're watching a movie. Mr. Breadcraft is there," he added as an afterthought.

Fiona shuddered to think she would have to face him.

They sped up the long, winding driveway and Fiona was so relieved Jonathan had taken the road to the servants' entrance. The car stopped. Fiona didn't wait for Jonathan to open the door. She was out quickly, up the back step and into the kitchen. She nodded good evening to the chef and to Henry, who was drying and polishing the silver. He put down a knife and looked at her.

"Good evening, Mrs. Chase."

"Good evening, Henry. Where are they? Thank you for sending the car," and she shot out the words so quickly he couldn't answer right away. She was almost out of the butler's pantry and was going to pass through the dining room into the long black and white marble hall and she hoped up the winding staircase.

"Mrs. Chase. They're watching a movie. I believe your mother said *Blow-Up,*" he responded.

"Oh good," Fiona answered and she went into the dining room over the beige Savonnerie flowered rug. The candles hadn't been snuffed out too long ago. Fiona could smell the smoke.

The doors to the dining room were closed and Fiona wasn't going to open them until she made sure the way was clear. I just can't run into them now, not now with my face this way, she thought. She went to the mirror over the stone mantel. She stood tiptoe to see herself. There was just enough light from the paintings. She looked away with disgust. Her eyes were red, her hair disheveled. She felt the warmth coming from the burning embers. She turned around to the fire, leaned on the mantel and looked down at the hearth. That

251

fire is about the only warmth left in my life tonight, she thought, moving her arms against her chest.

Fiona still couldn't go through the door to the hall. She calculated, they will be in the library taking coffee. Soon they would be sitting down watching the movie. Then she could escape to her room. Really, there was no escape. There wasn't any way out, she knew that now. She would have to face all of them, even Breadcraft. He would delight in her agony. He would see the marks of violence on her face and he would tell everyone. He would write another book.

Maybe there was a way. She had thought before of going away, of starting over again—maybe in England. She would call that Englishman, Richard Talbott Ross, and then Richard might meet her in Paris. They could go to the sun. She dreamed of fleeing with him. That would show everyone she was free, gutsy enough to live her own way. She couldn't bear the humiliation of running to Mummy and Daddy. That was a mistake. That was weak. She must be strong. Make a clean break. Flee. Flee to Richard. But could she get out of the dining room without seeing them and climb the long, winding staircase? She saw the steps, hundreds of them, going up to nowhere. She would telephone Richard and tell him—what? She had left her husband and was coming to him. That sounded neurotic, but if he loved her still, and she was sure he did, he would meet her.

Fiona thought of Paris. He would be there at the passport gate on the other side. She felt her body chill. I will take off into the sun from Kennedy, but when I land at Orly there will be rain and fog. I'll walk down the sterile stone hallway, past all those shop cases full of perfumes and wines and idyllic travel posters. My passport will be stamped with a heavy thump. Then I will go through the black swinging gate to Richard. We will take the escalator down to the wet street. The black Rolls will be waiting. The chauffeur will slam the solid car door, enclosing us. We will speed along the autoroute, sending up a spray. Outside the grass will shine so green through the fog and rain.

Buoyed up on her dream, Fiona flung open the door. She was full of courage just at that moment.

She started up the stairs. The door to the library opened. Homer

Breadcraft stuck his head out. He saw her and pointing his finger said, "There she is. There she is, darling Fiona. She's here."

Mr. and Mrs. Stephenson came out of the library. Mrs. Stephenson rushed up the stairs, pulling herself by the banister. She stopped on the step below Fiona. "You're here, darling. Home. Are you all right? We were so worried."

Fiona's back was to her mother. She turned around to face her. Mrs. Stephenson put her hand to her mouth. "You're hurt. Walter, she's hurt. Call the doctor," she screamed and leaned back against the black railing to brace herself.

Homer Breadcraft started up the stairs to help Mrs. Stephenson. Mr. Stephenson rushed ahead of him and took Fiona in his arms and escorted her up to the second floor. He had his arm around her waist and was lifting her up each step. Her body was limp. She was glad to be in her father's arms, to be safe. He took her to her room and gently guided her onto the bed. He saw the red welts on her face, her eyes red, alarmed, confused. He felt her cold hand. He sat down on the bed next to her, stroking her head. He took her head in his arms and held it tightly on his lap.

"Now, what happened? Tell me, darling. Tell me."

Mrs. Stephenson and Homer were at the door, standing, looking in. Fiona saw them right away and turned her head. Mr. Stephenson felt her body quiver.

"For God's sake, leave us. Leave us, Martha. Go away," he yelled, getting up from the bed. He kicked the door closed right in their faces. Mrs. Stephenson started to weep and they could hear Homer, after a long pause, escorting her down the hall.

Fiona took her father's hand. "I'm all right. Don't worry, Daddy," she said tenderly.

Mr. Stephenson sensed the honesty in her voice. He admired the way she had composed herself. Not at all like Martha, who was always getting hysterical.

"Now, tell me," he said again, "tell me everything."

"There's nothing to tell. We had a fight, a bitter fight. I'm leaving him tomorrow. I'm going away," Fiona said.

"That won't help. You'd hurt yourself running. And hurt all of us. Think about that. Now I think you should get some sleep," he told her, as he started pulling down the bedspread. He put her head on the pillow. Fiona thought of Cain. How she had held his head as he was dying.

"Where is Michael?" Mr. Stephenson asked Fiona abruptly.

"At the Jordans, where I left him," she answered.

Mr. Stephenson thought that was unfortunate, so unfortunate they had all been together. He would have to act quickly.

"I'm all right. No, Daddy, really. Go see the movie. Don't upset Mummy. Tell her I'm just exhausted and want to sleep," and Fiona dropped his hand, relieved to think she would be alone in her own bed.

Mr. Stephenson kissed her on the brow and brushed back her hair. He examined closely the marks on her face. He guessed Michael had struck her. He wasn't shocked. He felt weak inside. He knew that he had once struck Martha and he had paid dearly. She had never let him forget it. He must save them both from further suffering, Mr. Stephenson was convinced, as he closed the door.

"Good night, darling. It will all be arranged. Good night. I love you."

Fiona turned her head to the blue silk wall. Tomorrow—tomorrow she would run away. To England. To Paris. Somewhere. The blue room seemed to close in on her. She curled up tightly in the warm bed. The trouble was, she'd be taking herself along, wouldn't she?

Michael fumbled with Uncle John's key chain. He couldn't turn the key in the lock. He rang the bell to their apartment. He heard the bell sounding shrill inside. He tried the key again. He looked through a crack between the doors. No lights. Fiona must be sleeping. He turned the key again. It worked and he rushed in. Behind, the key chain, with Uncle John's inscription, dangled in the lock.

He went to the bedroom without turning on the lights. He felt the bed all over. Empty. He went to the living room, the library, his dressing room, back and forth, up and down the hall. No one. Empty. So empty, only objects sitting all about—lifeless, meaningless without people in the rooms, without Fiona. He sat down on his couch, threw his head back into the pillows and then remembered. Of

254

course, Fiona wouldn't be here. She never would. The servants were off for the weekend. How stupid.

Then he wondered where she really was. He suddenly panicked. No, she must be safe. She wasn't driving alone. She wouldn't go home to Mummy. She wouldn't do that. She had always said she didn't want to be with her parents. She didn't want to be like them.

Then, Michael realized, where else could Fiona turn? If he called Brooks Farms, he surely would have to speak eventually to Mr. Stephenson. They probably wouldn't let her go to the phone.

He got up and paced the floor and each time he passed near the bar he hesitated and then went on. Finally he gave in. He flung open the door. There he was, Michael, fully reflected against the crystal glasses in the mirrored wall. He couldn't look at his face. He took a large glass and a whiskey bottle, and fled back to the couch. He removed the cork with his teeth and poured halfway to the top. He took a long sip and leaned back again and looked at the ceiling. I just can't sit here and do nothing. I can't bear the silence, he thought, pouring in more whiskey. There's too much at stake. I'll throw away everything, my reputation—and Michael saw the image that he really didn't have, destroyed. Uncle John, what will he do? And he shuddered to think.

He paced the floor again and flicked on the radio. The music blared. He turned up the volume, hoping to drown out his own thoughts. He couldn't stop drinking. He knew he should. The more he drank, the more his mouth drooped. His lips curled up into a cynical smile. He sank back into the couch and buried his mouth in the pillows. He could feel the wetness of his lips running onto the silk.

He moved over to the other side and picked up the phone. He dialed. He hung up the receiver. He had dialed the wrong number. He dropped the receiver with a bang onto the glass table and the dial tone buzzed. He went to turn down the radio. He dialed again. He looked at his watch. After midnight. So what. She was always up late. He smiled to himself. She was the gay one in Paris. I remember the night when she went home with André on the Vespa. Yes, I remember, and his smile turned to a sardonic smirk as he let the phone ring. She's got to be there, he thought.

"Hello, hello," Michael said quickly. "Catherine, I'm so glad to get you. I need you right now. I hope I didn't wake you up. I've got something important to tell you." Michael paused, then went on, "I've left Fiona. We had our last fight." Michael reached out for the whiskey glass. By now his hand was trembling. He took one sip after the other.

"I've left. Yes, I have. I have and I'm glad it's all over. You know we never got along. You remember the night, that night that Paul—" and he stopped just before he was about to say died. He waited. He couldn't think of what to say next.

"Catherine, darling. You know I love you. Yes, that's it. I love you. And the child, I can help you bring up the child. I do love you. I'm coming to see you now. I want you tonight. Catherine, are you listening?" Michael waited. There was no response, but he talked on. "You see, Catherine, I can give you everything you had before. I can take over where Paul left off. I mean, take his seat if I'm elected. Then we can start afresh, both of us. You need me. I need you. With your support, imagine the tide of sympathy. You're so popular and I'm . . . I'm so . . ." and he couldn't finish. He put the glass to his lips and drank again. The glass rattled against the phone. He waited, holding the receiver tightly to his ear. Michael frowned and dropped the phone onto the glass table. He could hear the buzzzzzzzzzzzzzzzzzz of the dial tone. He fell asleep.

20

ARRANGEMENT

Uncle John had just returned from the club. He had won the back-gammon, hands down, and he took out the loser's check from his pocket, looked at the amount, and then entered the ten thousand dollars in his check book. He was about to check his balance when the phone rang.

The phone was next to his Louis XVI trictrac table, where he worked and played backgammon. He picked up the receiver.

"Hello, Walter. What's on your mind at this hour?" Uncle John asked.

"Fiona has come home to us. She's in a bad state. I don't want to go into any details," Mr. Stephenson said, pausing and picking his next words carefully, "but I think we have to act quickly to ar-range the situation. Their separation, even if only temporary, would be scandalous for both families."

"I agree. Immediately," said Uncle John looking at his watch. "Where is he?" he asked.

"At the Jordans," Mr. Stephenson shot back and continued, "and John, before you do anything, just remember about your wife."

Uncle John couldn't answer right away. He thought of his wife, away, upstate in an institution, put away by him, because she suf-

257

fered from nervous depressions brought on by his lack of real feeling and affection for her. He excused himself, because he really had no affection for anyone. He sat down in the wicker chair and held his hand to his head.

"Walter, I'm going to get him right away. Leave it to me," and Uncle John hung up the receiver and adjusted his glasses on his nose.

He dialed the Jordans. Georgette answered.

"No, he's left Uncle John, in our car. He's gone to get Fiona in New York. He's at the apartment, I'm sure. I don't know what happened. Really, I don't know. We had some drinks and then the evening seemed to fall apart. Go quickly. Find him before there's trouble," Georgette pleaded.

Uncle John reached into his pocket and changed his reading glasses for driving glasses.

He drove his black Mercedes out of the private garage on Sixty-third Street and turned up Park Avenue. He parked in front of Michael's apartment.

Uncle John hesitated before Michael's door. What was he going to say to the boy? What was he going to do? He saw the key and the square gold piece with his inscription dangling in the door. He couldn't remember exactly what it said—something like, "Your fate lies not in the stars, but in you," paraphrased from Shakespeare, *Lear,* possibly, he thought, as he went down the long corridor past their bedroom.

He hadn't been in the apartment since the night Cain had died. He could still see all those dressed up, elegant people pushing their way toward the room to see a dying man. He remembered how Mr. Stephenson had closed the door and taken charge while he was left outside, shoved up against the wall. I'm responsible now, he thought.

Michael was sprawled out on the couch. Uncle John went over to him. He saw the whiskey bottle, the empty glass, and the telephone off the hook. He replaced the receiver and sat down next to Michael. He hoped the weight of his body on the couch with Michael would awaken him gently. Michael slept on. Uncle John tapped

258

him on the arm. He still didn't move. He shook his arm again and again. Michael opened his eyes, looked up and closed them.

"Get up. Get up, my boy. Wake up. I'm taking you back to your wife. Let's get up now."

Michael stirred and finally recognized Uncle John. He turned his head away, burying his face into the pillow. He was trying to hide like a child.

"No. No, Uncle John. Go away. Leave me. Please go," Michael pleaded.

"I'm here to help you," Uncle John said firmly.

"You can't," Michael answered.

"Where are your guts? Come on, up on your feet," said Uncle John, as he grasped Michael under his arms and lifted him up. He let go and Michael fell to the floor.

"I'm going to be sick," Michael said.

Uncle John acted quickly. He took Michael by the arms and dragging him across the floor, kicked the door to the bathroom open and with one final tug placed his body next to the toilet. He grasped Michael by his hair and placed his head over the bowl. Michael vomited. Uncle John closed the door and went to the couch, picked up the glass and whiskey and put them away in the bar.

Uncle John and Michael were up early. They had breakfast at the club.

"It was an excellent breakfast, Uncle John. Thank you," said Michael, looking down at his shoes.

"That's all right. We had better be going," Uncle John said firmly.

"Do you suppose," Michael began as he got up from the table, "I could get a shine?"

"Downstairs," Uncle John told him.

Michael watched the colored man putting the black polish on with his bare hands. The strength of the hand slapping against his shoe and the rag snapping across the leather calmed Michael's nerves. He must keep busy. Michael looked down at the shine. A good job, he thought to himself, as he signed the chit.

Uncle John drove quickly up the Connecticut Turnpike. Michael could think of nothing to say to Uncle John except thank you, but wouldn't that sound rather silly? He was concerned about facing Fiona, but Uncle John said it all had been arranged. Michael didn't want to know how. They went up the Brooks Farms driveway. Uncle John stopped at the portico.

"Let's get out," he told Michael.

Michael opened the door and stood alone in front of the big white house, waiting for Uncle John to come around from the other side of the car. Michael looked to the back of the house. He saw Jonathan sitting in the Stephensons' black Jaguar, ready to go somewhere.

Before they could ring the bell, Henry had opened the front door. They were in the marble hallway. Homer Breadcraft stood at the top of the staircase with Mrs. Stephenson. He gave a feeble wave to Michael and then gripped Mrs. Stephenson's hand. Mr. Stephenson opened the library door and came out, arm in arm, with Fiona.

"Good morning," Mr. Stephenson said to Uncle John. He stared at Michael.

Fiona looked at Michael blankly. Then she said, "Hello, Michael," like a shy, proper little girl greeting a playmate.

Michael smiled thankfully. He saw the welts on her cheek. He took his handkerchief out of his inside coat pocket, put it to his nose, returned it to his pocket.

Mr. Stephenson dropped his arm from Fiona. She walked to Michael.

Uncle John went over to Mr. Stephenson, shook his hand, and when their eyes met each knew all was arranged.

Uncle John climbed the stairway, perfunctorily took Homer Breadcraft's wet hand, and kissed Mrs. Stephenson's cheek.

"Stay for lunch. Please do, John," she said persuasively.

"I will," Uncle John answered.

Mr. Stephenson looked over at Fiona. She was at the front door. Henry opened it, letting in the first summer sun.

The black Jaguar was now in front of the portico. Jonathan opened the car door. "Good morning, Mrs. Chase," he said softly.

She climbed in and sat as far as she could to the other side. She gripped the leather hand pulley and looked out of the window onto the browning grass. There had been little rain that spring. Michael got in beside her and clutched the hand pulley on his side. The car moved slowly down the driveway, turned onto the main road. They didn't speak. Michael and Fiona were going home.